MW01222676

INGRAM MOUNTAIN

Best wishes John & Jennifer

Reg Johnston

REG JOHNSTON

MELANIE ZACHODA

1st WORLD
PUBLISHING

16 LRJ

Ingram Mountain

Reg Johnston - Melanie Zachoda

© Reg Johnston 2005

Published by 1stWorld Publishing
1100 North 4th St. Suite 131, Fairfield, Iowa 52556
tel: 641-209-5000 • fax: 641-209-3001
web: www.1stworldpublishing.com

First Edition

LCCN: 2005909211
SoftCover ISBN: 1-59540-972-6
HardCover ISBN: 1-59540-974-2
eBook ISBN: 1-59540-973-4

This material has been written and published solely for educational purposes. The author and the publisher shall have neither liability or responsibility to any person or entity with respect to any loss, damage or injury caused or alleged to be caused directly or indirectly by the information contained in this book.

The characters and events described in this text are intended to entertain and teach rather than present an exact factual history of real people or events.

For Layne

WE WISH TO THANK THE FOLLOWING PERSONS FOR THEIR ASSISTANCE

Thank you for all you have done.

SHAUNA CAMERON
PAUL CHRISTOFFERSEN
CHARLENE CHRISTOFFERSEN
CAROLE MCINTYRE
CONNIE BOBINSKI
PAUL NAPORA
FORT SASKATCHEWAN SPIRITUAL FREE THOUGHT
    STUDY GROUP

Author's Note

A closed mind or unwillingness to explore beyond traditional boundaries is among the greatest impediments to solving the problems facing humanity today.

Unless we are willing to step outside the confines of the "traditional box" and examine firmly entrenched beliefs and behaviors with ruthless objectivity, the human race is in for a very rough ride and possible extinction.

Tragically, warnings of this nature are so common place they either fall on deaf ears or are shrugged off as the "cry wolf" syndrome, resulting in a complacency that could soon backfire with savage and deadly results.

Planet earth is at a critical crossroads. In the writers opinion, which is shared by a bevy of experts in the field, we have one option left and that is to completely discard the old system which has been monopolized by incompetent governments, greedy corporations and emotion controlling organized religions.

If this is to be accomplished we have a momentous task ahead of us but the time has come, if it hasn't already slipped past, for every capable human being to take up the cause in an attempt to halt our downward spiral into oblivion.

This book was written to be another wake up call of a different flavor but the message is the same; make the reader realize we must view the present outmoded system as no longer a system at all but a serious threat to our survival as a species.

The following story is offered as a guide to making both a personal and social change of direction.

If it resonates with you in any way then you are urged to take up the cause and convince as many others as possible to do likewise because we have only one hope left. We must achieve no less than critical mass that might still tip the scales in favor of the human race.

CHAPTER 1

"Do you think it is really that bad Wes?" Adam asked when his friend finished revealing some of the most unsettling news that Adam had ever heard.

"It's at least that bad. There is so much information suppressed by both government and industry that the average Joe seldom knows more than a smattering of the true picture."

Adam shook his head a few times and stared out the window of the posh clubhouse that had come to feel like his second home since his divorce some two years earlier. He finally took a long drink of his favorite rye and water from the glass he had held poised in mid air when Wes Scott began telling the disturbing story. Doomsayers were nothing new. They were on every street corner and thrived on predicting everything from nuclear annihilation to invasion by aliens who would enslave the entire human race. Adam paid little attention to this sensationalism chalking it up to the useless drivel that helped keep tabloids in business but this sobering news coming from a highly esteemed and long time friend was not so readily dismissed.

Wes had called the previous evening suggesting they do one last round of golf before the course closed down for the season but had made no mention of the real reason for the invitation. What he was now revealing sounded like science fiction but if it contained even a few kernels of truth, it painted a gloomy picture for the human race.

"The group I've joined is strongly committed to this cause. We're affiliated with six or seven other groups across the country and have connections to similar groups in the U.S. We hope that through combined efforts we'll be able to dig up previously distorted facts and spread them far and wide as quickly as possible."

"If it's as bad as you say, it might be better to leave it alone. Disclosing what you've told me could cause a whole lot of panic over something we can't do much about anyway."

"Everybody deserves to know the undiluted truth, Adam—if we can find it. This potentially affects every person on the planet and all should have the right to deal with it in whatever manner they choose. But if all they're getting are half truths or downright lies, then that right is being denied them."

"Well you've got me in a sweat right now and I've sure as hell no idea what to think or do."

"How about joining our group?"

Adam stared hard for a moment at his longtime friend then turned away and exhaled slowly through pursed lips.

"Membership isn't open to just anybody," Wes Scott continued. You have to be recommended by an existing member who, in your case, is me and then attend a meeting to see what your reaction is."

"God I don't know Wes. I've been so damn busy lately…"

"No you're not Adam. You flung yourself into your work because of your son's death and I don't blame you for that. But this group might just be the diversion you need right now."

"I'm not so sure of that. I've been living in doom and gloom for the past year and now you're suggesting I take on some more."

"Adam, one meeting can't hurt. If you decide against it after that then you won't hear from them again."

"Give me a chance to sleep on it Wes. I'll let you know in a day or two."

"Agreed. But please don't take a bit longer than necessary. Time is one luxury we don't have."

The urgency in his friend's voice was disturbing, Adam thought, as he drove back to his penthouse apartment. Wes Scott was one of the most stable persons he had ever known and certainly not prone to sensationalism. Adam would not treat his request lightly.

Once settled down, for the evening, in his favorite easy chair he began mulling over the disconcerting news Wes had given him. Foregoing his usual stint in front of the massive plasma TV, he poured himself a small measure of Canadian Club hoping it would digest the sumptuous meal his housekeeper Hilda had prepared for him. She always countered his objection to all the rich food by insisting "we gotta get some meat back on those bones, Mr. Finlay. It's a wonder you can even fight off a cold."

He never won the argument with her but he really wasn't trying to. Her food was irresistibly delicious.

Since the loss of his son Jeffery in a car accident a year earlier, he had been fighting an uphill battle with his emotions and excessive weight loss was one of the more obvious symptoms.

Now Wes Scott had dumped some new and unsettling news on his lap just when his life had started approaching normal once again. Did he want to get involved? On the other hand, if the environmental situation was half as bad as his friend had indicated, could he afford not to. According to Wes there were only a few isolated groups around the world who were willing to critically examine the seriousness of the situation and they needed all the help that anyone was willing to offer. Besides there was apparently even more disturbing news which would be revealed if he attended the meeting.

Finding time away from his property development business really didn't pose a problem. He had used it as a crutch since the death of his son. He had a very efficient manager who was more than capable of taking over in his absence.

Drawing his gaunt six foot frame out of the chair, he wandered across the thick carpeted living room to stare out through a huge picture window at the Edmonton skyline.

Catching a vague reflection of himself in the window, he surveyed the image for a moment. 'What lie in store?' he wondered. Would it add a few more lines to the lean face? Some more gray to the once dark brown hair. Maybe, too, he was blowing it all out of proportion. It might not amount to anything more than some community work aimed at increasing the environmental awareness of as many citizens as possible. But his instinct told him otherwise. There was much more to it than that for a stable man like Wes Scott to take up the cause with such dedication.

But what environmental problems could this group reveal that most people were not already aware of. Could they be more serious than acid rain? Clear cutting forests? Extincting plants and animals? Attacking the ozone layer? Global warming?

He wanted to talk to Wes once more before committing himself so he arranged another meeting for the next afternoon. He arrived before Wes and settled himself into his favorite spot to sip on coffee. A few die hard golfers were trickling in from what was likely their last round of the season.

He watched them absently as they ordered drinks and compared score cards. Most were wealthy businessmen and like himself probably had given little thought or even cared very much about the environmental problems descending on the planet. Problems Wes had made him painfully aware of when he wanted nothing more than to smooth out his life that had been full of potholes for several years.

Still watching the club members seated across the room, he realized that what really mattered to most of them was that they were comfortable today, tomorrow's outlook was pretty good and next year was shaping up not too badly.

"The environment? Oh I don't think the problems are as bad as they make them out to be. Besides with today's technology they are able to fix practically anything. But hey what about our junior hockey team knocking off the world championship. They were never behind once during the whole tournament."

That could have been almost any one of them talking. He'd heard the idle prattle a hundred times over and until now had been a participant himself.

Reflecting on what Wes had told him, he realized how minor any problems were compared to possible disasters as a result of environmental breakdown.

"Wes why aren't they shouting these problems from the mountain tops. Giving them to every newspaper that would print it. Haranguing government officials feeding it to TV stations and anything else they could do to make it public," he asked when his friend got seated.

"They have done it all with results ranging from mild interest to complete brush off. They have presented their findings to every government official, industrial mogul and newspaper in the country and really got nowhere. Now they've chosen to engage a select group of highly credible persons who may not be so caught up in the culture trap that they could, if appealed to, see through the veil of profiteering and recognize what dangers lie beyond."

"How do you know I'm not one of them Wes? I too have a hell of a lot invested in the economic trends of the country."

"So have I Adam. But if our planet is heading downhill as fast as I'm told it is, the economy soon won't mean much to anybody."

"Maybe it's just a bunch of scare mongering? This sort of thing is nothing new. They could be just another group of environmental extremists who have something to gain if they pull off this caper."

"How long have you known me Adam? Over twenty years now? Remember I have a business to run too and any down turn in the economy will affect me as much as you or anyone else. I viewed it with a hell of a lot of skepticism at first myself until I met the group and that was the biggest eye opener I've ever experienced."

Adam nodded his head slowly and emptied his coffee cup then said as he sat it back on the table, "Okay I'll give it a try."

CHAPTER 2

The meeting was held in the home of a group member. Adam couldn't help noticing the modest character of the house as he entered. It was functional and well cared for but he certainly didn't sink into the carpet as he was led into the dining room with a large table in the center. The rest of the group was already seated when he and Wes arrived so introductions were brief and straight to the point. Each one in turn gave their name and occupation. One, a middle aged man, was a physicist. Two others, a man and a woman, described themselves as spiritual practitioners. The fourth one, a woman, was a biologist and the fifth a male psychic.

This seemed like a strange cross section of occupations, but Adam had little time to mull it over because the biologist, who seemed to be the leader, wasted no time in driving straight to the core of the reason for the existence of the group.

"Mr. Finlay. We came together as a group about a year ago initially to explore methods to help salvage a seriously ill planet. Our focus has shifted somewhat since that time. We've found an equally, if not more serious problem exists because much information is either so diluted or completely withheld by governments that the average person is largely in the dark. When we began investigating this issue, we were told that information was withheld to avoid panic amongst the masses. After much probing, however, we've concluded that the real reason is to protect industry whose profit margins shrink in proportion to imposed environmental controls. This area is very shady. It's difficult to identify where governments really stand on environmental issues. As often as not they say what they think the public wants to hear and then hope that we'll leave it alone. For this reason we've circumvented government and industry and through independent research have arrived at a few reliable conclusions.

The environmental situation is much more serious than most people are aware of. The earth is facing a crisis unprecedented in our history and if it continues unabated the result could be the extinction of human life."

"Pardon?" Adam said almost before realizing he had spoken.

"I know that's a bold statement," she said. "But just hear us out and you'll understand."

"Of course," he answered. "I'm sorry for interrupting.

"That's quite alright. Environmental problems are nothing new. Practically anyone can list some of them, but in order to get up to speed I'm going to repeat the commonly known ones. Air pollution destroys the ozone layer that filters out dangerous rays from the sun causing the greenhouse effect due to a planet wide temperature increase which severely disrupts weather patterns. Acid rain is one result, which is extremely harmful to plant and animal life and causes serious respiratory disease in humans. Plants and animals are becoming extinct at a faster rate than any time in recorded history and that in turn undermines the ecosphere upon which all life depends. The sea and land environments are poisoned by the dumping of dangerous industrial waste which includes mercury and nuclear waste as well as non-degradable packaging and other disposable products. Soil erosion is occurring in various locations all over the world and is the result of inappropriate land use such as clearcutting forests, misuse of dangerous pesticides and chemical fertilizers as well as land over use resulting in soil eroding at a rate faster than it can replenish itself."

She stopped talking and glanced around at the other group members. "Does anyone want to add anything?" she asked.

When they all shook their heads she turned to the scientist and said, "Carl would you take it from here?"

The slightly overweight man who appeared to be in his mid-fifties shifted his position in the chair and stroked a short gray beard for a moment. "As Angie said," he began. "The situation is far more serious than what most people are aware of or are prepared to accept. She was just setting you up for the kill Mr. Finlay. I have to do the dirty work."

Adam glanced over at the biologist. It was the first time he had noticed anyone in the group smile and even then it was so faint, it hardly rated as a smile.

"What we're finding is that we could have much less time left than what we once thought before our climate becomes unbearable," Carl continued. "And this is for several reasons. Firstly buried in the arctic tundra is a potential time bomb from the global warming viewpoint. There are enormous quantities of naturally occurring gases trapped in the ice like structures in cold northern muds and possibly in the bottom of seas. These mud structures contain in the range of three thousand times as much methane as is already in the atmosphere and methane is twenty times more potent than carbon dioxide. As long as these gases stay locked in the ice, we have no problem. But this almost certainly is not going to happen. A temperature increase of even a few degrees could cause these gases to volatize and discharge into the atmosphere further raising temperatures and releasing more methane which heats the earth even more rapidly and in turn releasing still more methane. Once triggered this cycle could result in runaway global warming that would be more apocalyptic than anything man has ever before experienced and the frightening aspect is this event could be right on our doorstep."

"My god!" Adam blurted before realizing he had spoken.

"That was my first reaction too," Wes Scott said.

"It sounds like we've already gone beyond the point of no return. Is there anything at all that can be done to reverse that trend."

"Stabilize global warming right where it's at and that might not even be enough," Carl said. "Another phenomenon of a similar nature that is creating a lot of concern among scientists is a sudden jump in atmospheric carbon dioxide levels when there has been no increase in emissions from the usual sources that cause it. The fear is that this abrupt speed up may be the dreaded climate change feedback mechanism. This can happen when global warming breaks down the earth's natural systems for absorbing carbon dioxide to such a degree that a compounding affect occurs. Warming then increases more rapidly than before and continues to increase at an accelerating pace because it is now feeding on itself. What this boils down to is that instead of decades to bring global warming under control we may have only a few years."

Adam was temporarily lost for words. He glanced at Wes Scott who shrugged his shoulders and said, "at least you understand why I made it sound so urgent.

"Another serious issue of a different nature is the fact that many American politicians are also fundamentalist Christians and they are completely united in their opposition to environmental protection."

This statement came from Gina, one of the spiritual practitioners who looked young enough to be Adam's daughter.

"They claim," her male companion continued, "that we are living in the end times and any concern for the future of the planet is pointless since the Son of God, will soon return at which time the righteous will be taken to heaven and sinners sent to hell. They believe, along with millions of other fundamentalists, that environmental destruction should actually be welcomed because it signifies the return of Christ."

"The U.S. swings a mighty big axe in the world," Angie continued. "If they were to get on the bandwagon our chances would be increased perhaps tenfold. But let's keep in mind we all have a responsibility. I once heard a Canadian lumberman make the comment that when he looks at a tree all he sees are dollars. That is a very dangerous and pathetic attitude."

"It sounds to me as though time is a deciding factor," Adam said. "Do we have time enough left to implement any effective remedies?"

"There is yet time," the psychic finally spoke. "But none to be wasted.

"Even if that's so, what do we do?" Adam said. "We still have to find a solution in a hell of a hurry."

"What I've presented," Carl said, "is the worst case scenario. It may take much longer than I estimate. It may not be as intense as I think and it may not happen for many generations to come. We could destroy ourselves with nuclear weapons or terrorist warfare before a vindictive environment has the chance to do the job.

The point is there is sufficient evidence to push alarm buttons. I'm afraid I personally don't share Eldon's views that we still have enough time to make significant changes," he said nodding toward the psychic. "But I do hope he is right."

"I've often heard," Wes Scott said, "that the planet has a built in regulating system that could adjust to compensate for the extensive misuse. It would become a different world that humans would have to adapt to but it would still be habitable. Instead of the various cultures that now exist, there would be a complete paradigm shift. Cultures have come and gone in the past. Maybe this is just the beginning of one of those phases."

"That is a possibility," Angie said, "and if so it could happen despite every counter measure we now undertake because we may have already pushed ourselves beyond the point of no return. It almost certainly wouldn't be a slow transition meaning we would be in for a very rough ride. The difference between the present threat and the demise of earlier cultures is the total impact we now have on the earth. In ancient times the downfall of a race was restricted to a small section of the planet with little effect on the rest of the world. All that has changed. From now on we take what mother earth hands us because in the final analysis which is where we are at right now, mother earth is the big boss and she will decide what happens to her inhabitants."

"Why," Adam asked, "isn't this information being disseminated by every means possible? Shouldn't we be shouting it from rooftops? Treetops? Mountain tops?"

The scientist smiled faintly and said, "that has been done Mr. Finlay. You may be assured that we and all other environmental groups have used every possible method to warn governments, industry and anyone else responsible with success ranging from mild to none. Some leaders are more receptive than others, but as Angie emphasized they are hamstrung by pressure from industry who dangle the specter of economic downturn in front of them. Besides these same corporations have often contributed enormous sums of money toward election campaigns. If the candidate they have supported gets elected it's a foregone conclusion that the contributing group will receive many more concessions than they otherwise would. To repeat what Angie said the information flow from scientists to the public is screened so that the average citizen only hears what the government wants them to hear. To me this is a criminal offense. If everyone was fully aware of the gravity of the situation, we might have a fighting chance to unite in a common cause to halt the destruction or at least slow it down."

Adam could only shake his head in disbelief. He had been aware as had most, that the planet was facing environmental problems. But what he was now hearing was difficult to accept.

"We've already acknowledged the various ways we've desecrated the environment," Wes said. "The solution to that would appear to be simple; stop doing it. But obviously that won't happen. It seems as though we must search for some deeper cause."

"Precisely," the psychic chimed in. "We began violating sacred laws at a certain point in our history and all along most of us believing we were doing the right thing."

"When we made the transition from hunter gatherers to communal living," Angie continued, "it seemed to be a good industrious thing to do. But right then and there is likely where we introduced unnatural conditions into our methods. In order to establish settlements we began to manipulate our environment to conform to our needs rather than work cooperatively with the environment. In other words we set out to conquer nature believing this was what we should be doing."

"So that's probably when we made a wrong turn and there's no way of reversing it," Adam said looking at Carl.

"Nothing we're presently aware of. Just stabilizing it will be a massive job and that can only happen if enough of us get on the same bandwagon. We will never reverse the trend. Stabilization is our only hope to leave us with a habitable world."

"Part of our mission," the biologist said, "is to ensure that we don't make the same mistake the second round if we do manage to survive the current threat."

"It seems to me," Adam said, "that the answer is simple. You're telling me that when we formed settlements, we began violating sacred laws by manipulating nature for our own benefit. If we learn the laws and live by them wouldn't that get us back on track?"

"That's partly true," Gina said, "or perhaps I should say it's part of the equation."

"What's the rest?"

"Well first of all we've probably gone beyond the point of no return. But what would you do Mr. Finlay, if we did have the opportunity to start over knowing what we know now. What would your recommendation for our behavior be?"

"I just said it. Learn the laws and live by them."

"Define living by the laws."

"Off the top of my head, I'm not sure. It would be a re-educating process. One we would have to all participate in, if we were to avoid the same mistake."

"Give us an example of a law you think we should observe."

"Simply respect the environment by not violating it as we have done."

"Very good. But everyone else would have to do the same."

"Well I should think they would want to after having experienced the mess we've already made."

"Can you be sure of that?"

"I couldn't guarantee it, but they'd have to be insane not to want to."

"What about the fundamentalist Christians I mentioned earlier? How would you persuade that group to change their behavior when their theology has them convinced that environmental breakdown is part of a divine plan that they believe must not be tampered with."

He looked at her for a moment, a faint smile playing at the corners of his mouth. "Alright," he said. "You tell me."

"Mr. Finlay," Angie broke in. "None of us have the answers, which is precisely why we formed this group. We have brainstormed for the past eleven months and although we've come up with some pretty good ideas, they are only partial fixes. There are always obstacles, such as the one Gina has just presented you with.

We've always planned to gradually expand the group with highly intelligent persons such as yourself and Mr. Scott thereby adding to the brain pool and hopefully in time identify the core problem if in fact that can be done at all. We believe searching for answers is of foremost importance in our life and should be in everybody else's because if a solution isn't found and implemented very soon, the planet will not sustain life. Everyone sitting at this table agrees and has made a firm commitment to that cause.

Some of us such as yourself and Mr. Scott are financially independent and probably could devote all the time necessary to the mission while others, which includes me, have jobs but only because it enables us to continue our participation in the group. We feel, and I think I speak for everyone, that there is no longer anything else on earth as important as this. If a viable solution to the environmental breakdown isn't soon found then all other activities will gradually become pointless. Are we extremists? Maybe we are. Nothing would make us happier than to be proven wrong. If we're right then at least we can say we gave it our best shot."

Adam was nodding slowly as she finished talking. "I'm starting to see where you're coming from," he said.

He glanced at the rest of the group to find that all eyes were fastened on him. Looking at the backs of his hands he asked, "how often do you meet?"

"At least weekly," Angie answered. "More often if anything comes up that we feel we should discuss."

"If you decide to join us," Carl said. "We've agreed on a few basic and simple rules which I'm sure Mr. Scott has already versed you on."

"He has but I'm curious about the emphasis on secrecy."

"There are powerful forces out there Mr. Finlay who would go to any lengths to completely neutralize groups such as this if we started to make any real progress toward changing the attitude and behavior of the majority. Now when I say any lengths, well —use your imagination. Consequently we commit to complete secrecy more for our own safety than anything else. When someone has been recommended for membership such as yourself, you may rest assured that they've been thoroughly investigated. We apologize for infringing on your privacy, but…"

"I understand," Adam said. "But I have one more question. What makes you think this group might be able to find a solution to the ultimate problem facing the human race when some of the best minds on earth haven't been able to." Quickly realizing what he had said he began an awkward attempt to correct his blunder.

"Excuse me," he said. "I didn't mean to imply that there aren't great minds in this group."

"I think we understand what you meant Mr. Finlay," the psychic spoke up. "What I'm reading in you is a healthy skepticism which was not intended to offend but to explore all avenues before you commit to something."

"I agree with that," Carl said, "and your question is a valid one. The answer is really quite simple. In the past many groups that attempted to find solutions were usually all of a very scientific mindset which meant their focus was from a rather singular viewpoint. They were and are experts at determining the cause and seriousness of the problems. But any proposed solutions were also from that focus. Our group and others like us, by contrast, represents a diverse cross section of persons and if you join it will add to that diversity. We will continue to follow this format for as long as there is some chance that we can turn the tide. If we can't, well…we should at least get an A for effort if there's anybody left to grade us."

Adam glanced around the table again and found that all eyes were still fastened on him. What he had heard left little doubt in his mind that he would participate but he wanted another day to think about it.

"Of course Mr. Finlay," Angie said when he made his request, "and thank you so much for coming tonight."

After handshakes all around he and Wes Scott took their leave and made their way out to Adam's black Mercedes. Once seated in the car Wes asked, "Wanna swing by the club for a drink?"

With both hands grasping the steering wheel Adam said, "Yeah I do and I'm starting off with a double."

CHAPTER 3

After a restless night, there were no doubts about his association with the group. The meeting had jolted him like few things ever had before. Reports on environmental problems were always hanging around in the background, but he viewed them as mostly scare mongering to appease the objectives of left wing environmentalists.

Now he was seeing this issue differently and after a hurried breakfast in the high rise café, he gave Angie a call to confirm his membership in the group.

"That is wonderful news, Mr. Finlay. We'll be meeting again at my house next Thursday and bring along any topics for discussion you may have. No idea is discounted. We give credibility to every idea anyone has and, by the way, when you've settled in and clearly understand our philosophy, we would gladly welcome any new members you might recommend."

"Sounds great," he said. "See you Thursday."

After a brief visit to his office to inform his manager he would be absent for the day, he began giving some thought to what his next move should be. Search the internet? Visit a library? A bookstore? What seemed most important was to get a more thorough background on the whole environmental issue so he could offer something useful to the group.

On impulse he phoned Wes Scott to see if he might be free for a few hours to talk more about what had been discussed the previous night.

"Meet you at the club for lunch," Wes responded. "By the way did you remember the annual hunting trip we scheduled for the weekend."

"Oh dammit," Adam said. He had become so consumed with the group and their objectives that it had completely slipped his mind. "Okay, lets talk about it over lunch."

By the time he reached the posh building, he had decided to pass up their annual big game hunting excursion in favor of doing enough research to at least be conversant about environmental problems.

Wes Scott was already seated when Adam arrived and he immediately detected a look of concern in his friend's face. Although five years younger than Adam, his thinning blonde hair and proneness to worry combined with a noticeable middle age paunch caused him to look older.

"What's up?" Adam asked removing his overcoat and draping it over a chair.

"Willis and Leo just left and they're still hell bent on the hunting trip. Will says he's holding us to it because we all confirmed it last month and he's made special arrangements to get away. I didn't know what to say. Since joining the group everything else has become secondary to me and running around the mountains chasing after some big game that I wouldn't kill anyway is the last thing I want to do right now."

Adam couldn't help smiling at his friend's last remark.

"I'd made up my mind on the way over to pass too," he said. "I wanted to learn as much as I possibly could by next Thursday's meeting so I could at least join in the discussion."

"Will you be having lunch too Mr. Finlay?" a waitress interrupted.

"Yes please Karen. My usual soup, sandwich and coffee.

After the waitress left Wes said, "something did come up

during our conversation that you might want to think about. It's seems we'll be going into a different area this year because Will got a tip from somebody that moose are more plentiful there. But here's what's really interesting. There are several parcels of land in the area that for some mysterious reason haven't fallen victim to clear cut logging. Usually logging companies make such lucrative offers that owners finally can't refuse but from what Leo was saying not a tree has been touched on this area and nobody seems to know why. It might give us a chance to look this spot over and who knows maybe get a chance to talk to the owners and find out more about it. They might just be some old folks who no longer have need for money. But, if so, when they pass away that land could be up for grabs and in all likelihood end up being clear cut. I was thinking if we could get in touch with the owners and explain our objectives, they might be willing to consider selling."

"There's a quite a few if's there," Adam grinned at him.

"Maybe but Leo is already checking into it and you know Burns, he doesn't do anything unless there is a dollar to be made. If he got his claws into it, he'd sell every goddamned tree on the property to the highest bidder."

Adam stared out the window overlooking the eighteenth green. His thinking hadn't even progressed to the idea of purchasing land just to preserve it.

"If we did go on the trip it would at least give us a chance to have a close look at it," Wes continued. "I understand it's a size-able chunk still in it's original state. Preserving that kind of property certainly has to be in line with our group philosophy."

"If there's any possible way of doing that I'm with you. Okay let's do the trip. At least now we have more reason to. Besides we've been doing it for the past ten years. I guess we owe it to them just for that reason. But I'll be making it clear that this will be my last one."

"It will be mine too. I'll call Will and confirm it tonight. Oh we're leaving Saturday morning in Leo's SUV and should be back sometime Wednesday."

That's the only stipulation," Adam grinned. "I'm going to be back for Thursday's meeting if I have to walk.

CHAPTER 4

They had been on the road for over eight hours when Adam decided to question Leo Burns about the location.

"Understand it's privately owned," Adam said. "Did you get permission to hunt on it?"

"Couldn't find out who to ask," the stocky Burns replied. "I tried all the usual sources but I just drew blanks. Didn't have enough time to keep digging, so I thought we'd chance it anyway."

"Well let's hope to god they don't rattle us with a trespassing charge," Wes said. "You should've made damn certain we had permission before we left."

"Well what the hell was I supposed to do?" Leo fired back. "I checked every source I could think of. The B.C. land titles office weren't even able to dig it up when I called. Said they'd get back to me but we were leaving. I couldn't wait."

An animosity had always existed between these two and at times such as this it would come to a head. Adam often wondered why they continued keeping the same company since they disagreed on almost everything.

Wanting to head off a full blown fight Adam quickly intervened by saying, "I hear it's raw timber covered land that hasn't been touched by loggers."

"Yeah that's right. We flew over it about a month ago," Leo said and after staring out a window for a few seconds added, "a person could make a killing if he owned that chunk of ground."

"Yeah and help kill the rest of the world," Wes Scott blared at him.

"What the hell's with you Scott? Wife kick you outta bed last night?"

Adam quickly interrupted again. "Thinking about trying to buy it Leo?"

"Oh who knows. I'd first have to find out who to make an offer to and right now that's a mystery."

Adam realized that Leo's response really meant he was carrying out an aggressive investigation and if the land was available he would purchase it. He was a ruthless businessman who had made a fortune on land speculation and one could be certain if he was considering anything at all it had a lot of profit potential.

His thoughts were interrupted by Wes pointing out that they had just entered a heavily logged area. Dozens of clear cut strips dotted the mountainsides like giant golf course fairways.

"That is a pitiful sight," Wes said. "We're heading down the tube at breakneck speed and the bastards just keep pressing on the accelerator."

"What the hell's wrong with progress?" Leo said. "That stuff'll regrow."

"Not before we all suffocate," Wes shot back.

"Hey look," this time it was Willis Clarke who broke into their bickering. "Check to the northwest. That must be the area you two are fighting about. Notice how the clearcutting stops near the edge of it and if my map's right, that's right where we're hunting too."

A few minutes later he swung the SUV off the main road and on to a rough rutted trail that took them right into the heavy forest. For the next twenty minutes they drove through the thickest woods Adam had ever seen in his life. At times the mass of evergreen boughs overhead blocked out the sunlight completely lending a kind of surrealness to the atmosphere.

"This is pure beauty," Wes Scott said. "I've never seen anything like it."

"It's a pure fortune," Leo grunted. "Let's find a campsite before Scott's romanticizing makes me puke."

"For Christ's sake break it up you two," Adam barked finally losing his patience. "If you keep this bullshit up we might as well turn around and head home right now."

For some reason that Adam never understood they both respected him and when he lost his cool it seemed to be all that was needed to pour water on their fire. They both nodded in agreement and lapsed into silence.

CHAPTER 5

Since they were unfamiliar with the area, they decided to set up a campsite that would be visible no matter which way they went. They finally found a suitable spot at the base of a small cliff with several large pine trees growing on top.

"Those trees should be visible for two miles in any direction," Willis Clarke remarked after they got settled in. "I bet everybody is ready for a good stiff drink," he added pulling a bottle of whiskey from his backpack.

"None for me," Adam said.

"Me neither," Wes said.

"What the hell's with you two? You haven't reformed on us have you?"

"No," Adam laughed. "I would just like some supper first. A drink on an empty stomach would knock me for a loop."

"That was the idea."

"Well go for it, I'm going to fix us something to eat."

The next morning dawned crystal clear and warm for mid-November.

Adam had always enjoyed getting out into the wilderness and immersing himself in natural surroundings. The smell of frying sausage and eggs and the aroma of coffee on a campfire added to the pleasure of the experience although, this time, his enjoyment was tainted by the distressful news the environmental group had revealed two days earlier.

Wes Scott had arisen early too and was helping with the preparation of breakfast when a badly hung over Willis Clarke managed to drag himself out of his tent. He and Leo had caroused late into the night arguing over everything from government spending to golf scores and disposed of two bottles of whiskey in the process.

"It's mostly your fault," Willis slurred as he poured himself a cup of coffee and used both hands to prevent spilling most of it before he got it up to his mouth. "If you two would've helped us out with the drinking, we wouldn't had to do it all by ourselves,"

"I'd say your aim might be a little off right now Will," Adam said between bites of his breakfast. "Sure you don't want to crawl back in the sleeping bag a little longer."

"Sounds like a plan," he said shaking his head to clear away the cobwebs. "Besides I'll likely have to give Burns artificial respiration to get his heart started again. You two go ahead and when we're ready we'll radio you."

He finished the coffee and squirmed back in through the tent flaps and within minutes was snoring again.

Wes shook his head and said, "they do it every year. I've often wondered why they bother to bring their rifles along."

"I hope to god they don't try using them in the shape they're in," Adam answered as he began clearing away the breakfast utensils.

"Adam if you want to head out I'll finish up here. You made most of the breakfast anyway and I kind of think those other two are going to need one of us here to remind them who they are when they do finally get up. Besides I could even slap Burns around for a while and he probably wouldn't remember it."

"Sure you don't mind?"

"Slappin' him around? Hell no, I'll enjoy it."

"You know what I meant," Adam answered laughing.

"Yeah I do. But I bet the goddamned sidewinder knows more about this land than he's letting on. He's likely already been talking to the owners and then peddled us that bullshit about not being able to find out who they are."

"Maybe," Adam said. "But this time he might have some competition. I'm interested in it too."

"I'm with you. Now why don't you head out and take a look around. Give me a shout on the radio later and we'll make arrangements to connect up somewhere."

Adam was grateful for the opportunity not only to examine the countryside but to be alone for a while. A hundred questions about the environmental issues were buzzing around in his brain and quiet time in the forest would give him a chance to do some concentrated thinking.

The beauty of this wilderness was intoxicating. The area was genuine old growth forest and in his mind it would be criminal to cut down even one tree. There were heavy stands of both evergreen and deciduous trees interspersed with an occasional glade. The undergrowth was lush and varied even though it was November. Moss covered boulders were numerous often serving as a perch for an indignant squirrel scolding Adam for intruding on his domain. This kind of natural beauty was constantly under threat by profit hungry logging companies who cared only for the dollar value of a tree.

As he walked along soaking up the tranquility of his surroundings, he became even more committed to playing an active role in preserving what was left of nature.

The squelching two way radio shattered his peaceful reverie. It was Wes Scott calling to say he had finally revived their two companions but it would likely be a while before they could walk straight, so they would hang in at camp until Adam returned.

"I'll be back around noon for some lunch," Adam replied. "I

didn't bring any food with me."

"See you then."

He made his way to a nearby knoll and after a quick scan of the horizon, spotted the landmark that identified the camp location. Checking his watch he found it was only nine so he decided to keep going for a while longer. He was seeing the wilderness from a much different perspective now and wanted to stay immersed in it for as long as he could.

Tree covered valleys and hills punctuated by ponds and streams; even a few small waterfalls greeted him as he continued along. Occasionally a startled deer would vanish into the thick forest and once a lone moose casually walked away as though annoyed by Adam's intrusion.

Birds seemed to be everywhere filling the air with a symphony of sounds that he was hearing for the first time. The lure of the forest caused him to lose track of time and upon checking his watch again found it was nearly twelve. "Damnit, where'd the time go?" he wondered. Climbing on top of a huge boulder to get his bearings revealed only solid forest. The landmark was no longer in sight. Digging in his backpack he pulled out his binoculars but found they were of little value giving him only an enlarged view of trees. The sun had disappeared behind thick dark clouds that had come up suddenly between mountain peaks making him uncertain of his directions. He scrounged in his backpack for his compass but after a thorough search realized he must've forgotten to bring it.

"Wes, do you read me," he spoke into the radio. Do you read, Wes?"

After his third call, he received some squelching crackles and then silence. Several more attempts produced similar electronic crackling but nothing coherent. "Damnit!" he said outloud angry at himself for not paying more attention to the time."

He climbed down off the boulder and started back in what he thought was the right direction, but after several hundred yards realized he was lost. A pang of fear nudged the pit of his stomach. He tried the radio again but this time it was completely silent.

"The cell phone," he thought digging the small instrument out of his backpack. But after several failed attempts he realized he was probably tucked in an area between mountains that blocked off any link to a tower.

Heavy clouds were moving in more rapidly and the temperature was starting to drop. "Of all the goddam stupidity," he thought.

Walking faster now he searched his surroundings trying to discover something he recognized. A clump of trees that he might have passed, a stream, a glade, but the more he searched, the more confused he became.

The wind had picked up suddenly and dark clouds now blanked out the blue sky completely.

"Calm down Adam," he said to himself. "This is no time to panic." But panic was exactly what he was starting to feel. Suddenly remembering his rifle, he unstrapped the weapon from across his back and quickly got off three S.O.S. shots then listened for a response but all he could hear was the loud rush of the wind through the trees as it picked up speed. He fired three more shots, but realized it was a futile effort. The wind was roaring now and bringing with it driving sheets of snow.

He huddled down behind a huge boulder for protection trying to decide his next move. Fortunately he had dressed himself in appropriate clothing that included a light hooded parka and he knew there was a liner for the parka in his backpack. After zipping the liner in place and drawing his hoodstrings in tight, he stood up to face what had now become a blizzard. Blinding white sheets of snow raced among the trees reducing his visibility to only a few yards. He dropped down behind the protection of the boulder again and sat staring at small drifts starting to form against tree trunks and in dense undergrowth. The storm seemed to have come up suddenly from out of nowhere. They had checked on the weather forecast for the area before leaving Edmonton. It had predicted cool temperatures but clear skies for the entire weekend.

Desperate now, he realized his choices were limited. He could stay put and hope his companions might come searching, but that would be unlikely since they would get just as lost as he was. Besides he would get dangerously cold by sitting idle in one spot for any length of time. He had no choice. He must keep trying to find his way back. He guessed that the storm had approached from the west and he knew he had gone south from the campsite, so with the wind on his left, he should be going north. It was a gamble, but he had run out of options, so after pulling on a pair of gloves and strapping his rifle and backpack on again, he started out praying he had made the right choice.

He was grateful for the protection of the forest. Walking in open country in a blizzard of this magnitude would've been unbearable. Snow was piling up rapidly making walking more difficult. He stopped occasionally to catch his breath and reconfirm wind direction, but quickly resumed travel again. Being stranded in the wilderness overnight in a blizzard would likely be fatal. He tried to keep that thought out of his mind, but as he struggled along through the ever deepening snow, it was all he could think about.

He checked his watch to find it was nearly 4:00 PM. It had taken him three hours to get out to where he decided to turn around. He knew the return trip would be slower because of the storm if he was indeed even going in the right direction at all. If he was he should soon encounter the camp. Another half hour of trudging revealed only more of the same solid forest within his limited range of vision. Exhausted he stopped and leaned against the tree that provided some protection from the storm. He was fighting panic now knowing that if he gave into it, his chances of survival would be slim. The blizzard had continued increasing in intensity until it seemed like all hell had been unleashed. He allowed his body to slide down slowly against the tree trunk until he was sitting in the snow. Is this where it ends for Adam Finlay, he wondered. This seemed like an ironic twist of fate. Would his life be snuffed out just when he discovered a cause had really made it worth living. He sat motionless watching the snow build small drifts around his high top hunting boots when suddenly a noise loud enough to be heard over the roar of the wind caused him to struggle back up to his feet.

He couldn't be certain which direction it came from and it might have only been a falling tree, but then it might also be a gunshot made by a member of his hunting party.

"Is anyone there?" he called as loud as he could. He waited for a few moments and called again. "Is anyone out there?"

After his third attempt he heard another loud report and this time for an instant thought he caught sight of something through the dancing snow.

"Hey is anyone there?" he called charging toward the vague form. After only a few yards he had to stop and gasp for air. Other than a small accumulation of deadfall directly ahead of him, he could see nothing else. Breathing heavily he removed a glove and wiped the mixture of snow and perspiration off his forehead. Panic started to creep over him as he strained once again to probe his white surroundings. The panic increased and he had to fight the urge to start running and to continue running as far as the deep snow would allow and when he could go no farther, collapse into the snow.

Wiping his forehead again he replaced the glove and took several deep breaths in an attempt to calm down. He realized he must get a grip on himself if he had any hope of survival. Adjusting his backpack he resumed trudging through the snow finding it now more difficult than before.

Every few minutes he called out the names of members of his group but in this wild blizzard he could hardly hear himself.

After another hour of struggling he started to become aware of another problem. With only breakfast in his stomach, exhaustion from the lack of food was beginning to overtake him and he knew fatigue was soon going to terminate the distance he could go. He pulled back his sleeve cuff to check the time. It was after 5:00.

He must find shelter. Further travel would sap his remaining strength greatly reducing any chance of survival he had left. He resumed slogging forward searching now for a spot that would at least serve as a windbreak. The wind began to slow down but along with it came a sharp temperature drop increasing the urgency even more to find some shelter. His strength was diminishing with every step and he fell heavily into the deep snow several times. Each fall presented a greater challenge to get back to his feet and he knew he could go little farther.

A nearby thick stand of evergreen trees loomed in front of him and appeared as though they would at least afford protection from the wind. He struggled toward the trees half walking and half crawling when he heard the loud crack as the tree snapped from the force of the wind and began to fall. It had been off to one side and he saw nothing until it was too late. Fortunately it was only the top portion that hit him as it came crashing down but that was enough to knock him heavily into the snow and momentarily unconscious.

He lay motionless for a few moments then slowly regaining his senses called out as loud as he could through the maze of spruce bows but all that he emitted was a raspy squawk. Sharp pain shot up his right leg when he squirmed to free himself and he had to stop to retain consciousness.

With his one free arm he managed to push aside some of the thorny branches that were scratching at his face and then tried twisting his upper body to see if he could move at all but the fallen tree had him pinned securely beneath its weight.

Wild panic gripped him and he began thrashing wildly but this only brought on more pain. It was excruciating this time and he had to stop as quickly as he started to avoid losing consciousness once again.

Everything had happened so fast that the first few moments were vague. But now he began to realize just how serious his situation was. He likely had a broken leg. His left arm was pinned under him and he was unable to move it. There was pain in his right arm but it was not immobilized. His left leg seemed to be okay but crisscrossed spruce bows held it captive.

Wracking his brain in despair he realized his only hope left would be to attract the attention of somebody else if there happened to be anyone out there near enough to hear him. It was a slim chance and he knew he would have to work fast. The intensity of the wind had lessened even more which was in his favor but the rapidly dropping temperatures would soon incapacitate him completely eliminating his one last glimmer of hope.

He began tugging with his right hand at the shoulder strap that he hoped his rifle was still attached to. His glove made the work awkward so he seized the tips of it between his teeth and yanked it off. His fingers were becoming numb from the cold but he managed to slip his thumb under the strap and by tugging and twisting his body as much as he could he felt the weapon move. A few more desperate tugs brought it free and he stopped for a moment to catch his breath. It was completely dark now so he had to feel up and down the length of the rifle to determine which end was which. Struggling with all the strength he had left he managed to pull the gun barrel up through the maze of branches with his one free hand and stand the stock as firmly as he could in the snow. His fingers were now so numb they would barely move. With agonizing slowness he released the safety latch and inserted a finger into the trigger guard. It was an expensive automatic rifle and he got off three S.O.S. shots without difficulty.

The wind had dropped now to little more than a breeze and the shots reverberated eerily through the dense forest. He listened for a moment not really knowing what he was listening for. Then he began firing the gun again and continued until the clicking hammer indicated the chamber was empty.

Knowing he could do nothing more he let the weapon drop away and laid his head back against a bough. If nobody was close enough to hear the gunfire then this spot in the snow pinned under a fallen spruce tree would be his deathbed.

He made an awkward attempt at crossing himself with his one free hand and began saying a prayer but before he could finish the unconsciousness he had been fighting off now engulfed him completely.

CHAPTER 6

"Can you hear me Mr. Finlay?"

The gentle female voice seemed at first to come from a distance and then draw closer as she repeated the question.

"Mr. Finlay, can you hear me?"

He struggled to open his eyes but the heaviness of his lids resisted. Her outline was vague, appearing at first as nothing more than one of many shadows in the room. The pale orange flickering light coming from some unfamiliar source on a wall was inadequate to reveal anything in detail.

Slowly he coaxed his eyes fully open and was able to identify the woman separately from her surroundings. She was hovering over him but in the dim light the softness of her features made him wonder if she was real or had he died and was now in some other place.

"Where am I?" he finally managed to ask in a raspy whisper.

"You're safe and you're going to be okay. Just relax."

"But what…" he stopped talking abruptly and winced from the sharp pain in his leg. Then the memories came flooding back; trying to find shelter from the raging storm, being trapped under a fallen tree and the struggle to get out. Knowing now he was still very much alive, he asked again. "Where am I?"

"This particular spot is called Ingram Mountain but you won't find it on any map. Prince George is the nearest large center and it's about a hundred miles away. May I ask where you were going?"

"Hunting big game. I was with a group of four."

Feeling nauseated and weak, he stopped talking and closed his eyes.

"There's no need to explain right now," she said. "You've had a rough time. You need rest."

She placed a hand on his forehead and he managed to open his eyes just enough to see her looking down at him with concern.

"When we first brought you in you couldn't stop shivering," she said. "But now you're a bit warm."

She dipped a face cloth into a bowl of water sitting on a night stand and gently sponged his face.

"Do you feel like eating anything?" she asked repeating the process.

He shook his head. "I'm thirsty."

She poured a glass of water from a large porcelain jug and held it up to his lips. After several swallows, he leaned back and closed his eyes again.

"That's a nasty break you have. It's going to take some time to heal. I've got it in a wooden support for now. We'll splint it as soon as the swelling goes down.

"Splint?" he repeated in a weak voice wondering if he had heard right.

"Just relax Mr. Finlay. We'll talk about it later. You're going to be okay. You have a few other bruises and some frost bite. Nothing too serious, but that leg could be painful for a while. Here's something that will help and I've left a bottle of aspirins by the water jug. Don't hesitate to use them."

The pain in his leg had worsened and he was vaguely aware of pain just under his right collar bone. He swallowed the small brown tablet without question then quickly drank another glass of water to rid his mouth of the bitter taste it left.

"Good medicine always tastes terrible," she said with a smile. "But it should help. It'll make you drowsy, so don't fight it. You need the sleep."

The woman's gentle voice was soothing, but feeling too sick to care about anything he paid little attention to her or his surroundings. At that moment he wanted nothing more than to fade into a deep sleep and stay there.

Drowsiness soon descended on him from the unfamiliar medication which also seemed to lessen the pain in his leg. He wondered hazily about his three hunting companions. His last thought as he succumbed to the potency of the pill was hoping that they had not attempted to search for him.

CHAPTER 7

He was awakened by a noisy clatter coming from across the room and raised his head just enough to see an elderly man hunched down in front of a wood burning heater cranking vigorously on a handle. It was broad daylight now and he could easily make out what had only been shadows when he was last awake.

Showers of sparks and small puffs of smoke escaped through the top of the antique pot bellied device with every turn of the crank filling the room with the pungent odor of burning wood. Finally satisfied with his efforts the man pulled his lean frame up to a standing position and glanced over at Adam. He was dressed in a plaid shirt and dark trousers held up by a pair of wide suspenders.

"Morning," he said in a gruff voice. "Name's Andy."

Adam nodded in silent response wondering what his connection was to the woman he'd first met and how many other persons might be living in this primitive dwelling.

"Brought you some warm water and towels," he said pointing to a large metal pan and jug sitting on the night table.

"Toilet's in here," he added opening a narrow dark brown door beside the heater. Then crossing the room to a crude home-made cabinet he pulled out a pair of crutches and leaned them against the wall near the bed.

"Ever use these things?" he asked running bony fingers through a thick mop of unruly gray hair.

Adam shook his head.

"Ain't hard to handle. They were my Pa's 'fore he died. You'll need em to git around."

He stared down at Adam for a moment from under bushy eyebrows. His eyes were deep set in a lean chiseled face that appeared to be permanently etched in an expression of grimness. A heavy stubble of whiskers suggested he didn't place much importance on shaving.

"Well gotta finish chores," he said unhooking his thumbs from under the wide suspenders. "Anything else you need?"

"Could you tell me what time it is?"

"Around nine."

"Nine?" Adam repeated to be certain he had heard right.

"Yup."

"Uh, okay. Thanks."

The old man turned and quickly walked out leaving Adam shocked at the length of time he had slept.

"Must've been one hell of a potent pill she gave me," he thought.

The sun streaming through one of the two windows in the room signaled the end of the storm, but even from his reclining position in the bed he could tell that huge amounts of snow had fallen. The cedar trees visible through the window were heavily blanketed in the soft white fluff reminding him of an oil painting that had once hung on his office wall.

"Hope they've graduated to motorized snow plows in this part of the country," he thought grinning wryly. "They're sure gonna need them."

Deciding to attempt a visit to the washroom he struggled to a sitting position on the edge of the bed. It seemed that every inch of his body was in pain and unexpected dizziness from his weakened physical condition forced him to drop his head onto his knees. The feeling soon passed but he decided to remain sitting before attempting the trek on crutches across the shiny linoleum covered floor.

Although only mildly interested he was struck by the antique nature of the room and its contents. It had ridiculous looking high baseboards above which the lower half of the wall was covered in a coarse green material and the upper half an off white wallboard or plaster. Enveloping the entire room near the ceiling was a dark stained narrow molding from which was suspended several black and white portrait style pictures. He was able to make out the details of the one nearest him that revealed four persons; two men and two women dressed in clothing reminiscent of the 1920's. Both men had handle bar mustaches and were seated while the gowned women stood behind them. All wore sober expressions appearing as though the picture taking session was an ordeal, they had to suffer through and would be relieved when it was over with.

He had seen pictures like this but seldom so prominently displayed.

Shrugging his shoulders he reached for the crutches and made his way slowly and cautiously to the washroom. Once inside the tiny candle lit cubicle he was faced with more surprises. The only thing recognizable about the toilet was the seat. Otherwise it was nothing more than a dark metal container with a pipe running up through the ceiling and in place of what might have been a sink stood a wooden stand with a large porcelain bowl and water jug sitting on top.

"My god," he thought grimly. "Maybe I did die and I still don't realize it."

A large rectangular mirror hung on the wall over the small stand and when he looked into it he was in for another shock. The only features familiar were his gray speckled brown hair and brown eyes and even they were severely swollen. He parted his bruised lips as much as he could to check his teeth but they seemed intact.

"Guess I'm lucky to be alive at all," he thought as he ran his fingers gently over the scratches and bruises on his face.

Struggling with the antiquated utensils he managed to complete his washroom needs and make his way awkwardly back to the refuge of the bed.

Still groggy from the pill the woman had given him the night before he began dozing but was soon awakened again by noises coming from some other part of the house. Doors opened and closed several times accompanied by the clanging of metal against metal.

"Mr. Finlay," the woman called knocking on his door. "May I come in?"

"Yes. Come on."

"Good morning," she said cheerfully pushing the door open with one hand and balancing a tray on the other.

"I took a chance that you would like some coffee. Did I guess right?"

He smiled faintly and nodded

"How do you feel this morning?" she asked filling a cup from a gray metal pot.

"Sore."

"I'm sure you are but you look much better. Did you sleep well?"

"I slept very well but I could pass for a circus clown without a costume. I made the mistake of looking at my face in the mirror," he said sipping the dark brew.

"Oh that will all heal. They are just bruises.

"Let's have a look at that leg," she said pulling back a corner of the blanket to expose the injured limb.

"It's still quite swollen. It'll take a few days to go down so we'll just let it be. Now I think it's time we got properly introduced."

"My name is Jennifer Ingram. My brother Andy and I live here.

I know your name is Adam Finlay and you're from Edmonton. I hope you'll forgive us for checking your wallet. We thought we should just in case we had to … notify someone."

"I understand," he said looking into her hazel eyes for a moment. Then turning away said, "I'm indebted to you both. I likely wouldn't be alive now if you hadn't found me."

He paused and took another sip of coffee then asked. "How did you manage to find me. I thought I was done for."

"Andy heard your rifle shots. He was out doing chores. Actually you were only a few hundred feet from the yard. He couldn't pry you lose from under that spruce tree by himself so he came back and got me, an axe, and the toboggan. It was a little awkward in the deep snow with only lantern light, but he managed to cut off the section of the tree that had you pinned down and then we pulled you free. We towed you in on the toboggan and thawed you out," she said smiling. "The rest you probably remember."

"Vaguely. Thanks for the pill. It was a potent one. I slept right through until I heard your brother doing something with that heater."

"Oh you've already met Andy. I'm sorry I meant to be here to introduce you. I was out gathering eggs. I thought he was still outside too. Anyone who doesn't know Andy might find him a bit backward. He's quite a loner. Would sooner be out tending to animals than talking to people."

"No problem," he said and for the first time took stock of the woman. She was probably in her late thirties and like her brother wore a plaid shirt and dark slacks.

"Must be this years style for mountain dwellers," he thought sarcastically. At least it looked better on her than him. Her cheeks, still red from the cold outdoors, lent a wholesomeness to her overall countenance and her full figured body was in sharp contrast to the coveted slenderness of most style conscious city women. Despite that she possessed refined feminine features that he found attractive.

"I'll bet you're ready for some breakfast?" she said. "How does ham and eggs sound?"

"Good. Thank you. Look I will certainly pay you for my lodging and any other costs…"

"Oh you will, will you? Well now let's just see what we can come up with," she said with an impish smile. "As soon as you're up and around you can help Andy milk cows, feed pigs and clean barns. I can use a hand canning vegetables and then there's wood to be split and eggs to be gathered."

"Okay, okay," he said unable to suppress a chuckle. "Would you just settle for money?"

Definitely not. You must at least learn how to milk cows before you leave."

"Well then I pity the cows."

"Don't worry. They can defend themselves."

He laughed out loud. It just happened before he was fully aware of it. She laughed with him and for a brief, strange moment everything about the whole scene felt familiar.

After their laughter had subsided she looked at him with a gentle but penetrating gaze that seemed to reach right through his tough exterior and touch a spot in him that even he didn't know existed.

"I've just had payment enough Mr. Finlay," she finally said and slowly picked up the tray. She looked at him for a moment longer then turned and walked out.

He stared at the closed door and shivered slightly. Something had been stirred inside him that felt familiar, but yet stayed just outside his grasp. He struggled trying to retrieve it but without success. It was a fleeting memory that teetered for a moment on the edge of total recall only to slip back into oblivion again. He shuddered at the strange haunting feeling that accompanied it and wondered if this whole weird experience was starting to affect his sanity. The feeling gradually subsided and after eating some breakfast he relaxed and dozed off to sleep.

He awakened with a start from a dream that had him battling

the blizzard in the forest once again and trying desperately to reunite with his companions. Momentarily forgetting his broken leg, he sat up quickly but dropped back on to the bed just as quickly from the pain.

Shaking the sleep out of his head, he realized they would have a search party out looking for him which up until now he hadn't thought of.

"Miss Ingram," he called loudly. "Miss Ingram."

She quickly appeared in the doorway with a look of concern on her face.

"I'm okay," he assured her. "But I need to use your phone. I must let someone know Im safe because they'll be out searching for me."

"We don't have a telephone, but Andy can go down to our neighbors on horseback and have them place a call for you."

"You don't have a phone?" he blurted. "My God," he thought. "I've gotta get the hell out of here as quick as I can. This is worse than dying."

Out loud he said, "would you bring me my back pack. I have a cell phone."

A quick check of the small instrument revealed that the battery was very low which meant if he could make any connections at all he would have to do so in a hurry. His mother answered on the third ring and when she realized it was him, she began crying and talking at the same time. "Thank god, Adam. Thank god. I've been nearly insane from worry."

"I've gotta make this fast Mom. My battery is very low. Now other than a broken leg I'm okay so don't worry. I was rescued by some folks who live here in the mountains."

"Oh I'm so relieved dear. I've been praying day and night for your safety."

"I'll call again in a few days and make arrangements to get back Mom."

The connection was cutting in and out now and he was only

receiving snippets of her response. Finally the crackling phone went silent indicating a complete discharge of the battery. Exhaling slowly he snapped it shut hoping that his mother had picked up enough of the message to eliminate the worry she was so prone to.

"If you're concerned," Jenny said after he told her about his interrupted conversation. "We can still have Andy go down to Hank and Beatie's and place another call."

"She knows I'm okay. That much I'm certain of. But perhaps when the snow is cleared away I could send out another message to let them know where I am and have someone pick me up."

"Of course," she answered smiling faintly. "Anything else you need right now?"

"Oh no and thank you so much for everything. I'm deeply indebted to you both."

"No more than we are indebted to you," she said in a quiet voice.

"Pardon?"

She looked at him for a moment, then without answering turned and walked out.

Baffled by her comment he stared at the closed door wondering just how they were indebted to him.

"Oh well," he thought. "I'll soon be out of here. I guess it doesn't really matter whether I understand anything about them.

CHAPTER 8

"How long do you think it will be before they snowplow your road out?" he asked her when she brought in his breakfast tray the next morning.

"It'll be a while. We're the only ones living up here."

"What if you had an emergency; illness or something?"

"Oh we keep in touch with the Meades, the neighbors I mentioned yesterday. They're a mile or so down the road from us. They farm in the valley. Young Henry, their boy, comes up regularly to see how we're doing and when the road is open I often go down in the cutter. They're great neighbors. Always ready to help out anyway they can. Beatie, that's Henry's mother and I often exchange baked goods. Her blueberry pie is the very best in the valley…"

"Excuse me," he interrupted. "What is a cutter?"

"It's a horse drawn sleigh. I prefer it to horseback, but right now the snow is so deep we can't use it. Andy rides out on Sampson if there's any urgency.

"You have only the one horse?"

"Yes, but he's getting old. We don't use him now any more than we have to. I guess we should get a young one but we've had him since birth and gotten so attached to him. He seems like family. It's going to be sad when he goes."

"My god," he thought. "I wonder if they even know what year it is."

She was giving him a smile and the penetrating gaze once again but wanting to avoid the strange sensation that it had brought on earlier he turned away.

"Would you like to hobble out to the kitchen later?" she asked still looking at him intently.

"I guess so," he said glancing back at her and thinking sarcastically maybe they just didn't see other people very often.

"Uh, I'll finish eating and then make a trip to the washroom and...

"Oh of course. I'm sorry," she said her cheeks reddening "And please forgive me for staring."

She turned and walked quickly toward the door but before exiting said, "Just call when you're ready. I'll come and give you a hand." She paused for a moment then added. "You must think we seldom see other people. That was rude of me."

Before he could respond she smiled and walked out leaving him looking at the closed door in bewilderment. It was as though she had read his thoughts. Shaking his head he scolded himself for such an idea. He had to get a grip on himself and start viewing things logically.

For some reason since he had regained consciousness in this unfamiliar place he felt as though he was perched on the edge of some sort of fantasy. That made little sense but it was the only way he could describe his feelings.

Feeling a flicker of the flame that had once driven him completely, he resolved to regain at least some of the composure that had been his trademark in the business world. Even though life had delivered a few crushing blows during the past two years he most certainly was not going to be intimidated by an archaic pair of mountain dwellers who seemed unaware of the outside world.

He would vigorously assert himself for whatever length of time he was stuck in this place that the creator had obviously forgotten about and in the bargain brighten up their vintage lifestyle by introducing them to the twenty-first century.

After eating his breakfast and taking care of washroom needs he decided to flaunt his independence by making his way out to the kitchen without her help. All went well until he attempted to open the door. Being inexperienced with the use of crutches, turning the knob, and pulling the door open all in one motion proved too much for him and he fell heavily to the floor. The racket and his instinctive yelp brought his benefactor running from some other room.

"What happened Mr. Finlay. Are you all right?" she asked kneeling down quickly and helping him in his attempt to sit up.

His pride suppressed any further outburst but the pain induced by bumping the broken leg as he fell was excruciating.

"Why didn't you call me to help you?" she asked examining the limb and making adjustments to the wooden support. "I hope you didn't aggravate that fracture. It's going to take long enough to knit as it is. What in the world were you thinking about?" she asked in an angry tone.

Gritting his teeth he just shook his head and clasped a hand over his mouth. With his eyes closed he rocked back and forth and moaned as inaudibly as he could. This seemed to arouse sympathy in her and she said in a more gentle voice. "I'm sorry. Don't try talking. Just stay where you are until you feel better."

The subsiding pain was replaced with anger and he cursed himself for his 'idiot blunder'. "That was an impressive display of independence," he thought. Exhaling slowly he reached for the crutches.

"Let me get those," she said retrieving the wooden supports and leaning them against a wall.

"If you're ready I'll help you up. Do you want to go back and lie down or…"

"The table," he said pointing to the large oval wooden structure in the middle of the room and with her assistance made his way slowly over to be seated in a high back wooden chair. She pulled a faded yellow footstool out from a corner and gently positioned it under his broken leg.

"Thanks," he muttered breathing heavily then added, knowing it was only a lame excuse for his accident. "That linoleum is damned slippery."

"Yes of course," she said placing a cushion between his heel and the wooden surface of the foot rest. "How do you feel now?"

"Alright, I guess."

"Well it's fortunate you didn't break anything else and I'm sorry for snapping at you. I was really concerned for a second."

"Forget it," he grunted still berating himself for his stupidity. Metaphorically Adam Finlay didn't make mistakes. He didn't fall. In fact he never even stumbled. He was always the one looking down on someone who did, but had never been as willing to help them back up as she just had.

I've made a fresh pot of coffee, are you ready for a cup?"

"Yeah. Thanks," he said wishing she wouldn't be so damned nice and understanding. If she would just bitch at him he could let off some steam. But aside from saying she would lay out mats on the slippery floor she made no further mention of the incident.

After pouring the coffee she said "if you'll excuse me for a while I'm going to finish washing dishes."

He nodded and sipped the dark brew which was tasty despite the fact it was made on top of a very old cast iron, wood burning cook stove. The antique appliance looked like it had been salvaged from a museum, but then so did all the furnishings.

He watched her for a few minutes fascinated by a process he had only heard his grandmother talk about. She deftly scrubbed the dishes in one metal pan then dipped them into another and finally out onto a drain rack perched at an angle that allowed excess water to run back into the first pan. She worked quickly and soon had the job completed.

"How about a refill?" she asked wiping her hands on a tea towel and bringing the coffeepot to the table once again. "I'll finish up and then I'll join you."

He nodded and watched as she began drying the pile of dishes on the drain board.

He shook his head in amazement. He had heard of persons still living this antiquated lifestyle but never thought he would actually meet any.

Having recovered somewhat from the demoralization of the fall he relaxed and began surveying the rest of the room. There was no evidence of a modern appliance or convenience anywhere. The entire kitchen and likely the rest of the house, could have served effectively as a prop for a western movie. A large box filled with blocks of wood stood in a corner and beside the stove a stand with a galvanized pail on top out of which she had dipped water to make coffee. Beside the pail was a white enameled hand washing dish and several brightly colored towels dangled from hooks in the wall.

His scrutiny of the room was interrupted by her brother coming in from outside carrying two pails of what looked like milk. He nodded briefly to Adam as he removed his heavy outerwear then carried the two containers through a door tucked into a corner of the room and pulled it shut behind himself.

"Separator room," Jenny said noticing his puzzled look. "We store milk and cream in there after it's been separated. Keep the door shut so the room stays cool. We sell cream to folks in town and have to make sure it doesn't go sour.

He wasn't sure whether he nodded or shook his head. It was likely a combination of both. His association with milk and cream was limited to cardboard containers of the stuff stored in the fridge which his housekeeper always took care of.

He was startled by something rubbing gently on his good leg and looked down to see an orange and white cat fearlessly caressing the leg with its sleek body.

"Trina come away," Jenny said catching sight of the cat and glancing at Adam.

"I'm sorry Mr. Finlay. She doesn't readily take to people but you seem to be an exception.

"It's okay." He had never been an animal lover. Pets were always something he could take or leave. He had inherited a small dog when his family split up which his housekeeper had become more attached to than he had. An occasional rub on the head was all the dog could expect from him. But this cat seemed to stir something inside him. He even felt an urge to pick her up and pet her.

"She knows Andy's in with the milk and she'll soon get a bowl of it."

As if on cue the old man emerged from the separator room and sat a small metal container on the floor outside the door.

Meowing faintly "Trina" quickly trotted over and began consuming the white liquid with relish. He shivered slightly at the unfamiliar feelings he kept having. He had no objections to a dog, but until now he never had any desire for a cat.

"We've had her since birth," Jenny continued. "And she's terribly spoiled. Andy loves her dearly but he tries not to show it. In the summer she'll even go out and follow him around the yard when he's choring."

She draped the damp tea towel over the top of a metal shelf rising from the back of the stove which he later learned was called a warming oven.

"Can't get much more basic than this," he thought watching her next remove a stove lid and insert several blocks of wood.

A few wisps of smoke escaped as she replaced the heavy metal disk allowing a faint campfire like odor to waft through the air.

"Sorry," she said glancing over at him again. "I hope the smoke won't bother you."

He shook his head and kept watching as she gathered the clean tableware and carefully replaced it in a white wooden cupboard adorning a wall close to his bedroom door. Cups hung from hooks in the ceiling of the antique cabinet and plates leaned side by side in an orderly row against a backboard.

A low muffled drone began emitting from the separator room and once again she answered his unspoken question by explaining Andy had started the separator.

"He has to get it up to the right speed before he opens the milk spout. Otherwise the cream would be too thin."

He had no idea what she was talking about and knowing any further explanation would likely be wasted, he nodded and turned his attention back to inspecting the kitchen.

Two windows were cut into opposing walls each one consisting of six smaller panes separated vertically and horizontally by narrow wooden frames. Frilly colorful curtains tied back at the middle hung over the windows reminding him of a teahouse he had once dined at.

The walls were decorated with bright colored paper right from the baseboard to the ceiling and equally bright linoleum covered the floor. An archway led into what appeared to be a living room and another door on the same wall was shut. A stairway to an upper level was tucked into a corner and even though now broad daylight outside, he had to squint to make it out.

Two lantern style kerosene lamps hung from hooks in the ceiling which he soon learned required frequent "pumping up" in order to keep shedding adequate light at night.

Despite the antiquated nature of the place, it was impeccably kept. The woman obviously was a scrupulous housekeeper and her brother, when he did come in, followed suit.

The separator must have reached its normal operating speed because the drone had now leveled off at a high pitch and remained that way for the next ten minutes or so.

After wiping a few spots on the walls and sweeping the floor, she poured herself a cup of coffee and sat across the table from him.

"How does the leg feel now?" she asked cautiously sipping the hot brew.

"Pain's gone," he said taking a sip of his own coffee.

"Good. Perhaps we can try for the living room later. I'll stir up the fireplace and you can relax on the chesterfield if you want to. There are shelves of books in there too. You might find something of interest."

"Thanks. Have you seen any sign of a snow plow yet?"

"Oh no. It'll be a while. Hank Meade will likely open our road with his tractor anyway. He has a small blade on it to clean out his own yard and he usually gets up to our place before a snow-plow comes along. He can only make a narrow trail but we can drive the cutter out on it."

"We could get out though," he asked thinking about the environmental group he had recently joined.

"We could but I certainly wouldn't recommend that you travel anywhere for a while yet."

She took another sip of coffee then continued. "We'll be okay. We had a good garden last summer. Got lots of vegetables in store. We could get by for a couple of weeks without going into town. Got plenty of flour and sugar. I'm going to bake bread and churn butter today. Should bake a few pies too."

He decided not to ask how she "churned butter" knowing he probably wouldn't understand anyway, but he found their self sufficiency both intriguing and puzzling. It was a total departure from the only lifestyle he had ever known and he was curious as to why, in this day and age, they clung to it.

Just then Andy re-emerged from the separator room carrying the two pails he had taken in only now they were capped with fluffy white foam. Trina immediately jumped off Jenny's lap and ran over to rub against the old mountaineer's leg.

After donning his heavy parka he reached down and rubbed her head several times but abruptly straightened up and glanced over at Jenny and Adam. He quickly buttoned the coat and walked out with the pails leaving Trina sniffing at the closed door.

"I think it would devastate him if he thought anyone suspected he had some tenderness in him," Jenny said with a laugh.

"The cat seems to know it."

"So does every other animal we have. In the summer time he'll just milk the cows right where they happen to be grazing in the pasture and they quietly stand still and chew their cud until he's done."

"Must be very used to him."

"Partly, but most animals can readily sense the nature of a human.

Andy might fool us but he can't fool them."

Trying to sound as casual as he could he asked, "Is the power line close to your place?"

She looked at him with a puzzled expression for several seconds then answered.

"Oh you mean the electricity. I'm not really sure. I guess we've just never thought much about it. Anyway how about telling me something about Adam Finlay? I've told you about us. Now it's your turn."

"How could they not think about it?" he wondered when the rest of the country was almost totally dependent on electricity.

"I'm waiting Mr. Finlay," she said smiling sweetly.

"Not really much to tell."

"Oh I'll bet there is," she said and then quickly added. "We all have a story to tell."

He sighed and for a moment examined the red and yellow oil-cloth covering the kitchen table. The events of the past two days had shoved his other life into the background and he needed a moment to bring it back into focus. His struggle for survival out in the rugged wilderness had caused him to temporarily forget that he had made a commitment to help save it, but explaining that to these mountain dwellers would be redundant. They were already living in complete harmony with their surroundings.

"Well," he began slowly "the first half of my life was pretty regular stuff. I was heir to a property development company and after graduating university began working at it full time under my father's tutelage. Ten years later he developed a heart condition and had to back away from direct involvement at which point I assumed all management responsibilities. Dad passed away about six years later and I became sole owner and president of the company. Along the way I met this girl who eventually became my wife and we had had two kids: a boy and a girl. After fourteen years of marriage things went sour between us and we finally divorced. That's pretty well it.

"I'll bet there's more to tell," she said in a teasing voice.

For a moment he was tempted to ask her why the hell it should matter since they were total strangers, but he detected something more in her voice than just the usual female desire to have some gossip handy for when the girls got together if mountain women actually did that sort of thing.

"Mr. Finlay, I'm sorry," she suddenly blurted. "Your private life is none of my business. I didn't mean to pry. Please excuse me."

He studied her in silence for a moment. There was a certain uniqueness to this woman that he couldn't put his finger on. It was an ambiance that would not be ignored but also was not readily defined.

"No reason to apologize," he spoke quickly as she stood up from her chair. "I really don't have any objection to revealing my past. I guess I'm just curious as to why you would be interested. We are complete strangers."

"Yes of course," she said adding more wood to the cookstove and then kneeling down to squint at the heat indicator on the oven door. "Old gauge isn't too reliable anymore," she said smiling back at him. "I burned more than one batch of bread before I got used to it."

How quickly the tables had turned. Now he found himself wanting to tell her his story when the opportunity to do so seemed to have passed. Hoping to revive the conversation he asked, "You've lived here all your life?"

"All of it," she nodded pulling pans and trays out from a cupboard.

"Any siblings besides Andy?"

She stopped in the midst of dipping flour out of a bag and stared out the window for a moment. Finally resuming her work she said, "we had a younger brother Clarence. He died from leukemia when he was ten."

"Oh god I'm sorry," he said feeling uncomfortable. "Now it's my turn to apologize."

"Don't apologize for asking. It's been over twenty years since he passed. But at the time that the heartache was almost unbearable."

"I know the feeling well," he said.

"I know you do."

"Pardon?"

"You've lost someone close to you, haven't you?"

"How do you know that?"

"Well just now you said you know the feeling well, but besides it shows."

"Does it show that much?"

She nodded and said, "want to talk about it?"

He stared out a window wondering if reliving the story would revive memories of the heartache he had suffered back then. It had been devastating and he shuddered at the thought of telling it again.

The uniqueness of this woman, however, seemed to urge him to speak more openly than he ever had before.

As though sensing his conflict she spoke again, "I believe you took evasive action after the mishap and by that I mean you may have thrown yourself into your work or some other mission in an attempt to suppress the grieving as much as possible when you should have faced it headlong."

She stopped talking and after adding more ingredients to the large pan turned to face him again with a smile. "Don't worry I'm not going to preach to you. I won't mention it again if you prefer I don't."

"Actually I prefer you do. You've already told me things that no one else has. I would like to understand more about facing my sorrow head on. It seems pretty damned hard to avoid it when it consumes you."

"Adam. May I call you Adam?"

"Please do."

"There is a difference between allowing it to consume you and facing it objectively. Suffering over the loss of a loved one is normal, but surrendering completely to it means you are subconsciously allowing your sorrow to exert a negative control over the rest of your life. This often manifests as prolonged depression that may actually worsen as time goes on or alternately cause one to dive head long into their work or some other activity that buries the sorrow in the back of their subconscious. But it is always lurking there ready to resurface if you let your guard down. In either case you spend the rest of your life running away from the tragedy or running headlong into it although you may not think so. Now," she said looking up from mixing the bread dough. "You can tell me to stop and I won't be offended."

"Are you a psychologist by any chance?"

"No," she shook her head and laughed. "Life throws us a lot of curves. It's just a matter of learning how to field them."

"I don't think it's quite that simple. You must've had some wicked curves to have acquired that knowledge."

Looking at him again she answered, "we all have a story to tell.

Some are more harsh than others."

"Whew," he said under his breath. For the first time in his life he had met someone who saw through a tough exterior that he was certain no one could ever penetrate if he didn't want them to. He watched her as she added more wood to the cook stove.

She had struck a nerve that brought unhappy memories into focus again and for a moment he was angry. "Why the hell couldn't she have just let it alone? How many times did he have to re-experience the heartache? She was right about one thing. He had talked very little about it to anyone, not even his mother."

"I have to heat up the kitchen so the bread dough will rise," she said adjusting dampers on the stove. "It will get quite warm so we should take refuge in the living room for a while."

Once seated on the couch with a fresh cup of coffee his thoughts wandered back to her comments about suppressing his sorrow over the loss of his son. Talking about it again couldn't hurt anymore than he had already been hurt and she seemed to be willing to listen.

Seated in an easy chair across from him with Trina purring contentedly on her lap she asked, "are you comfortable there?"

"Yes, thank you."

He stared into the cup for a moment then looked up to find her gazing gently at him. He looked away and rubbed the back of his neck for a moment.

"Adam, do you want to talk more about it?"

"Yeah I guess I do and you had it pegged. My son Jeffery was killed in a car accident over a year ago now and I admit I've really been having a difficult time coping with it."

"I'm so very sorry."

"It's been rough. He was only eighteen. We had a great relationship, and I guess that's what really hurts. Often times fathers and sons can't see eye to eye at all. But Jeff and I didn't have that problem. We agreed on most everything. He had a cool level head and was very interested in the family business. He was enrolled in law at the university and would've been quite capable of taking over when I retired."

He paused and stared at the floor, the all too familiar hurt creeping over him again.

"For three months afterward I was completely crushed. I couldn't do anything at all. Spent most of my time sitting in my apartment staring at the walls. Gradually I began feeling bitter and angry, but it didn't replace the sorrow. It just added to it. I vacillated between lashing out at everybody and everything, to wanting to die myself.

That phase finally passed but then I immersed myself in my work to the extent that I practically lost touch with the outside world. Some friends of mine, business associates, talked me into this hunting trip. Otherwise I suppose I'd still be sitting behind my desk."

He had deliberately omitted his connection to the environmental group realizing now that he had taken up that new cause partly because he believed in it and partly to immerse his mind in a constant whirl that kept his sorrow at bay.

He looked up in time to catch her wiping tears away. "I'm sorry," she said dabbing her eyes with a handkerchief. "It's a woman's privilege and obligation."

He smiled sensing in her compassion that he had always considered a sign of weakness. It had no place in the business world where one's success could be measured, in part, by someone else's failure. Right now all that seemed so meaningless. He felt as though he had been playing some pointless game all his life in which everybody ultimately lost no matter how successful they might have been. His involvement with the environmental group had seemed like a saving grace, but strangely even that no longer felt as urgent as it first had.

She was smiling at him gently now and he found himself unable to resist smiling back. Not the artificial response he had perfected over the years, but a genuine warm smile that had its origins in some atrophied corner of his emotions.

"Thanks for listening," he said.

"Talking about it always helps and besides, that's the most you've said at any one time since you got here. That alone is an achievement. Anyway I must go right now and tend to the bread making so there is some ready in time for supper.

CHAPTER 9

He was eagerly looking forward to more talk with her the next day. But before she had cleaned up after breakfast, the roar of a tractor outside sent her scurrying to a window.

"It's Hank," she said. I'll get some more coffee brewing. I kinda thought he might be up today."

"I'll go back to the bedroom," he said reaching for the crutches.

"Oh won't you please stay? He and his wife Beatrice are dear friends. I'm sure you would like them both."

He shrugged and sat back grateful for the invitation mainly because it was easier than struggling to the bedroom.

She wrapped a shawl around her shoulders and stepped outside the door. She returned in a few seconds saying she had ordered him to come in for coffee and cake before leaving.

Adam smiled faintly but suspected that no coaxing was necessary. Her food was as tasty as any he had ever eaten and guessed that the neighbor would have plowed his way up for that reason alone.

Hank Meade was a big, good natured, ruddy complexioned farmer whom Adam liked immediately. He appeared to be in his mid forties and seemed to spend most of his time helping everyone else. Between mouthfuls of Jenny's chocolate layer cake he brought them up to date on the state of everything and everyone in the valley.

The day before he'd hauled a load of wood over to the widow Larkin's because she was laid up with her rheumatism and on his way back had checked in on young Ben and Lydia Rafferty. Lydia was expecting her third and since their phone was out of order he felt he'd better keep a close eye on them. Then there were the Chomsky's who'd taken Elsa into town for her piano lesson just before the blizzard hit and had to night over with Mrs. Hartz the music teacher. He'd helped Fergie Donovan pull his pump out and replace the piston leather yesterday and on the way home stopped at the Chomsky's and stoked up their furnace so their place wouldn't freeze up on them before they got back.

"Now Andy," he said wading into his second slice of cake. "You come on down and get chop anytime you want it. Me and young Henry crushed up a good sized batch the other day so we've plenty to spare. The cows'll eat more in this kinda weather so don't you go running short. Soon's the snow's cleared away a bit more we'll pull the crusher up and do enough to keep you 'til spring. Oh Jenny, Beatie told me to tell you she'll send Henry up tomorrow with some material. She said to just tell you that and you'll know what she meant by it."

"Right. It's complicated woman stuff that you men would never understand," she said with a laugh. "How about more coffee?"

"I've long ago learned it's best never to try," he said shoving his cup forward to be refilled. "And Jen I think your chocolate cake gets better every time you bake one."

"Thanks Hank. But it's not a pinch better than Beatie's blueberry pie."

"Speaking of that she's bakin' a bunch today. Said she's sending up a couple with Henry tomorrow."

"You've a treat in store," Jenny said to Adam. "You haven't lived until you've eaten Beatie's blueberry pie."

"Sounds great."

"Andy tells me you're over from Edmonton Mr. Finlay," Hank Meade said turning his attention to Adam. "What brought you out our way?"

"Hunting; big game. I got separated from the rest of my group. Then the storm caught me…I guess you've heard the rest of the story."

"Yeah, Andy told me. Sorry about your mishap. You're darn lucky you were near the yard. A person wouldn't've lasted long out there."

"Indeed not."

"Well gotta be goin," he said pulling his overshoes on and snapping buckles shut.

He stood up and donned his heavy faded brown parka then paused and said, "oh have you heard about the strange happenins over at the church during the last couple of weeks?"

Jenny and Andy both seemed to freeze on the spot and stare at him shaking their heads slightly.

"Well the story started with old man Lithgow but nobody paid any attention to him cause he was likely pickled every time he went past the church so he could'a bin seein just about anything. Anyway he'd bin tellin the story in the beer parlor in town to anyone who'd listen. He said that several times when he passed the church on his way home at night there was a light on inside and he swore he saw Dodds through a window prancin around and wavin a bible just the way he used to. Everyone pretty well ignored him believing it to be liquor talk but then last Sunday Tom and Helen Spangler was doin the clean-up after the evenin service and just when they was getting ready to leave, Dodds, or something that looked like him appeared standin up on the altar with a bible in his hand. Scared the daylights right outta both them and I guess they headed for home as fast as they could go. Now when the story comes from reliable folks like them it makes you wonder what is goin on."

"Old son of a bitch!"

The sharp retort came from Andy and all three of them turned and looked at him in surprise.

Dead silence hung in the room for a moment then Hank Meade began babbling in an apologetic tone.

"Jenny, I'm sorry. I wasn't thinking. I didn't mean…"

"It's okay Hank," she said walking over and placing a hand on his shoulder.

"No harm done."

"Oh god I feel awful."

"Well don't. As I said no harm done. I think it bothers everyone else more now than it does me."

"Rotten old son of a bitch," Andy repeated as he dressed to go back outside.

"That goes for you too Andy," Jenny said. "That was probably just some pranksters over at the church."

"Now Hank you scat on home and tell Beatie we're looking forward to some of her blueberry pie tomorrow and Andy I'll come out and take care of the chickens. You'd better go sit in a snow bank and cool off."

Andy finished buttoning his coat and stomped out without saying anything more.

She looked at Hank Meade in silence for a moment then suddenly wrapped both arms around the burly farmer and for a moment held him tight.

"Now be off with you," she said "and thanks a million for plowing us out of the snow."

Looking as though he wished the floor would open up and swallow him he nodded to Adam then turned and quickly walked out.

After his departure Jenny stood staring out a window in silence. She just stood motionless apparently so caught up in her thoughts she was oblivious to her surroundings.

It was obvious, Adam thought, that there had been some tragic event in the past that traumatized the whole valley but then in a small backwoods community like this if someone's cow died it would likely be traumatic.

He emptied his coffee cup and reaching for his crutches said, "I'll go into the living room for a while."

She came quickly out of her trance like reverie and with an apology came over to assist him. Once he was seated on the couch, she added several blocks of wood to the fireplace and then swept up a few ashes that had fluttered out onto the floor. After replacing the broom and dustpan on the wall where they always hung, she stared silently at the crackling flames that had started consuming the fresh supply of firewood.

Any hopes he had about further conversation with her were quickly dispelled. After staring into the fireplace for a few more moments, she turned to face him and speaking slowly said, "I will be away for the rest of the day, Adam. There's plenty of food already prepared and Andy will be in at mealtime to set it out and help you to the table."

She looked at him for a few more moments as though trying to decide whether or not to say something more, but then turned abruptly and walked out.

A few minutes later he heard the outside door open and close and guessed she was probably having her brother hook the horse up to the sleigh. The tinkling of harness bells and the dog barking confirmed his assumption.

Human nature is a strange thing he thought as the sounds of the bells gradually faded off into the distance. At first he wanted no part of anything that might have happened in this remote hinterland, interested only in getting out as soon as possible. But now he wanted to hear more of what this unique woman had to say. He sensed she was also suffering emotional distress for some reason and he found himself wishing she was still there so he could console her.

'Careful Adam,' he thought. 'Be very careful. You've no place in your life for this. The sooner you're out of here, the better.'

The day seemed to drag on endlessly. As she had promised Andy came in at mealtime and after setting out food that had been kept warm in the oven, he helped Adam to the table. Despite the tastiness of Jenny's food, he was able to eat very little. Try as he might he couldn't shake off his concern about her and Andy's only response when he questioned him about where she might have gone was, "don't know."

He spent the afternoon trying to interest himself in one of the many books that lined the shelves in the living room but to no avail. On one occasion he thought he heard harness bells and without thinking jumped quickly to his feet only to fall back just as quickly onto the couch from the pain in his broken limb. He sat in silence listening intently for more sounds that would signal her return, but finally chalked it up to his imagination.

The evening meal came and went with still no sign of Jenny. Andy's apparent indifference about his sister's well being began to annoy Adam.

"Don't you think you should try to find out if she's okay?" he finally asked.

"She kin handle herself out there as well as anybody can. No cause fer worry," he answered as he cleaned away the remnants of the evening meal. "Gotta finish up some chorin'. Anything you need right now?"

"A helicopter would do nicely," Adam thought but shook his head in silence as the old gent walked out carrying two pails of something Adam didn't recognize. He had taken a lantern with him so Adam assumed he would likely stay out to unharness Sampson and feed him when Jenny returned.

Two more hours passed when Andy finally walked back in obviously this time to stay. He removed his heavy outer clothing and sat two empty pails in the separator room.

"No sign of Jenny," Adam asked.

"Nope." He turned and looked at Adam for a moment then

added, "if it gits too late she might just night over at some-body's place. Happens all time round here."

"I guess I shouldn't be surprised at that," Adam thought but he did feel relieved. He also felt perplexed over his concern for her well being and redoubled his conviction to put her out of his mind and escape this country as quickly as he could. He had brought his book with him when he came out for supper know-ing that the kitchen with its two kerosene lamps would be the only place in the house he could read. Even though feeling less anxious about Jenny, he was still unable to regain interest in the book.

"Gotta put a new handle in this axe," Andy said going over to a corner where a sturdy looking table sat. Adam had earlier wondered what the purpose for this table was because he had never seen Jenny use it.

"Havta do a little drillin' and raspin'. Hope the noise won't bother you."

"It won't," Adam said closing the book and turning to watch the process.

"In summer I'd do it out in the old shed," Andy said struggling to retrieve a heavy vice from a shelf under the table and then bolt it to the table surface. "No heat out there," he added as he locked the axe head still containing splintered remains of the old handle into the vice.

Adam watched with fascination as Andy hand drilled several holes down through the portion of the handle still anchored in the axe head and then using a hammer and punch tapped out the pieces. He next clamped the new handle in the vice and tried the axe head on for fit. Obviously dissatisfied he removed the head and vigorously hand rasped a few spots on the handle and tried the head on again. This time it seemed to meet with his approval because he tapped the head on until a portion of the handle protruded up through the top. Next he repositioned the axe in the vice and sawed off the protruding piece of handle and then drove in a wedge shaped piece of wood to anchor the handle in place.

"Hear they's making wedges out of steel now," he said as he

surveyed the finished product. "Gonna try to pick some up. They's bound to hold better."

Adam shook his head as much in admiration as amazement. His only association with an axe was a small hatchet he usually took on camping trips and he never paid any attention as to how it was put together.

After sweeping up wood chips and returning all tools to their place, Andy entered the washroom that seemed designated to that side of the house and pulled the door shut.

The fascinating process Adam had just witnessed had temporarily taken his mind off Jenny, but now he began to wonder about her again. The temperature had dropped sharply with the onset of nightfall and he hoped she would stay with someone and return in daylight.

"Well think I'll turn in," Andy said emerging from the bathroom and drying the back of his neck with a towel. "If you want to stay up longer I can git one of them lamps down and set it on the table."

"No," Adam shook his head. "I'm going to bed too."

"I'll stoke up yer heater before you do. Gonna be a chilly one tonight."

Sleep eluded him as he knew it would. It was past eleven o'clock and normally he couldn't have kept himself awake beyond that time. He wished he could have the same confidence about Jenny's well being that Andy had. But try as he might he couldn't shake off his concern for her.

Finally drowsiness began descending on him and just as he started dropping off to sleep a faint noise by his bedside jolted him wide awake again. The bright full moon shining through the window lit up the room well enough to make out everything, but he couldn't see anything that didn't belong there. Guessing he must have been dreaming, he laid down again and began pulling the covers up over his shoulders when he heard Trina's faint meow. This time he looked out over the edge of the bed to see the cat staring intently at him. Chuckling he said, "you miss her too, don't you. Okay come on up here. We can at least keep each other company." The cat needed no second invitation. She immediately jumped up and snuggled in close to Adam and began purring. Perhaps Trina was a reminder of Jenny. With the cat beside him on the bed he relaxed and fell off to sleep again. He didn't know how long he had slept before he was awakened this time by the dog barking. Then he heard the harness bells in the distance and in a few minutes Andy's footsteps descending the stairway from his bedroom.

Adam breathed a sigh of relief and checked the clock. It was 1:35 AM.

Andy was outside by the time Jenny made it to the back door and after some muffled talk she entered the house as quietly as she could.

"Hi Trina," she whispered to the meowing cat who had immediately jumped off Adam's bed when she heard the dog barking.

Unable to contain himself he sat up and pulled on his housecoat and hobbled to his bedroom door. "Are you alright?" he asked quietly.

"Oh hi. I'm sorry for waking everyone. Of course I'm alright. Why wouldn't I be?"

She had lit a candle and even in the dull light he could see the redness of her cheeks.

"Well I was just wondering. It is pretty chilly out there."

"It's invigorating," she said with a laugh. "Did Andy take good care of you?"

"Yeah, he did. Well I…guess I'll go back to bed then."

"Are you okay Adam?" she asked placing an ice cold hand on his arm.

"I'm…alright. It just seemed quite cold for anyone to be out there. Andy said you might even stay over at someone's place."

"I'm so sorry. How thoughtless of me. I guess I disrupted the whole household."

She squeezed his arm and smiling asked. "Am I forgiven?"

"Oh nothing to forgive."

She continued smiling at him for a moment longer and then said, "as soon as Andy gets in we'll refuel the heaters and then perhaps we can all get some sleep."

"Yes of course. Goodnight."

CHAPTER 10

The next morning at the breakfast table he announced his decision to return to Edmonton as soon as arrangements could be made. He felt he had imposed on them long enough, and besides he was still running a business that would need his attention."

"You know you're not imposing on us," Jenny said. "But if you've made up your mind to leave we'll do what we can to help. Andy's going down to Hank and Beatie's either this afternoon or tomorrow. He can have them place another telephone call for you."

Instead of feeling relief at the prospect of finally getting out and going home he felt a tinge of remorse. He knew he was starting to have feelings for her that were more than just friendly but also felt he must keep them in check. A week earlier he had made a firm commitment to an environmental group to contribute everything he could to their cause. Now he was having romantic thoughts about some mountain dwelling woman whose lifestyle ran counter to everything he had ever known or valued.

Since his divorce some six years earlier he'd rarely had any desire to date another woman. Now, for reasons that completely baffled him, he found himself attracted to the most unlikely woman he'd ever known and he'd only known her for a few days. The situation seemed so absurd that he resolved to place a closer guard around his feelings until he was on the road home and then he would put the whole strange experience out of his mind for good.

Determined to square up with them in every way he would insist once again on paying for all the care he'd received and indeed for saving his life. He had always been able to settle any score with money and he wasn't about to leave without settling this one. Getting her to accept was quite another story.

"Dear Adam," she said after he had announced his intention "it always boils down to money doesn't it?"

"It has always worked well for me. Now Jenny I am going to pay you. If you won't tell me how much I owe then I'll…"

"Adam, Adam," she interrupted. Sighing heavily she turned her attention to Trina who was engaged in a boxing match with a string dangling from a cupboard drawer. "I know you mean well," she resumed. "And I also know that beneath your tough exterior is a tenderness that has been petrified by your perceived need for success at almost any cost. If you were to stop for a moment and ask yourself exactly why success and money were so important, you would, in truth, be unable to come up with a practical answer because there really isn't one. No human being should become so obsessed with amassing wealth that they lose sight of the true reason for their existence. The inhabitants of this community experienced a harsh tragedy during the past few years that no amount of money could have averted or corrected. Money played a certain role in the nasty drama, but only in the sense that the distorted value placed on money was exemplified.

Offering unconditional help to someone in need benefits the giver as much as the receiver because we are all parts of a greater whole and therefore inseparably linked to each other. A gift to any part is a gift to all parts including ourselves so I thank you Adam for an opportunity to give. Payment of money simply complicates the matter because it then becomes an issue of who should pay who. The only thing anybody truly owes anyone else is compassion and understanding, and if we all began disseminating that in unlimited measure the axiom 'it is better to give than to receive' could be changed to read 'to give is to receive'."

She reached across the table and squeezed his arm lightly.

"I'm glad you've been here Adam and when you're home again I hope your memories of us will be happy ones."

She stood up and pulled on her coat and gloves.

"Jenny…"

"I have a few chores to do outside. Be back in a while."

He sat staring at the closed door for several moments after she had walked out. He was only vaguely aware of Trina jumping up on his lap and pushing her head under his hand for some petting. Finally he looked down to see her looking back up at him.

"Kitty," he said exhaling slowly while rubbing her back. "I want you to explain a few things to me since I seem to be missing the boat myself. For starters how come our Miss Jenny all of a sudden talks like a college grad when up to this point she sounded like a hillbilly high school dropout? And just what the hell did she mean by that garbled abstract talk of everything actually just being some part of a greater whole? Whole what?"

Trina had begun purring contentedly as he continued posing questions to her.

"Why is it I keep feeling there is something mysterious about our Miss Jenny…and about this place? Something behind the scenes that I'm not seeing and worst of all why am I starting to like her… a lot?"

"Answer me Trina," he said standing the purring tabby up on her hind feet and looking into her partly closed eyes. "You don't know either? Okay that's it. When Miss Jenny walks back in through that door we are going to set her down and she is going to answer some questions for us. Are you with me?"

CHAPTER 11

You have a degree in biology?" he repeated, the astonishment registering in his voice.

"Yes."

"Any you...I mean why...?"

"What am I doing living out here in the wilderness when I probably could be earning a good salary somewhere else," she said laughing at his babbling attempt to ask the obvious question.

"Well it would make one wonder."

He had broached the subject as subtly as he could when she returned from the hen house with her payload of eggs.

"If you won't let me reimburse you for my stay here," he had said "then you must agree to answer some questions for me. Is that a fair trade?"

"Sounds like it is," she said smiling gently at him as she carefully transferred eggs from the basket into a pan of water for washing.

"You did say you've lived here all your life?"

"Right."

"Were you...uh...ever married?"

She stopped washing eggs and stared into the pan for a moment. Then looking at him soberly said; "I was engaged a few years ago but it ended very tragically."

"Oh I'm sorry. Care to..."

"Mind if we skip that one? It's a bit of a sore spot."

"Of course. I didn't mean to get personal."

"That's not the point. It's just that I'm still struggling with it. It not only left me decimated but it also left a many unanswered questions that I'm still piecing together."

"I understand. Willing to go on?"

"Yes."

"Great, let's see. Oh. How about your education?"

"Are you really interested in that?"

"Yes I am."

"The usual. Elementary school in the valley and high school in town."

"Any post secondary?"

She stared into the pan again appearing as though the question was also a difficult one to answer. After a short silence she replied, "UBC: four years"

"University...for four years?"

"Right."

Noticing her hesitancy again, he said, "look, if that's also something you prefer not to discuss..."

"I don't mind Adam. It's just often difficult to explain to anyone why I would attain that level of education and then appear to do nothing with it. I never had any intentions of gaining financially from my degree. I use that knowledge for reasons that would make little sense to most people. Consequently I avoid talking about it as much as I can. I told you simply because I agreed to answer your questions."

He had always held, in high regard, anyone with a university education. To him they rated a few notches above the average person and deserved to be treated with the respect that years of dedicated study had earned them.

Jennifer Ingram, however, was in a different category. It was obvious she would never flaunt her achievements even though he sensed that she had the capability to achieve any level of knowledge that she chose.

"I'm a naturalist because of a very deep love of nature and an innate sense of responsibility toward the environment. Learning all I could provided me with an understanding of natural laws and how everything fits into a much larger and perfect scheme."

"Excuse me," he interrupted but are you telling me you are an environmentalist?"

"I guess you could say that. Why?"

He shook his head and chuckled. What were the odds of meeting an environmentalist after he had joined such a group.

"Adam?"

"Oh I'm sorry please continue."

She stared at him for a moment as though piecing something together in her mind, then resumed.

"Initially I tried to gain this awareness from the church; the one Hank Meade spoke of earlier but it did little more than confuse and disillusion me. In the years since I've come to a point of clarity that no religion could have provided. I've learned of the important role we all play in creation and the potential disaster in shirking our sacred responsibility. If any of that makes sense to you then you understand my reason for studying biology."

For someone whose every activity in life had been geared toward making money, it didn't. Thirty years in the property development industry had honed his business ability to a razor sharp edge and he couldn't conceive of someone expending the energy to earn a degree and not profit financially from it. Strangely, however, this unique characteristic increased the attraction he felt towards her and he wanted to know more.

"That tragedy you spoke of, was someone killed?"

"Yes, but…"

"Someone close to you?"

"Yes, but we agreed that was a taboo subject didn't we?"

"Oh right. Right. I'm sorry."

"I think you were cheating."

"Can't blame me for trying," he said with a grin. "I thought I could sneak a few past before you noticed."

"That's an evil tactic and you nearly succeeded," she answered smiling back but her expression quickly sobered as she continued. "Please understand Adam that incident is still rather fresh in everyone's mind and right now most of us want to push it as far into the background as possible. I'm not being evasive. I just want to give a nasty wound time to heal.

Practically everyone in the valley was adversely affected by it one way or another. It was a nightmare that most would like to forget about. I was more directly involved than anyone else so I have more poignant memories. I even seriously considered moving away after the whole mess was put to rest. But then I realized that no matter where I went the memories went with me and besides this was my home. Nothing was going to force me out."

"I'm sorry," he said. "I can understand how you felt about losing someone close to you. I haven't talked much about my son's death either although I've had many tell me I should."

"You belong to the Catholic faith don't you?"

"How did you know?"

"Your crucifix," she said pointing to the small cross dangling from a chain around his neck.

"Oh right."

"Did your church not offer you counsel?"

"Yeah," he said sighing. "The parish priest talked to me on several occasions and he seemed genuinely concerned but frankly it didn't help at all. In fact it raised a number of questions I had never really thought about before which simply added to my bitterness."

He stopped talking, feeling once again the heartache and anger that had once plagued him mercilessly.

Wanting to put it out of his mind he said, "We've strayed off course. I was asking you questions, remember?"

Appearing not to have heard him she said, "you are still very angry about your loss aren't you?"

"What makes you say that?"

Ignoring his question she continued, "Likely God is on top of your list for allowing Jeff to be taken at such a young age, angry at what it's done to your plans for Jeff. Angry at yourself for things you either did or didn't do. Why you're likely even angry at Jeff because he could've avoided the accident if he stayed away from that party and…"

"Wait a minute, how did you know about the party? I never mentioned it."

"Just a guess. Young men his age often party a lot. But the point I am trying to make is you are harboring bitter resentment that you should release."

If she had been searching for the trigger to set him off she finally found it. Everything came flooding out as though a large valve inside had suddenly been snapped open.

"Well what the hell am I supposed to do? Yeah, you're right I was mad and still am. I'm pissed off at anything and anybody I can blame. I know it doesn't help. Nothing is going to bring him back. But it just seems so goddamned unfair for a bright promising young man to be snatched away at that age while on the other hand some worthless bag man or lady parades up and down back streets until they're ninety, and when they do die the city has to cover their funeral costs."

He tossed his hands up in exasperation.

"I know people die all the time. Parents lose kids, kids lose parents. But I guess you never think much about it until it strikes home and then it's all you do think about. After a while your thinking starts taking weird twists and you begin to question everything and anything and before long nothing makes sense anymore.

When I was younger, it all seemed so simple. You went to college, got married, had kids, strove for success in work. Then came the grandchildren and later retirement during which you sat back and enjoyed the fruits of your labor. All nice and tidy, but then that cozy agenda gets interrupted and after enough interruptions you begin wondering what it's all about. It started with my marriage break up and then I lost my son. Hell my daughter has even turned away from me, saying Jeff might still be alive if I'd allowed him to make his own career choices. Maybe she's right, who knows."

"And so you plan to spend the rest of your life beating yourself up over it?"

"I don't know. Maybe I do. It's been over a year but anytime it comes up again I feel the same anger and sorrow that I did back then."

"Do you have any plans for your future?"

"Why bother? Planning hasn't worked! I had plans coming out of my ears and I provided everything to ensure those plans would succeed. That's what you do isn't it? Provide for your family? Tell me, was that wrong? Or maybe I'm being punished for an over indulgence in materiality. Maybe that's it. After all everyone in my family has, or at least had, their own car and space in the garage. Then there was the motor home, the swimming pool, the house at the lake and on and on. What did all that accomplish? We might as well have lived in a cabin in the wilderness. The result is the same. We die off after a life of constant struggle and heartache and if we're lucky we might come to our senses long enough during our last few breaths to wonder why we struggled as we did, which could just be the most intelligent thought we'll ever have."

"It's a blessing everyone doesn't look at life that way."

"Well, what are we struggling for? Money? I've got lots of it and I've never felt worse. Fame? Glory? I'll never have any and even if I did it really won't matter much after I'm gone will it? To leave an inheritance for your kids? Great if they stay alive long enough to inherit it. To make this world a better place to live? Very noble, but then there's a larger segment of humanity that keeps trying to destroy it."

"How old are you Adam?"

"Forty-six."

"That's in your favor."

"My favor. What are you talking about?"

"You still have plenty of time to take advantage of your opportunity."

"My opportunity. Haven't you heard anything I've said? I'm groveling away in the bottom of the misery barrel and you make it sound like a new lease on life."

"Which is precisely what it is."

"Did I miss something somewhere?"

"Only that you fail to realize you've finally put life into perspective."

"I have?"

"Yes. Oh you're taking an extremely negative view right now, but even that has it's purpose."

"Suffering has a purpose?"

"And you gain immeasurably from it once you understand why."

He stared at her, a smile playing at the corners of his mouth. He expected her to burst out laughing and tell him she was joking but after a moment of silence he realized she wasn't going to.

"Well I'll give you an A for uniqueness," he said. "Let me see now, I'm going to do a quick review. First of all my son is killed in a car crash and then in an attempt to mitigate my grief, I dive headlong into my work. I did talk briefly to my doctor, the parish priest, a grief counselor, close friends, a psychiatrist, some relatives, even the dog when I came home drunk one night and with the exception of the dog who only licked my face, the rest all told me after a certain grieving period I would gradually return to normal and be able to get on with my life. I know now that none of that really worked at all. Anyway I came up here because some friends talked me into it. But I get lost in a snow storm, a tree falls on me and breaks my leg. I damn near freeze to death, get rescued by some mountain dwellers who don't even have a telephone, we're snowed in for God knows how long and you tell me I've finally hit the jackpot."

"You've summed it up very well."

"Quite a sense of humor you have."

"Thank you."

"Well you do have my attention. Care to tell me just why it is that I'm so fortunate?"

"For starters you've just released a lot of pent up anger but as I've said you've started to put life into perspective."

"I have?"

"Yes. For one thing you've begun to realize that the material things we collect along the way are just tools we use to assist us on our journey. They are a means to an end not an end in itself."

"A means to what end?"

Adam I'm not trying to counsel you. I've made my point."

"Then I missed it."

"What part did you miss?"

"All you said is the acquisition of material things is a means to an end. A means to what end?"

"That is my point, a means to an end. The particular end I'm talking about would likely conflict with your religious belief."

"Try me."

She stared at him for a moment as though debating with herself. Finally shrugging her shoulders she resumed. "It is a means to achieving much loftier objectives."

"Such as?"

"Our spiritual development."

"I thought any strong emphasis on material goods was in conflict to spiritual development."

"Well if you think so why did you struggle to acquire so much stuff?"

"I guess I'm asking myself that now, but at the time I was always able to justify it one way or another."

"The challenge is to place the correct value on materiality. It does serve an indispensable purpose."

"An indispensable purpose."

"Right. Now let's leave it there. Obviously you've already had a glut of would be counselors. You don't need another one to add to your confusion. I suggested you should try to release some pent up anger and you did. I guess I inadvertently injected some of my own beliefs into the discussion but it was intended to keep you talking not convert you."

He smiled faintly and turned to gaze out a window. She had seated herself at the table now and out of the corner his eye realized she was studying him intently once again. The uncomfortable feeling that accompanied her penetrating gaze started creeping over him and he quickly brought his eyes back to meet hers. This seemed to shatter the strange atmosphere that she somehow created. He was certain it was unintentional because she would quickly respond with embarrassment when becoming aware of her behavior and apologize. This time was no exception, but the experience always left him shaken and he was at a loss to understand why. The only reason he could think of was because she seemed to be probing depths of his being that no one else ever could and probably had never wanted to. The total control he had always exercised over himself was an essential ingredient for survival in the tough business world but in her presence all the rules changed. The domineering self-confident Adam Finlay, was replaced by someone he hardly recognized. What was more strange, he felt comfortable in that new role.

Suddenly remembering that the conversation had gone astray he said, "Just a minute Miss Ingram. I started asking you questions a while ago. How did this get turned around."

"It's a technique I learned from a politician."

"And it almost worked, but don't think you're off the hook."

"It worked for a while. You see the objective was to make you forget the original question allowing me to divert the conversation to another topic."

"Sorry but I do remember where we left off. Now it appears that breaking away from your church actually expedited your spiritual quest which seems contradictory. Would you care to explain that?"

"There are several reasons," she answered looking at him soberly now. "But an important one for me was to isolate myself from the external distractions that interfere with our inner search. I didn't realize how much I was influenced by people and situations in my life until I withdrew from them. I don't mean we should become a recluse and take up residence in a cave somewhere, but we do need a sabbatical that allows us to clear our mind and recognize what our inner voice is trying to tell us. Finding solitude was easy for me. It's in my back yard," she said motioning toward the mountains behind the house. "I simply went farther up that way and stayed there until I began to hear the divine voice that is within each and every one of us. It will speak to us all when we are ready to listen and lead us on a pathway of self discovery that is exclusively our own. Does that make sense to you?"

"In a way," he said rubbing his chin. "And I expect it is contrary to just about everything my church espouses. But you seem to have gained a certain kind of contentment through that experience. You must have found something very precious."

"I have gained a huge measure of contentment Adam. Much more than I thought I could have in this life time and it doesn't stop flowing as long as one doesn't stop accepting it."

"Now that will need some explaining but I don't want to get off track. Was it that tragedy that set you on the pathway?"

"Primarily."

"Would you suggest the same for me?"

She chuckled slightly and stared at the floor for a moment, then shaking her head said, "no not right now."

"Why not?"

"Adam a detailed explanation would be very lengthy and likely something quite foreign to you. But trust me when I say the signals you are presently sending out make it very clear that you would probably even resist the very things that I've come to embrace."

"Didn't I hear you say something about an inner voice that will speak to us all?"

"When we are ready to listen and right now you aren't. You want to lash out and blame something or somebody for your plight and exact justice by devastating some phantom enemy."

"Wouldn't your method of isolation help me past that attitude?"

"It must be your method Adam. Could you really see yourself alone in the wilderness for two weeks at a time? But haven't we strayed again? I promised not to counsel, remember?"

"No. You're being evasive again."

"Not deliberately. I am explaining what worked for me. No two people are alike. In our quest for spiritual enlightenment, we must each find a pathway that is exclusively right for us. Sooner or later you will encounter some new action that will resonate with your purpose. If you are vigilant enough to recognize it, then grab hold and don't let go."

"I think I already have."

She gave him a look that appeared to be expressionless and said nothing.

"I didn't tell you everything before," he continued. "I joined an environmental group just a week before coming on this hunting trip and found out things about the deterioration of the environment that really shook me up but also charged me with motivation to do everything I could to help. From what you've been telling me, I could conclude that this is a true direction for me. I actually became so excited about it that a close friend who also belongs suggested that we should take advantage of a hunting weekend that would give us the opportunity to look at the wilderness we are trying to preserve. Does that sound like it could be my pathway?"

"It is your pathway Adam. Does the group yet have any solutions to offer?"

"No at least nothing practical. We are affiliated with a number of other groups and hope that by putting many heads together we might formulate something worthwhile. But then even if we do there are always the governments and industry who seem to oppose just about any suggestion that might interfere with the economy."

"Indeed. But you must not allow that to dampen your enthusiasm. You have embarked on probably the most urgent quest facing the human race. If we fail in this endeavor then we fail in everything."

"Some of the members made that very same comment. You obviously believe it's quite serious too."

"Far more so than most are aware of."

"You seem to place much emphasis on spirituality though. Which one is more important to you?"

"There is no difference between the two Adam. They are as connected as breathing is to life."

"I don't recall hearing anyone in the group even mention the word spirituality. Now you're telling me they are practically inseparable."

"Depending on your viewpoint, yes."

"Could you be a little more specific?"

"It's a long story that would require much more time than you have left here Adam. It's probably best not to get started."

This was a brand new twist on the environmental issue at least for him. There were two spiritual practitioners at the one meeting he had attended and they had made no mention of spirituality in connection with environmental problems. Did this mountain dweller know something that had eluded the so called experts? That was ridiculous thinking he decided. She might be a biologist but since her life appeared to revolve around these mountains and the valley below, how could she have anything useful to offer to something as profound as a major threat to the human race.

"I must go and finish up bread making but we can continue later if you wish."

CHAPTER 12

He had noticed mild chest pain and shortness of breath on several earlier occasions but this time it was much more pronounced. The exertion of making his way from the kitchen table to the living room couch after the evening meal brought on severe discomfort that left him perspiring and weak.

A pang of fear nudged the pit of his stomach. His father had died from a heart attack and the symptoms the senior Finlay had complained about were similar to what he was now experiencing.

The pain gradually subsided but his concern about it didn't. Later in the evening he mentioned it as casually as he could. He only wanted them to be aware of it not set off alarms, but there was no suppressing Jenny.

"That could be serious Adam and we're going to get Doc Greer up to check you out as soon as possible. I'll have Andy go down to Hank and Beatie's tonight and call him. For something urgent like this he'll get here as soon as he can."

He started to protest saying it was probably nothing to be concerned about but as he had already learned when Jenny made a decision any attempt to oppose her was useless.

"You just shush," she said with a faint smile and when you're ready we'll help you into bed. You musn't exert yourself at all."

"Okay Dr. Ingram"

He laid awake for a long time after getting settled into the bed. Mild pain was still noticeable in his chest and arm and he knew his concern about it was contributing more to his insomnia than the discomfort was.

The pain continued to subside and he was able to relax, but sleep still eluded him. His thoughts wandered back to the discussion he had had with Jenny earlier and to her comment about the direct link between spirituality and the well being of the planet. She had obviously experienced some tragic event in the past which seemed to precipitate a turning point in her life. Maybe her new found optimism led her to believe that she could conquer anything including the decimation of the planet.

Finally sleep began descending on him and his last thought before drifting off was the hope that he would be around long enough to witness a reversal in the destructive pathway humanity was on.

He didn't know how long he had slept but he found himself suddenly wide awake and certain he could sleep no more. He pulled himself up to a sitting position then stood up and took several steps from his bed before realizing he was walking. Something was very strange, he felt no pain or discomfort in his leg. In fact it felt better than it ever had.

Right then his bedroom door burst open and both Jenny and Andy clad in nightclothes and carrying candles hurried over to his bedside.

"Hey what's going on?" he asked walking back toward them. "I'm sorry if I've wakened you, but I didn't think I'd made any noise…"

He stopped talking suddenly realizing something was very much amiss. They paid no attention to him at all but were concentrating instead on his bed. He moved quickly around to the opposite side and then saw the reason for their frantic actions. There was a body lying on the bed and it was his.

"What the hell is going on?" he blurted out, but still neither one gave any indication that they heard him, continuing instead to shake the body and call his name.

"Hey I'm right here," he said again but to no avail. Andy was now checking a wrist for a pulse and Jenny was peering into an eye. Finally they both straightened up and stood motionless looking down at the inert form.

"My god," he thought. "I don't believe this. Did I...die? That's my body but, I'm not...in it." He was shocked but at the same time felt a strange sense of elation. Then he started, slowly, to lift off the floor. It was an effortless motion that felt natural and he knew he could resist if he wanted to but chose, instead, to go wherever he was being taken. He was nearing the ceiling when Jenny suddenly turned and looked up in his direction.

"Jenny," he spoke again certain now she was seeing him. "I'm okay. I'm just not...well I'm okay. Jenny? Jenny?"

She stared straight at him but still didn't respond. He looked helplessly back at her not knowing what else to do to make contact. He called her name several more times but she wasn't hearing him.

Strangely he felt no remorse but rather felt very peaceful and free.

Free seemed to be an odd way to feel but that was what he felt, wonderful freedom.

Suddenly, Jenny who was still looking up in his direction, smiled then raised her hand and waved. "Go to where you must, Adam," she said. He heard her words but he didn't know if she had spoken out loud or just transmitted her thoughts. It no longer mattered. He felt completely released and once again began floating up. He moved easily through the solid ceiling and then up and away from the old house and out into black empty space. Complete blackness surrounded him but it was warm, soothing and seemed to caress him with feelings of euphoria.

Soon he noticed a light in the distance. It appeared at first as just a pinhead but slowly enlarged as he floated closer. It was the brightest light he had ever seen and he began fearing he couldn't look at it without damage to his eyes. His fears were soon dispelled. He not only looked at it with ease but gently merged with it and found himself in a place that seemed to be all light. It was unlike any light he had ever known. Brilliantly bright yet gently soothing. Then from out of the misty distance two figures appeared and slowly moved toward him. They were vague impressions at first but began assuming specific shapes as they drew closer.

"Jeff! Dad!" he called out and ran to meet them. The feeling of love and happiness was all consuming as he embraced them both. Jeff looked exactly the same but his father looked much younger than when he died.

"Is this what it's really like here?" he asked in an excited tone or is this some beautiful illusion."

"This is the real thing Adam," his father replied. It took me a long time to finally accept that because I too expected something quite different. But you don't have much time. You are only making a short visit to gain some clarity about certain things and then you must return."

"Return? But why? I don't want to leave this place. This is home isn't it?"

"You must Dad," Jeffery said. "You still have important work to do on earth."

"But I'm here with you now and I've never felt such joy and peace. Earth life has become nothing but pain, suffering and sorrow. Why do I have to go back?"

"It will be easier Adam," his father spoke again. "For now you know that Jeff and I are safe and very happy and your sorrow over Jeff's death can end."

The scene behind his father and son had changed and he turned to gaze at it.

It was a meadow filled with flowers of every imaginable color. The plants seemed to glow softly from an internal light and defied any description he was capable of.

In the background was a lush green forest; a greener green than he had ever seen and behind the forest rose majestic mountains shimmering in the beautiful ubiquitous light. The whole scene had a sharp clarity about it that enabled him to see detail that he had never before witnessed. This was the kind of setting he would often imagine himself in on earth when the pressure of his daily life became overwhelming. Now it was here waiting for him and he wanted to walk out in its midst and stay there forever.

"Dad," his son's voice broke into his reverie. "You cannot go beyond this point for if you do, return will be very difficult but return you must. There is very little time and we want you to understand some things before you go back."

"We cannot tell you much Adam," his father continued "for you must gain understanding through experience in the physical realm. We are permitted only to point out the direction or pathway you must take if you are to fulfill your purpose for the remainder of your time on earth. Accept the guidance and counsel of Jennifer Ingram because she is a highly advanced soul. It is no accident that you have made contact with her. You and her are bonded in a manner that will only be revealed to you if you willingly embrace her teachings."

"There is much about ultimate reality you have not understood as we once didn't," his son said. "But if you choose you can correct that when you return. You have an accumulation of negativity from past lives that will nudge you toward balance and which balance must be attained before you can once again move forward on your spiritual pathway. Should you choose to defy the laws and remain locked in your erroneous beliefs your progress will be delayed until you finally decide to embrace the light of truth."

Then his father spoke again, "we are all some part of the greater one Adam and therefore one with each other but individually and totally responsible for our own behavior and its consequences. What we now are and have been is solely the result of choices we've made over many thousands of years and many physical lives.

The world is at a crossroads and decisions made by the human race are critical. You made a choice prior to entering your present physical life that you would be one of the leaders in this final attempt to reverse the self destructive direction the human race has taken. But this can only happen after you've cleared up some residual negative karma of your own."

"I came back to earth only long enough to assist you on your true pathway," Jeffery continued. My death in that car crash caused you to turn away from everything that had once been important and to realize there is something more. If you are to comply with the soul agenda you've set up for yourself in your present physical life then it behooves you to turn your back on everything you once valued and search out the ways in which you can conform to the purpose you yourself chose."

"That's all we can reveal Adam," his father said. "You must go back now. To remain longer increases the difficulty of leaving. At some point in your future you will return for a permanent stay and then we can continue on our journey together in this realm which is our true home."

Knowing he had no choice he embraced them both and immediately found himself back in the confines of his pain wracked body. There was no experience of a return trip. He was just suddenly there again.

"Adam? Adam? You're back with us. Oh thank God we thought we'd lost you."

Jenny was speaking in excited tones as he slowly opened his eyes to see her looking down at him with concern.

"This is getting to be a habit," he said in a weak voice and managing an equally weak grin.

"Just take it easy," she said smiling back and squeezing his hand. You've probably had a heart attack. We did get a message to Doc. Greer but it is snowing heavily again. Hank told Andy as soon as Doc got to their place he would plow the road up right ahead of him and then stay and see to it he got back again."

"Thanks, Jenny."

"How are you feeling now? Any discomfort, anything

you want?"

He shook his head. The soothing tone of her voice and the warmth of her hand clasping his was sufficient right then and he closed his eyes and drifted off to sleep once more.

What seemed like only minutes later, she was calling his name again and he slowly opened his eyes this time to see an elderly man hovering over him.

"This is Doc Greer Adam. He's going to examine you."

Still wearing his dark felt hat and a scarf, the old physician was already listening intently to Adams' chest with his stethoscope and for the next few moments checked various points in silence. His sober expression gave no hint of what his findings might be. Finally straightening up and removing his hat and the stethoscope he said in a tired voice, "Jenny could we open the window for a few minutes? We want to ensure a good supply of fresh air."

"Of course Doc."

"Now Mr. Finlay," the white haired physician said turning his attention back to Adam. "You've had a heart attack but it does seem to be a mild one. Only minimum damage as near as I can determine. There is no arrythmia that is, no heartbeat irregularity but it is most important to have complete bed rest for at least the next week, maybe longer. Convalescing in a hospital would be the desired treatment but the stress of getting you there in this kind of weather may do more harm than good. Anyway you're in good hands right here. Jenny has helped nurse many folks back to good health and besides she's a sight nicer to look at than me, so you just mind her and I'm sure you'll be fine. Now are you diabetic and do you smoke?"

Adam shook his head.

"Your blood pressure is slightly elevated right now but that's to be expected and you're certainly not overweight. Overall the prognosis is good. I'll get back in a week's time to check on you but until then bed rest is most essential."

"Now let's have a peek at that broken leg while I'm here," he said as he unwrapped his splints."

After a few seconds of feeling over the fractured area he said, "that tree did a nasty job but the leg is coming along nicely. I couldn't have done any better at patching it up than Jenny has. Don't put any weight on it for a few weeks yet and it should get right back to normal before too long."

"Thanks Doctor," Adam responded weakly and watched as the old physician tucked his instruments back into a tattered leather bag and picked up his dark, heavy overcoat off the back of a chair.

"While I'm here Jenny," he said hesitating at the door. "I'm going to check on Andy. Hank said he's been complaining of a stomach pain for some time now and about the only way we'd get him into my office would be in a straight jacket so I'll have a look at him before I leave."

"I appreciate it Doc," Jenny answered. "The old mule never even told me about it."

"I'm not surprised," the doctor said with a faint smile then nodding to Adam, walked out of the room.

"Well Mr. Finlay you heard the good doctor. I give the orders around here for the next while so no back talk of any kind, no exertion, no refusal to eat proper food and no flirting with the female staff."

"Can't agree to that last one," he said forcing another smile.

"Just keep in mind who's boss and we'll get along fine. Now I'm going out to see Hank and Doc off. I'll be back in a bit."

CHAPTER 13

His recovery was rapid. He felt better as each day passed and found it difficult to stay in bed for the full week that had been prescribed.

Blizzard conditions prevailed for two days following the doctor's visit but the third day dawned with a cloudless blue sky and little wind. Hank Meade made his way up once again with his small snowplow and before leaving popped his head through the bedroom door to inquire about Adam's health.

The sense of community was unusually strong in this back-woods country. Having a doctor making house calls was unheard of anymore, or so he thought. Out here it seemed no one had heard otherwise.

True to his word the doctor returned a week later and after a quick examination gave Adam permission to get out of bed and move around the house but cautioned him to limit his activities and not tire himself.

After passing along some medication for Andy and shaking hands with everyone, the old physician departed once again this time saying he would be back in two weeks.

The strange unsettling experience he had had during the time he was presumed dead was never out of his mind and now on his way to recovery, it possessed him completely. Every waking hour was spent trying to make sense out of it. Instead of fading away as a striking dream would, it became more imposing. A thousand questions flooded his mind. How could Jenny be any part of this fantastic drama? That made no sense to him and was the primary reason he believed the whole crazy incident should be written off as a hallucination. How could it be possible that someone he had never before heard of play any part in his life. Then there was the inconsistency of the experience with his religious teachings. He firmly believed in an existence after death but also believed entry to the heavenly realm was possible only through the auspices of the one true church. Any "temptation" outside these boundaries was the work of the devil and must be strongly resisted. However, the near death experience, although disturbing, contained no such fearsome undertones. In fact it felt so imbued with divine love and joy that any attempt to describe it was hopelessly inadequate.

For several days he struggled with an inner conflict that left him in a wretched emotional state. Finally forced to concede he must somehow deal with it to find relief he decided to approach Jenny.

Seizing an opportunity after breakfast on his third day out of bed he asked her if she would be interested in hearing a "ridiculous story" that she might be able to shed some light on. She agreed immediately and listened in attentive silence as he repeated the whole story with the exception of the role she was purportedly playing in it. He left nothing else out wanting to ensure she fully and clearly understood the depth of the experience and the profound impact it had had on him.

"I know it sounds weird," he said when he was done. "But that is exactly the way I remember it. It wasn't hazy or dreamlike. In fact I could perceive everything with a clarity and comprehension that I didn't know was possible. I've been struggling with the whole thing ever since trying to decide what actually happened out there. I mean is that the way... it really is? Or is it Satan up to some tricks? If that realm was heaven then I've been grossly misled for most of my life. Right now I'm very confused."

"That was a natural experience Adam. You simply paid a short visit back home."

"Back home?"

"Yes and you found out it was too soon to stay there because you still have important work to do here on earth so here you still are."

He stared at her in silence for a moment then blurted. "So you're saying you actually believe the story just as I've told it to you?"

"Every word."

"Whew," he said running his fingers through his hair. Somehow her willing corroboration was disconcerting. Had it been anyone else he would have been inclined to dismiss them as a thrill seeker wanting to indulge in sensationalism. But in her he sensed a wisdom that he couldn't just wave off and besides if she really was a vital link in this weird chain of events her participation might help clarify at least some part of it.

But how was he to engage her counsel without revealing the fact that his father suggested he should? He had purposely left that part out thinking it would eliminate the remote chance that she might cooperate just to validate his story.

A huge credibility gap still separated what he could accept and what this experience had revealed to him. His only reason for pursuing it was because he couldn't shake it off. It clung to him with a tenacity that was emotionally draining and he knew he could no longer ignore the numerous questions that it had spawned.

Had his father known Jenny while he was still alive? And why had his father urged him to be counseled by her? Had Jeffery known Jenny? How was that possible? What was the bond between himself and Jenny that his father had alluded to? Why had she not mentioned it? Had he somehow been destined to meet her in this unorthodox manner.

He even felt a tinge of anger because the whole experience had forced him into a situation he didn't want to be in. It had erased a portion of the old Adam Finlay leaving a vacuum in its wake.

He had always exercised total control over every aspect of his life but now something was being thrust on him whether or not he was willing to accept it.

"Adam," she broke into his thoughts. "Is there more you would like to talk about?"

"Yeah, a lot. But before I start, what alerted you and Andy to come and check on me that night?"

"Call it a sixth sense Adam. I knew you were in serious trouble so I called Andy and we rushed in."

"It was rather frustrating," he laughed. "I was right behind you and I kept saying everything was okay but you were completely unaware of me."

"I knew when you started to move up," she said. "Did you see me wave?"

"Yes and I tried once again to make contact but no luck."

"I did sense your presence near the ceiling."

"I should've guessed. Anyway we're off track. There is much more I want to talk about, but I'm not sure where to start."

"You have doubts about the authenticity of the experience don't you?"

"Yes, many."

"If it had unfolded exactly as Catholicism teaches would you still doubt it?"

"Obviously not."

"So it seems that Catholicism may not be the one and only true religion after all."

He shrugged but said nothing.

"Did you find out which one was while you were on the other side?"

"You already know the answer to that, but tell me this. If there is no special reward for a life of dedication to one's religious belief then what is the point?"

"Many reasons, Adam, but obviously none that you identify with. You see ultimate reality is much more profound than a simple reward system in which you gain certain credits proportionate to your behavior during this life."

"Okay but is there no benefit at all in being dedicated to the church?"

"Of course there is but you thought your good deeds would only be recognized if they were reported back to God through one very exclusive channel when the reality is something quite different."

He sighed heavily and stared at the floor. A few short months ago he would've snarled back some abrasive response and walked away. Now he was trying to find a discreet way to engage her counsel.

She was staring intently at him as though she was aware of his inner conflict and would patiently wait until he made the inevitable request.

"She knows," he thought. "Damn it she somehow knows what is going to happen, why the hell doesn't she just offer?"

Out loud he said, "Jen I realize that you are…well quite spiritually enlightened. I'm not sure of the terminology but would you…"

"I will teach as much as you're willing to learn, Adam. But if we do proceed, what lies in store is going to conflict, and conflict fundamentally at times, with your current beliefs. Are you prepared to temporarily suspend a lifelong belief system to explore a completely different form of spirituality?

Be aware, too, that this will take time and you do seem anxious to return to Edmonton as soon as possible."

He looked through the window out into the barnyard and for a moment absently watched Andy fork hay into a small corral that enclosed four hungry cows.

He realized that this was a major turning point in his life and instinctively knew that if he started down this road there was no turning back.

She had earlier mentioned that the environment and spirituality were an inseparable mix and for that reason she might be able to shed some light on the questions presented by the group he had joined.

Expecting her to quickly back off he asked, "can spirituality as you define it halt the destructive trend that mankind is presently following?"

"Yes it can Adam."

Taken back by the confidence of her response he stared at her for a moment, a faint smile tugging at the corners of his mouth.

"That's a rather bold claim isn't it?"

"No it isn't. I said adhering to spiritual principles can stop the destruction but we must have a majority exercising those principles."

Let's consider this. The human race is running out of options. Short of every person in affluent countries giving up their exorbitant lifestyle and reducing to basic needs, which they're not going to do, we've pretty well come to a dead end.

Following spiritual principles at the outset even as recently as the start of the industrial revolution would have averted the potential disaster we now face. But an obsession to accumulate much more than what any one individual needed soon began to predominate bringing us to the point we are at today."

"I always believed the lust for power was the major problem."

"A lust for power is just another form of greed. Dictators for example are taking more than what is rightfully theirs by depriving citizens of their freedom. Ruthless businessmen in democratic countries do the same by grinding their smaller competitors to death and controlling the market. If a certain product becomes popular, they charge the maximum the market will bear, simply because the product is in demand when they could charge forty percent less and likely still make a fair profit.

A formidable obstacle presently existing is that so few are aware of the seriousness of the problem or at least they don't want to be. Many more don't even think we do have a problem when in truth we are teetering on the precipice of annihilation."

"You make it sound worse than the group I joined."

"I hope I do. It is time for a very harsh wake up call. The only chance we have left is for enough persons of vision to hear and heed."

"I'm still new to all this but the limited amount of information I did dig up seemed to indicate some efforts are already underway to help turn the tide."

She had walked over and looked out a window as he talked. Then with arms folded turned to face him when he stopped but said nothing so he continued. "The most hazardous chemicals have either been banned completely or severely restricted by law. Oil eating microbes are now sprayed on oil spills which do a pretty good clean up job. Farming practices have changed with a switch over to low chemical agriculture and eventually to complete organic farming. In fact many organic products are already on the shelves in grocery stores. Oil companies have introduced cleaner burning fuels at least in heavy smog areas and improved public transportation systems such as light rail transits will help reduce air pollution. House plants do an excellent job of cleaning up indoor pollution."

"Adam," she said walking slowly back and seating herself again. "All those efforts you've just mentioned are commendable and will provide some relief but that is all. Relief. They are classic examples of closing the barn door after the horse is out. Let's start at the starting point. In an ideal world conflicts of all types including environmental issues could be resolved peacefully through dialogue and reconciliation but then in an ideal world we would have no environmental problems. As it now stands selfishness, bigotry and hatred are so powerful that disagreements and even outbursts of violence are inevitable. Conflicts that occur between nations, social and racial groups and between individuals are a reflection of conflicts that take place within ourselves. We will never have world peace until we have internal peace and we will not have internal peace until we start living in harmony with spiritual principles. That in a general way identifies the relationship between spirituality and the environment, but it is a vast subject. It would take several months just to overview fundamental principles."

"Several months," he said in a slightly raised voice. "You must have discovered the ultimate solution to everything."

"Nobody has made that discovery and on this plane of existence no one ever will. The truth is we are never finished learning or more accurately evolving no matter which realm we inhabit."

"Okay," he said with a chuckle. "You've already lost me. Obviously I'll need time to grasp even the basics." Exhaling slowly through pursed lips he stared for a moment into empty space.

"Several months eh?" he repeated. "I'll have to send out another message informing everyone that I won't be back for a while."

"Andy can do that today."

"I'll send it to my office this time."

"As you wish," she said handing him a pencil and paper.

"Are you sure you are willing to do this?" he said to her after completing a brief message to his manager. "It's going to take up a lot of your time."

"There is nothing in life more important than spiritual evolution, Adam. I evolve by assisting someone else to evolve."

Shaking his head slightly as he handed her the note he said, "I can see I've got a lot of learning in store."

"You've got a lot to remember, Adam. The knowledge is already buried within you. All I can do is help you bring it to the surface again."

"Again?"

"Yes, again. This is far from being our first round. But let's not get ahead of ourselves. I would like you to sleep on it and if you still are as willing to proceed in the morning as you seem to be right now, then we will embark on a journey that will challenge practically every spiritual belief you've ever held."

"Okay," he nodded in reluctant agreement. Now that he had made the decision he was anxious to get started. But she was likely right. He instinctively knew that this was a major turning point in his life and he knew he must not treat it lightly.

He laid awake thinking for a long time after getting into bed that night. Reviewing the events of the last two weeks he realized his focus had shifted from the concerns raised by the environmental group to his unsettling near death experience and he was now acquainted with a woman who claimed that the two were directly linked to each other. Besides if the near death experience had any degree of credibility about it at all, he then had some previous connection to this woman whom he had never met before.

His last thoughts as he drifted off to sleep was hoping she had answers because right now nothing made sense.

CHAPTER 14

"Are you all set?" she asked pouring another cup of coffee for each of them after breakfast dishes were washed and stored away once again.

"I feel like a lamb being led to the slaughter," he replied with a grin.

"I'll try to make it as painless as possible."

"I'm sure I'll survive. What's first on the agenda?"

She gazed absently out a window for a few moments. Then bringing her eyes back to meet his. "Adam have you ever questioned the many apparent injustices and disparities that seemed so prevalent in our world today."

Taken aback by what sounded like an irrelevant question he was silent for a moment. Then to be certain he had heard right he asked, "Would you repeat that I'm not sure..."

"You heard right," she said turning to face him again. "And the question is relevant. You see Adam before we can tap into truth we must face, squarely, what many would prefer not to and that's the degree to which our culture has either steered us away from truth or screened it from us. Evidence of this can be found anywhere we look and yet most of the time we really don't see it. The abnormal disparity in the distribution of wealth in the world is one example. The suffering and sorrow that seems to plague many, while others live a life of good fortune and good health is another. Then there is the perceived unfairness of a premature death compared to the long life of a centenarian. The cruel dictator or mob boss committing the most heinous of crimes imaginable and living in luxury while highly moral persons struggle along near poverty all their life. Have you ever had cause to question these things?"

"I think most of us have but some are inevitable. We certainly have no control over premature death or why misfortune always seems to plague some. And the uneven distribution of wealth is largely out of our hands too. These things have no solutions that I'm aware of."

"I wasn't suggesting that there are solutions. I was asking if you've ever questioned them."

"I have since Jeffery's death."

"Did you come up with answers?"

"What answers can we come up with? This is just the way things are."

"Which is precisely the way the culture keepers want us to think."

"The culture keepers?"

"I invented that term to describe the handful of persons who are the real rulers of our planet or a large portion of it. I'm referring to the financially elite who control the purse strings and hence set the tone of our culture. The term may not be applicable, but I couldn't think of a more appropriate one. The truth is they are only concerned about our culture insofar as the workings of it further their opportunity to amass greater wealth. Their greedy appetite for money and power drives them to manipulate the very cornerstones of society to ensure their continued stranglehold on a system that serves them well.

This is an insidious plague that has undermined the foundation of democracy and tragically the majority of people are completely oblivious to it."

"Jenny I have some problem here. How does this so called 'elite group' exercise that degree of control over the masses with so few of us ever being aware of it?"

"Various ways Adam. One that is very effective is through the media. Many newspapers are owned by wealthy moguls who will, when necessary, dictate what will be printed and how it will appear. They don't usually ignore issues that they may be in conflict with. They just downplay them. For example I once recall reading a brief article on global warming in a remote corner of a newspaper while two full pages were devoted to a major sporting event. This was some years ago but at the time I felt betrayed. Didn't our future as a species rate at least the same importance as the fact that your Edmonton Oilers had won their first Stanley Cup? And likely every person in Canada knew that the Toronto Blue Jays won baseball's highest honors two years in a row, but at the same time how many were aware of the serious threat to human life that clear cut logging posed? If the clear cutting was reported at all it was likely because of a conflict between environmentalists and some logging company with the conflict itself being the focus."

"Well I can understand one aspect of it. Canadians frequently lag behind in many ways. If we have made any achievement, even in sports, it is a newsworthy event."

"More newsworthy than the potential annihilation of the human race?"

"Of course not, but I don't believe you can blame newspapers entirely. Reader demands are a major influence on what they print. They would go down the tube pretty fast if they didn't cater to those demands."

"Agreed. But don't you think any newspaper also has a certain moral obligation to give at least equal and unbiased exposure to a topic that could adversely affect every human being on earth?"

"Well yes…"

"That exposure isn't given Adam because it would focus on more stringent environmental controls which, if implemented, could severely restrict the profit potential of the select few who continue to ignore what cannot be ignored much longer."

"This may all be fact but what does it have to do with my near death experience?"

"Much more than you think Adam, but for now I'm trying to make you understand that most of us have bought into social standards not of our own making. We've come to accept all manner of contentious issues with little resistance and unless you are now ready to question without compromise then anything I could offer would be of little benefit."

"I still don't understand."

"Adam do you remember saying some time ago that you had purchased all the material things that you thought should bring happiness? There was the motorhome, the house at the lake, the swimming pool and so on?"

"Yes."

"And do you also remember asking what did it accomplish and saying you might as well have lived in a cabin in the wilderness?"

"Yes."

"What does that tell you?"

"Well I suppose those material things didn't bring the happiness I sought."

"So why did you buy them?"

"I thought they would...at the time"

"Why did you think they would?"

"For one thing it was the trendy thing to do. Most of our friends had the same stuff and did most of those same things."

"In other words you eagerly bought into the system."

"I hadn't looked at it that way. I was just trying to bring some pleasure into our life."

"But did you really analyze what would bring pleasure?"

"We talked it over as a family. Everyone agreed, at the time, on the things we acquired. We all wanted that stuff."

"Why do you think everyone wanted it?"

"Okay it was in style, but…"

"Precisely. It was stylish, trendy, in vogue. You were keeping up with friends, neighbors, the Jones' and down near the bottom of that list, it's just possible some of your family members might have actually enjoyed some of it."

"That's not true. They did enjoy a lot of it."

"Well it's a blessing they did. At least you had some justification for the huge sums of money you spent. You're still missing the point. Whether you and your family enjoyed those things a lot or a little is secondary. You did exactly what the culture keepers wanted you to do. You bought into the current trend which indirectly added a bit more strength to their power base. Don't get me wrong, I'm not saying we shouldn't want or have those wonderful things that technology has made available assuming our budget allows for them. But it should be for the right reasons and in this society how often do we truly know what the right reasons are. We've become so accustomed to being told what we should like and how we should live life that we often don't really know ourselves at all. For example there are alternatives to the things you bought into and they certainly would be a lot less costly. If you were a family of swimming enthusiasts, the pool might be justified, but for an occasional dip in hot weather the local community facility would suffice. And did you really enjoy the cramped quarters of a motor home as well as all the upkeep associated with owning it? Maybe you did but for the eighty thousand or so that you probably spent you could have rented motels for the rest of your life. How often have we seen someone buy one of those things and for fifty out of fifty-two weeks it adorns the back yard. But once again owning the motor home was in style and the culture keepers snared another victim."

Exhaling slowly he said, "I never looked at it that way before. I guess most of us just go along with the current trends."

"That's no sin Adam. You simply fell into a fast moving stream, as so many have and you went with the flow rather than swim against it.

For a long time the problems associated with this condition have been more or less manageable. But we are fast approaching a day of reckoning that will force us to reverse this trend or suffer the consequences and they could be unthinkable. Humanity has, for too long, violated universal or spiritual laws and the negative results are popping up everywhere. We have environmental deterioration, social unrest, starvation, exploding population, crime, wars, disease, drug abuse all on an unprecedented scale and in the final analysis it can all be traced back to one human idiosyncrasy: obscene greed and lust for power."

"You also mentioned the unfairness of premature death and misfortune that seems to plague many. These things are beyond anybody's control."

"Keep in mind Adam I was only asking if you questioned the apparent unfairness of these conditions. You see the culture keepers have dulled our senses into an automatic acceptance of traditional explanations. For example what do you believe was the reason for the death of your nineteen year old son?"

"It was an accident," he shrugged.

"Why did the accident occur?"

"Why does any accident occur? It's just an accident."

"But at one point you strongly berated the unfairness of it right?"

"Yes Jenny and I still do, but that doesn't change anything. Jeffery's dead and it's due to an accident."

"Didn't Jeff say during your near death experience that his premature death was partly to get you back on track?"

"The jury's still out on that one."

"But you did say it seemed unfair but who or what were you directing that statement at?"

"Well…God I guess: the ultimate authority."

"And did God explain it to you?"

"Of course not. I mean is God really going to talk to me? It's just instinctive to take our sorrow to the higher power when it is beyond human understanding."

"So your instinct told you to talk to God about it, but you also believe God isn't going to answer."

"Jenny I don't see where this is leading. What is the significance of it?"

"Bear with me. Let's suppose a confirmed atheist had a similar tragedy. Would he or she ask God for an explanation?"

"Obviously not."

"Would they not be instinctively compelled as you were?"

"I don't know, but it seems unlikely."

"Then what's the difference between you and the atheist? Why do you think you turned to God and the atheist wouldn't."

"It's a fundamental difference in beliefs."

"And from what source did you acquire your belief?"

"The church.'

"The church. Right Adam. Finally we get to the root."

"Is there something wrong with believing in the church?"

"Certainly not, if you're satisfied with their explanation of things and right now you have doubts. What explanation did they give you for the death of your son at such a young age."

"It was God's will. God works in mysterious ways and we mere humans can't always understand his motives."

Did you feel better after that?"

"I felt…appeased."

"But you still didn't feel better?"

"No but grieving is natural."

"Of course it is. But wouldn't it lighten the load considerably if you felt free to explore that perceived unfairness and don't you now feel relieved after your near death experience?"

"How do you know I feel relieved? Right now I'm just trying to make some sense out of that incident."

"Adam your focus has changed completely. You are asking questions that you once wouldn't have dared think about. You do not yet have answers but if you stop for a moment and review your feelings you will find your sorrow has lessened considerably. It has been replaced with a curiosity about things that are fundamental to our very existence."

She was right he realized. In retrospect his sorrow over the loss of his son had largely disappeared since that strange experience.

"Okay but I still think we will never be privy to that information as long as we're alive."

"Why do you believe that?"

"Well I think most people do, at least most Christians do. It's a part of our teachings."

"Which you learned in church."

"Where else?"

"And they also taught that you can not or must not try to understand anything beyond what they permit."

"Jenny I don't think doctrinal restrictions are the issue. It's all we have available. The church uses the bible; the ultimate text book to guide them in this awareness."

"Correction Adam. They use their interpretation of the bible out of which they formulated doctrines that define what and how much you are permitted to know."

"Maybe, but I don't believe doctrines were formulated just to put a limit on our understanding of God and creation."

"Well in fact they were at the outset of Christianity, but that's a topic for another time. Right now tell me what you believe doctrines are for?"

"In general terms they are a statement of the churches philosophy or belief system."

"And if you subscribe to that belief system you wouldn't embrace any concepts outside of it."

"Not if they are extremely contradictory."

"Then the only explanation for your son's premature death is limited to what that system says you can believe."

"That system is all we need. Catholicism is the one true church; the keeper of the original revelations from Jesus."

"Do you still believe that Adam?"

"I guess I'm not real certain now," he sighed. "But it is an integral part of Catholic teaching."

"In other words it must be accepted just because they say so."

"Oh no. They are strictly guided by the Bible."

"Which I believe you referred to as the ultimate spiritual textbook."

"Yes."

"How do you know that?"

"How does anybody know it? It is just common knowledge. We are told that thousands and thousands of highly educated and intelligent persons have studied the Bible exhaustively over the centuries and have all reached the same general conclusion: the Bible is the irrefutable word of God."

"But that still boils down to the fact that the Bible is the absolute word of God only because the Bible itself says so?"

"At one time that was something we just didn't question any more than we questioned why the sun came up every morning. We knew it was going to happen without always asking why."

"Let me get this straight Adam. What we have is a church belief system built on the irrevocable word of God which they derived from a centuries old text book and based entirely on the fact the book itself says it is the word of God. That is what you are telling me isn't it? Now this church, along with many others, has formulated doctrines out of their interpretations of this book which subsequently became inviolable rules that followers are expected to abide by and admonished not to question.

Regardless of what their intentions were, and are, the existence of these rules, or doctrines, prohibits you investigating reasons for your son's death beyond what they have said you can know."

"I still don't think it's possible to know more because such knowledge just isn't available. And besides what if I simply don't want to know."

"Then there is no purpose in having this discussion."

"Okay, my mistake. Please go on."

"The point I'm trying to make Adam, is you are not even free to try to discover that fact for yourself as long as you conform to church rules. If you did make some attempt at doing so you would feel very uncomfortable because it violates a church norm which is nothing more than the culture keepers in slightly different form, imposing their will on us once again."

"Okay Jenny," he said with a sigh. I'm willing to give some validity to your views but how can they explain my near death experience?"

"They will if you can shake off social constraints long enough for us to carry out an unbiased and meaningful investigation of your experience."

"You make it sound as though we've been living an illusion all this time."

"Oh indeed we have Adam. Indeed we have."

"Okay I'm anxious to know more about whatever it was that I experienced back there so I'll do my best."

"I still have doubts about the authenticity of the experience and one of the reasons is because there was no mention of church or religion. From that I could conclude the church is of little use but that seems ridiculous. It's like saying democracy is worthless even though it has governed our country since its inception."

"That comparison is much more applicable that you think. But tell me this. Have you ever wondered why we exist at all?"

"Why we exist?" he repeated slowly. "Okay Jenny. Why?"

"Have you ever questioned the purpose for human beings? Do you feel we even have a purpose or are we just the evolutionary end product of a series of random cosmic events that started by accident?"

"We were created by God Jenny. I have no doubts about that at all."

"If we are divinely created beings then would it not seem logical that we must have some purpose?"

"Up until now I've always accepted the churches' explanation which says we are here to love and worship God and follow in His ways which have been revealed through the teachings of Jesus and if we were judged worthy at death we would be with God in heaven for eternity. If we choose not to follow in his ways we will be left in eternal alienation from God."

"That still doesn't answer my question."

"Why not?"

"You said we are here to worship God and follow in His ways. Have you ever wondered just why God decided to put us through this little exercise?"

"Well, no. But then does God really need a reason?"

"Well I do hope it's more than just a passing fad. If not the human race is on shaky ground."

"Okay. What I should've said is we don't know what his reasons are?"

"Why don't we?"

"Why don't we! Well now this may come as a surprise Jenny but God hasn't filled me in on this just yet and I don't think He's going to anytime soon."

"In other words we are an integral part of something God is doing but we are not permitted to know the reasons for it."

"I don't think it's possible for us to know or even that we should know."

"The point is you've accepted this as fact because your church told you so, which is just another facet of society, or the culture keepers, telling you what you can and cannot question."

"Jenny if God had wanted us to know why we exist we probably would. Since we don't He must have a very good reason for keeping it from us."

"Correction Adam. We are keeping if from ourselves."

"Oh really and just how are we doing that?"

"Simply by accepting without question what orthodox Christianity has preached to us during the past 1700 years or so. We could be excused at the starting point because the so called founders turned their belief system into the official state religion of the Roman Empire. Opposing it ultimately became a crime punishable by death and astonishingly, certain tenets established at that time are still practiced today. That ideology had little to do with authentic Christian teachings and a lot to do with what the emperor decreed which expanded his despotic control of the Roman Empire. Those times have long since passed but the influence they still have on modern day Christianity is astounding. For reasons that defy logic, many churches still cling to antiquated beliefs and practices that have no relevancy in this 21st century. The real tragedy lies in the detrimental affect they have had on our spiritual journey.

Nowadays we are free to choose our pathway without fear of persecution but we still have a residual unwillingness to question ancient beliefs that no longer make sense which keeps us trapped in the culture keepers iron grip. Expanding this fact out to embrace every aspect of our life we will find we've brought our planet and ourselves dangerously close to irreversible disaster. The majority of people still refuse to face squarely up to the causes, partly because it would transcend the boundaries of traditional thinking. The time has come to fearlessly question the status quo if humanity is to have a future and the logical place to start is where traditional belief systems had their origin: organized religion.

Now we can usually get general agreement on the fact that God is almighty, all powerful and with intelligence far beyond what any human can imagine so it would logically follow He must've had a good solid reason for bringing this physical realm into existence."

"I agree with that much."

"Your religion has told you that we are here to love and worship God and follow in His ways and if we don't succeed at this we are banished to hell which would indicate we are being put to some sort of test."

"I guess you could look at it that way."

"Then will you please explain to me why an almighty, all powerful and perfect God didn't just simply create perfect offspring that needed no such testing?"

"Well…"

"And can you tell me, Adam, what God is trying to prove by this exercise in which failure means eternal exile into some realm of torture too horrifying to contemplate?"

"But…"

"I mean doesn't it seem a bit odd for a perfect God to send His offspring out to take a test that wasn't necessary in the first place and then to really complicate matters those that fail are lost forever?"

"Yes, but…"

"Oh and then there's the worship you mentioned. Tell me why an almighty God who has and is everything needs His offspring to worship Him? In fact why does He need to be worshipped at all?"

"Okay! Okay! Slow down," he said with a grin. "Do I get a chance to talk?"

"The floor is all yours."

"First of all," he began. "Hell doesn't necessarily mean eternal torture. Just separation from God."

"That depends on which religious denomination you are talking about."

"Alright but I don't believe that myself.

"Much of Catholicism does."

"Well I don't and besides life on earth is not just a test. We are also here to gain the experience necessary to help mold a character that is worthy of returning to God's presence."

"Adam think about that statement. It's like saying we came from perfection to be perfected so we could return to perfection. It makes no sense. To gain experience in the physical realm? Great if it was unconditional, but it's not. In this scenario God is saying you may go to earth to gain experience but only those experiences that I've sanctioned. All others are a sin for which you will be punished. Is there any logic to that?"

"Satan plays a part in all this Jenny. He has a very strong influence on the events that take place on earth."

"Then why has God allowed his children to be exposed to Satan's temptations?"

"For the same reason Jesus was tempted in the desert; to see if he could resist the temptation. All of us are prone to Satan's lure, some more so than others. We become worthy of inheriting part of God's kingdom by proving our love for God through our capacity to resist Satan's temptations."

"Adam you're still evading the 'why' behind all of this and besides what you've said seems to imply that God has some agreement with Satan."

"How is that?"

"He must have engaged Satan's services to provide temptations for us to see how well we could resist them."

"God is not going to make deals with Satan, Jenny."

"Then how do you explain the fact that Satan seems to be free to roam around the planet tempting us with every kind of evil act that is in opposition to God's will?"

"Satan is a fallen angel. God didn't give him power. He has always had it but he chose to use it for evil, which finally got him banished from heaven. So he came to earth where he had free reign."

"I know the story, but it is saying God's power is not absolute. Satan seems to be equally powerful."

"Just here on earth."

"I thought God created earth."

"He did."

"Then He either allowed Satan in or didn't have the power to keep him out."

He tossed his hands up in frustration. He wasn't used to losing arguments, but right now he certainly wasn't winning.

"Adam there is much more depth to the creator and its creation than what we've just been discussing. But for now let's deal with those conflicts that are common to orthodox Christian faith."

"Okay Jenny," he said exhaling slowly. "Where is this leading?"

"Going back in history for a minute, it is readily evident that humanity has made astonishing progress in practically every aspect of life isn't it?"

"That's obvious."

"We can, as one example, call someone on another continent through a small wireless communicating device no larger than a bar of soap.

Our forefathers, on the other hand, had to dispatch a runner with a hand written message just to invite nearby neighbors to dinner and there was no way of knowing their response until the runner returned if he did at all. Being way laid by a band of outlaws or becoming a meal for some wild animal was all part of the cost of maintaining this crude communicating system.

Examples of progress are endless and amazing. We still keep mementos of bygone eras in museums that not only amuse us, but are a physical reminder of the lifestyle our ancestors lived. Older persons may view these relics with a certain nostalgia but likely few would want to return to a time and place in which they were still in common use.

The same can be said for understanding our world and the various forces that cause it to function the way it does. There were numerous beliefs brought into existence by our ancestors in an attempt to explain a world that they inhabited but didn't understand. They once thought, for example, that the sun was towed across the sky each day by a giant horse drawn chariot.

The sky itself was thought to be the blue interior of an immense inverted bowl; the top side of which was the realm of God or heaven. If God was angry with his children, He stomped around up there making loud frightening noises that we now call thunder. He would also fling deadly bolts of fire earthward and if one struck and killed somebody it was believed that somebody must have committed a terrible sin which God would not tolerate. Some held there was a trap door at a strategic point in the sky that opened up to admit us through at death assuming of course, that we weren't sent down through the other trap door to hell.

Earth was a flat slab of ground between these two regions and if we traveled too far in any one direction we would fall off. These beliefs were consistent with a race in its infancy. We can reflect back on them now realizing they were stepping stones on our evolutionary pathway. But right here is where logic flies out the window. Most of the time everyone readily accepts new concepts that displace outmoded beliefs simply because the evidence supporting the new discovery cannot logically be denied." She stopped and asked, "Are you still with me Adam?"

"I think so but I've no idea where you are going."

"You must've drawn some conclusions from what I've been saying."

Shrugging his shoulders he said, "Evolution is happening and it's a natural process but that's not really a startling new discovery."

"No it's not is it? And here's another one. Museums are filled to overflowing with archeological finds that prove, almost beyond any doubt that our planet is several billion years old. Pre-humans may have walked the earth between two and three million years in our past and actual human beings emerged about fifty thousand years ago. But you are aware of that aren't you?"

"I went to school for a few years."

"So you accept these theories as the most logical record of our history?"

"Who am I to argue with archeologists?"

"Why do you accept them?"

"For the same reason anyone else does. The supporting evidence is so strong that it would be foolish to oppose them. But isn't this rather elementary? Most of us know something about our beginnings."

"What does your church tell you?"

He looked at her with a faint grin playing at the corners of his mouth. She smiled back sweetly but with a look that demanded a response.

"So everything you've been talking about for the last few minutes has been leading up to this?"

"What do you think?"

"I think you're a master at answering a question with a question. why didn't you just ask me in the first place what my view was?"

"Which view would you have given, the religious or the scientific. I know it's elementary stuff Adam but for some reason that defies logic, certain Christian denominations still hold to the belief that somewhere between six and ten thousand years ago God created the world and everything in it when evidence refuting that idea is practically undeniable."

"Yes but we cannot always comprehend God's ways. They may not appear logical to our limited human brain, but in His great scheme of things they would make perfect sense."

"Adam if that were fact then all those events once considered to be miracles may never have been explained in purely scientific terms. Earthquakes, volcanoes, hurricanes, floods, fires previously thought to be God or gods expressing their dissatisfaction with us are now easily understood natural phenomena. Try to visualize a modern day jet plane somehow straying back in time to the twelfth century and flying through the skies. Would not observers on the ground think this to be a miracle? It would likely be seen as God demonstrating His almighty power by defying the law of gravity with this strange and fearsome aircraft and everyone would have probably ran and hid somewhere in fear. But to us in the twenty-first century it is an everyday occurrence that we pay little attention to. Most of us have some general idea of how and why an aircraft works and attribute it to technological achievement which is exactly what it is.

It is time, Adam, to stop trying to force fit first century belief into twenty-first century fact the way that many religious denominations do. In every other aspect of life we usually welcome new inventions and discoveries because they contribute to an improved quality of life but for some reason that is difficult to understand, the credibility of religion is seen to somehow increase in direct proportion to its age."

"It doesn't sound like you hold much hope for the future of organized religion."

"I don't hold out hope for anything that resists the natural process of evolution. When the 'horseless carriage' first appeared on the scene around the turn of the twentieth century it was considered to be nothing more than a worthless nuisance that would soon fade away. When the Wright brothers were involved in their initial tests to build a machine that would fly, skeptics everywhere said it could never be done. The only thing that cannot be done is stop the relentless thrust of evolution. We may slow it down as traditional Christianity has done during the past eighteen hundred years or so, but it will not be stopped."

"Taking that idea to its extreme it would seem to be saying we could ultimately replace God."

"We cannot replace what we already are Adam. God is having this evolutionary experience through and as us. We are one and the same and to the degree that we accept that truth is the degree to which we will understand those things that you refer to as divine mysteries."

"That really flies in the face of tradition. They believe that not only can we not know God's plan, at least not in it's entirety, but it is dangerous blasphemy to try. Now I find this mountain dweller recklessly breaking all the rules without apparent fear of reprisal. Ten years ago I would've ran for my life so I have to ask myself what has come over me?"

"It's called awakening."

"Have we really been that sound asleep? I have to admit what you say makes sense, but it also contradicts much of what millions have always believed. I still can't help feeling, for example, that when we die there will be some form of punishment for a life lived in opposition to God's will."

"Adam we are all God's will…"

"Jenny," he interrupted. "I don't understand exactly what you mean by statements like that. It sounds like some new age garble that I always thought was never really meant to make sense."

"It will become clear to you but one step at a time. Please bear with me."

"Okay," he said sighing heavily. It's just that this whole issue of God, creation and all the rest can be very frustrating. Why I remember times when I wondered what really is out there after death. Was it just possible I was on the wrong pathway? Or maybe there was nothing at all. Maybe we simply faded away into oblivion when we die."

"So you are saying that somewhere deep inside yourself lay a suspicion that the afterlife could have been something different from what your belief told you if indeed there was anything out there at all."

"Yes. But where does that leave us? It's a pretty desperate feeling to think we really have no idea what is beyond this life."

"Then strong belief in any religion would seem like a precarious balancing act if, as you say, we really don't know what lies in store for us anyway. Despite this, however, many denominations still declare their way is the only right way which, by implication, says all others are off track which must also say those others will be punished because they failed to guess which one was right."

He shrugged his shoulders.

"And yet it's possible that none of them really know what's in store at all."

"Congratulations you've just cast more doubt on an issue that's already cloudy. I've usually always accepted the church's explanation of the afterlife and I guess I never really thought much more than that about it."

"Adam you accepted what you thought you should believe otherwise a few doubts would've crept in."

"If that's so how can anybody, including you, be certain of what's next."

"Because I don't believe what society says I should believe, but what is true for me. The afterlife cannot be proven by any method but that's not really what's important. If it was, many of us would spend our life wallowing in apprehension about our ultimate fate. We can all dispel with doubts and fears and, as I've done, gain the only peace and contentment that's available to us in life. This is a very simple, but for many, a very challenging process that they will have to struggle with. I repeat a very simple but challenging process. Now I think we've gone far enough for today. I have some other work I must do but I would suggest you think about what that process may be and we'll pick up on it again tomorrow."

He nodded in reluctant agreement. He had become so

consumed by the topic that the sudden halt left him feeling as though he was groping around in the dark.

She had an ingenious way of leading him to conclusions rather than imposing her belief on him which kept him reaching for more.

Lying on the living room couch in the afternoon he began turning over, in his mind, the details of their discussion and the question she had left him with. What would one have to do in order to attain the peace that she appeared to have captured so completely?

To be contented in this wilderness environment seemed like a paradox but then maybe the isolation itself was the secret. Whatever it was there was a serenity about Jennifer Ingram that was not readily defined and thinking about it seemed only to take him further away from an answer.

CHAPTER 15

"Well Adam," she said as they resumed the discussion the next day "do you have an answer to the question I posed yesterday?"

"No but I have more questions. I tried but I really couldn't identify any one thing that might bring us genuine and lasting contentment in this life. I do know it is something different than what I've already experienced because in retrospect I realize I've never known what I would label as peace. Yesterday you mentioned something about doubts creeping in if we subscribe to beliefs that we haven't analyzed. Analyzing a firmly established church tradition seems sacrilegious and I'm sure is the reason why most of us wouldn't do it or haven't as yet. However, if you are right then traditional church beliefs are actually one cause for unrest. I do hope you will start revealing cures because right now you have me questioning every religion I've ever heard of."

"Adam there is something I want you to take and tuck firmly into a corner of your mind where it can always be accessed and that is just this: nothing, no thing, is valueless because absolutely everything is some part of the creator showing up as those things. Therefore no one religion is the only right one and none are wrong. To even think in those terms is absurd because it would mean God pitting some part of itself against another part. All religions are experiences that God is having through and as those religions. Different denominations help supply the variety that the creator is seeking on this experiential journey and I'm sure at times He or She must view, with amusement, the constant disputes over which one is right."

"Earlier it sounded as though you condemned religion but now you are saying they all are some aspect of God."

"Everything is some part of God including our freedom to express our disagreement. I disagree with the restrictive nature of traditional religion, not religion per say. Now here is where the basic reason for the physical realm comes into play. The conflict created as a result of differing opinions supplies the diversity necessary for evolution. Old outmoded beliefs should be dropped by the wayside when they can no longer stand the test of evolution. If new discoveries and revelations upstage them we then have a more solid foundation on which to build our knowledge."

"Are you saying we should eventually discard organized religion or that it will disappear?"

"You keep missing my point. Let me explain it another way. Most religions have done some good in the world and a few have done a lot. But radical changes in their philosophies will be required if they are to survive."

"What kind of changes?"

"All organized religions are institutional in nature. They have adopted a set of dogmatic doctrines that followers are hesitant to challenge if they want to remain a member in good standing. Think of any church service you've attended. The minister or priest stands up on the podium and delivers a sermon that all are expected to passively accept. There is no room for debate or discussion. They impart their interpretation of the bible which the congregation swallows without question. Many followers are probably impartial. They feel they've done their duty simply by being in church which they believe should gain them favorable standing in the afterlife. This format has changed very little since the beginning of Christianity even though the rest of the world we now live in would be unrecognizable by early Christians."

"But you did say that religions have done good in our world."

"Indeed they have and that good is a foundation upon which they can broaden their horizons. This is what must happen and what they are not doing. It would be foolishness to completely phase out a religion and start over with something brand new to replace it. Pull out the positive aspects of the religion and then expand on that base, but ensure that the expansion is in no way restricted by inflexible dogma. Delete those beliefs that evolution has shown to be in error but retain those that serve them well.

By way of analogy modern aircraft builders did not ignore everything that the Wright brothers discovered and put into practice. They took that valuable foundation of knowledge and built on it until we have the magnificent aircraft of today. Religion could've done the same thing and if they had the world scene would be very much different. Future religions must allow, indeed encourage, us to be true to ourselves which leads us back to your question from yesterday.

In order to attain the only genuine and lasting peace available to us in this life requires that we be *scrupulously true to ourselves.*"

"Be true to ourselves."

"Ruthlessly so."

"Is it really that simple? Just be true to ourselves?"

"It is that simple but remember I also said difficult."

"Well I'm lost. I believe I have been true to myself most of the time and I sure as hell haven't found much contentment."

"Have you really Adam? Let's consider this. There is a truth that we create for ourselves which is largely a product of our society and our ego and then there is our spiritual truth, the real truth of our being. For many the latter has lain dormant most of their life but for an increasing number including Adam Finlay, they are starting to dredge that truth up from the muck and wash it off so that it can be seen clearly once again. I'm sure this truth will contradict almost every principle that has ever guided you and this is why I'm saying it could be enormously difficult for now you will be viewing life through entirely different colored lenses.

I'm going to start with a story of a very wealthy man whose daughter I became friends with while attending university. She was studying commerce at the time and this particular incident was relevant to her studies. It started when her father, a hard nosed businessman had the opportunity to buy out a struggling company on the verge of bankruptcy. She relayed to me, with pride, the fact that he had made a major business achievement by negotiating the lowest possible price for this near defunct company. A price so low, in fact, that even his competitors had to hail it as a significant feat.

My friend, laughing, mentioned that her father had generously offered the two ex-owners employment with his now much larger firm. She even joked about the fact that they would probably have to accept his offer since they had a heavy debt load left as a result of the demise of their fledgling organization. This she attributed to incompetent management which resulted in a happy ending for her and her family."

She stopped talking and looked across the table at him. After a few moments silence he asked. "Is there more to the story?"

"Do you think there should be?"

"I don't know but it sounds like dad had a good business head and daughter was following in his footsteps."

"Yes indeed. They ranked high in the eyes of their industry. They had pulled off a business deal of which they could be justly proud."

"I agree. What's your point?"

"What about the plight of the previous owners who were left with debt simply because they were forced to sell out at an obscenely low price?"

"Jenny business is business. The deal wasn't dishonest or illegal, was it?"

"What about immoral?"

"That's a matter of opinion. We often find we must re-define morals in the business world otherwise we simply do not stay in business."

"Firstly you seem to be saying it's okay to have two sets of morals and secondly this man wasn't just staying in business Adam. He was already enormously wealthy and was gaining a great deal more at the expense of those other two men who ultimately had to file for bankruptcy simply because they couldn't handle the debt load on salaries alone. It's one thing to be competitive but quite another to grind your competitors to death just because you can do it."

"And what does Jennifer Ingram suggest?"

"Now here, Adam, is where you can dig deep within yourself and bring to the surface that truth I alluded to earlier. What, really, would be the truly moral and spiritually motivated action for my friend's father to have taken? Actually ex-friend. I didn't associate with her much after that."

He looked at her with a sly grin for a moment then answered in a sarcasm tainted voice. "Pay them fair market value."

"Right Adam," she said dragging the words out slowly for emphasis. "Fair market value and possibly even a few thousand dollars more because these two men who were honest, hard working citizens deserved at least that much and could have retained their dignity by avoiding the demoralization of bankruptcy. But more importantly we would be abiding by the God truth that underlies all things by responding to a brother with a loving compassion that overshadows the materialistic egoism still dominating the human race."

"That kind of talk causes me pain."

"I'm sure it does and it will continue to be painful for as long as you cling to socially motivated principles. But if you've truly embarked on a change of direction that old thread bare belief system is going to be exposed to some brutal attacks."

"I'm starting to see the challenges you mentioned."

"There's more coming. Now let's expand on the truths that up to now you've embraced and held in high esteem. These probably include hard work, success in business, financial gain, material wealth, social status and I'm sure there's more but you get the idea."

"I've lived them most of my life."

"Indeed but now we're going to do some very serious soul searching and we're not stopping until we've assisted you in adopting a belief system that is correct just for you. Uncertainty will finally be eliminated if you can, without hesitation, claim that what you believe is truly and exclusively yours. This will require a fearless and sincere search of the deepest recesses of your being and bring to the surface every facet of your current beliefs so that they can be held up to the light of uncompromising scrutiny. In the incident I just related you knew, when pressed, what was morally correct and in fact we all know if we probe the spiritual depths of our being.

Many will resist this exercise because the socially motivated desire to gain at almost any cost is a powerful persuader. There are numerous incidents in which immoral acts are considered achievements. Slipping an item or two past the checkout clerk at the supermarket. Accidentally damaging a parked car with your own and feeling as though you've gained because you weren't caught in the act. Feeling a smug sense of satisfaction because you received too much change when paying for something, cheating on income tax, lying about a child's age to gain free admission to some event. These are all examples of immoral and in some cases unlawful acts that much of our society has come to view as acceptable. In fact many will accuse you of stupidity if you don't take advantage of these so called opportunities.

Learn this and learn it well Adam. Absolutely nothing, no act, no uttered statement, no thing at all escapes the omnipotent and ubiquitous laws of the universe. The human legal systems often falls pathetically short of meting true justice but no such deficiencies exist in the realm of the divine. Any and all acts are accorded irrefutable and unfailing consequences no matter how cleverly we feel we may have camouflaged them. Never make the mistake of thinking you've successfully cheated anything because the relentless law of karma will bring about balance at some point in your existence. So take every idea, conviction, doctrine and dogma that constitutes your present belief structure and review it ruthlessly. This will take time but eventually you will redefine your entire moral code in the light of spiritual truths that will likely bear little resemblance to what you once believed.

This transition must be thorough and complete and you will be able to gauge your progress to the degree that your actions resonate with the inner God truth that lies at the core of every human being. When any future challenge in your life creates an internal conflict, stop and examine it carefully because the conflict arises out of discordance between something in the outer realm and the unfailing truth of your inner self.

Logic mixed with unblemished intuition is really all we have to go on and up to now most have not engaged those faculties. At the present time there is a significant movement toward spirituality primarily because we've exhausted all other sources to finding peace, contentment and solutions to problems. When all else fails we instinctively turn to some perceived higher power and that is what is happening now.

We've brought our race face to face with possible annihilation precisely because we tried those other methods and they obviously haven't worked. Humanity is presently teetering on a precarious ridge. If and when we do back away and salvage ourselves it will be due to a spiritual awakening but the need then would be to channel it correctly and one of the things that we must do is to *recover our individual identity*. We must stop turning it over to someone or something else and reclaim the freedom to know ourselves for who and what we truly are."

"That would mean opposing firmly held traditions that in some cases date back hundreds of years."

"Try thousands, which is precisely why we must revolt against them. If humanity is to have a future on planet earth it is urgent to find new direction. At present we are opposing the natural process of evolution by clinging tenaciously to certain outmoded traditions that have no relevancy whatsoever to the present day. This is not only detrimental but insane. Most humans act as if they cannot think at all in matters of spirituality. They willingly submit to concepts that someone else has formulated which if analyzed from the perspective of an intelligent adult should cause them to seriously question their own mentality."

"Those are pretty harsh accusations. You'll likely get a lot of flack."

"I already have. Rattling cages has that effect. Wake up calls are uncomfortable because they threaten powerful empires built on the gullibility of human beings."

"You might find yourself on somebody's hit list," he said with a laugh.

"Indeed I could. That is the moral and mental status of the monsters who still hold powerful sway. They will go to whatever lengths are necessary to preserve their kingdoms and if need be assassinate another human being as readily as you and I would swat a fly."

"You're talking radical changes," he said after a thoughtful moment. "Assuming they can happen where do we begin? In the past the majority turned to the church for guidance but you are saying the church is part of the problem."

"In its present form it is. We must turn back within ourselves to where we each find that small voice that has been suppressed for the better part of the past two thousand years. Once you've come to terms with that inner voice, as we've been discussing, then you may want to seek some outside assistance. If you do this you *must* find an organization, group or person that resonates with you, with your intuition, with your belief and not the other way around. We've spent far too long adapting ourselves to someone else's philosophy. It is time to take back control of ourselves and ensure that what we associate with fits us perfectly and not us trying to fit ourselves to it."

"You keep referring to that divine voice within which I'm assuming you mean to be God but you haven't specifically mentioned God. How does the creator fit into the picture you've just painted."

"If we talk about anything at all Adam we are talking about

God, because everything is an expression of God. There is one first cause and all that exists is an outpicturing of that basic and original source. Therefore we cannot avoid talking about God. This is a departure from most traditional beliefs which hold that God is separate from its creation but if you are to gain the maximum from your spiritual journey then you must grasp this concept of oneness. We will expand on this later but right now it's essential to understand the implications of this truth. Most importantly *each and every one of us have equal access to God*. No one individual or group has a monopoly on communication with the creator. It can be beneficial to pray in a group setting because many energies are combined to increase the potency of the prayers but *God can only respond to you personally back through you*. It cannot do something for you through someone else which is why reclaiming control of our spirituality is so critical.

CHAPTER16

Days turned rapidly into weeks as she guided him ever deeper into regions he had never before explored. Re-evaluating firmly held ideals was an ongoing exercise that finally had him questioning everything he had once taken for granted.

Maybe it was his imagination but the whole process seemed to have a positive effect on his health. Although in occasional disagreement with her ideologies he began gradually to experience a peace that he had never before known. Did this contribute to the rapid healing of his fractured leg and an equally rapid recovery from the heart attack? He didn't know but Doc Greer on his fourth visit expressed his amazement at Adam's progress by saying he had never seen anyone bounce back quite so quickly.

His feelings for Jenny grew stronger almost daily, and he knew she cared in some way for him too. But for reasons that still remained a mystery she refused to display those feelings. Not wanting to jeopardize whatever connection did exist between them he tread cautiously doing a sort of emotional balancing act between his constant desire to cradle her in his arms and a fear of pushing her away if he tried. The intrigue of her teachings served as a sort of substitute for the intimacy he longed for with her but he knew if this strange saga could have a happy ending it would be on her terms.

"The splints come off today Mr. Finlay. Doc Greer said it's time to stop pampering you."

"Awe come on. Just another week."

"Absolutely not. You have to learn to walk again so it's time to get the lessons underway."

"That means you have to help me with every move I make."

"It means you can use my father's cane to help you," she said removing the wrapping that had held the homemade wooden supports in place for the past eight weeks."

"That is not the sexiest leg I've ever seen," she said when the still discolored limb was exposed.

"Well you see the universe has its ways of protecting a defenseless man. If the leg looked normal I'd have to fight off a sex crazed attack which I'm unable to do right now."

"Well put your fears to rest, I have no problem restraining myself. Now try putting a little weight on it," she said helping him slowly to his feet.

"Oh ouch," he yelped in mock pain. "You'll have to hold on to me for at least a month."

"Here's the cane, just hold on to it."

"Alright, but keep in mind I'm reporting this to the humane society at my earliest convenience."

"Well in the meantime, practice walking so you don't fall down trying to get through their door."

"Oh this is so cruel," he moaned as he walked awkwardly around the table with the assistance of the cane.

"That's enough for starters," she said after his second round. "How does it feel?"

"Aside from pure agony, not too bad."

"Good. Doc said it was healing very well. You'll soon be able to help Andy clean barns."

"It will never be that well healed."

"Then you can help me bake a Christmas cake. You see it's very important that you keep active once you've started."

"Regular journeys around the kitchen table will do nicely, thank you."

He did help her bake the Christmas cake and helped with a number of other chores in preparation for the holidays. The playful bantering that accompanied their every activity brought him a quality of happiness that he had never before known.

They had mutually agreed to suspend the counseling until the holiday season was over which he appreciated because it gave him time to digest the huge volume of new concepts she had presented. But there was another obvious reason for the interlude. She was out on numerous occasions delivering gifts of baked goods, canned foods and homemade clothing to practically every resident in the valley.

"For a non-Christian, you sure do a lot of Christmasie stuff," he remarked one day.

"Oh it's just an opportunity to help out when people are willing to accept. Doing so at other times isn't nearly as easy because everyone wants to feel independent. So I just take advantage of the holiday atmosphere."

He could only smile in silent amazement at her answer. Never had he known anyone to give so freely just for the sake of giving. Christmas gift exchange in his own past seemed more like a duty than a desire with the major emphasis on ensuring he hadn't forgotten someone and that all gifts were appropriately expensive. Jenny Ingram by contrast seemed to get genuine pleasure from the fact that what she gave really helped another person and with no concern about receiving anything in return.

This was one more departure from the traditional habits he was accustomed to. Rather than the snarling nerve wracking rat race that was common in his urban world, she turned the Christmas season into one of relaxed joy and pleasure.

How could he resist loving a woman with such qualities? How would any man be able to resist?

It was both thrilling and disconcerting at the same time. The reasons to be thrilled were obvious, but if she didn't feel the same way toward him then he was in for a rough ride. This was the only fly in the ointment during an otherwise happy holiday season and she must have sensed his camouflaged despondency because she immediately addressed it at their first session in the new year.

"Adam," she said, "there are many things about ultimate reality that you are not yet ready to tackle and will not be for some time. I know you become impatient and frustrated at times but this, in fact, is a sign of progress. When impediments to your understanding no longer exist we must then move to the next deeper level but be aware that this will bring on new and relevant frustrations."

Smiling at her he said, "you always know just when I need a boost don't you Miss Ingram. Yes I do get frustrated and yes I know that frustration is really a measure of progress but there is another aspect to my frustrations that…well…" He stopped in mid sentence instinctively knowing it still was not the right time to express his feelings for her.

"All in good time Adam," she said as though she was reading his mind once again.

He had gotten accustomed to her ability to answer his unspoken questions and said, "sometimes I think you know more about me than I do myself."

"Woman's intuition…and privilege," she answered smiling impishly. "Anyway you started to ask a question before I diverted the conversation. Shall we get back to it?"

"Right and if you can answer this one maybe humankind will finally understand women."

"Never. We won't allow it. But let's have the question anyway."

"Since you obviously don't subscribe to the biblical version of our beginnings, at least not the literal one, I would like to know how you think we came into existence."

"Well it goes like this. Several million years ago there were only storks on earth and they were very busy delivering bundles all over the world and…"

"And accidentally dropped a certain mountain dweller on her head. Now can I have your other version?"

"It's not as much fun."

"I'll suffer."

"Killjoy. However if you insist. We'll start with a conflict between what science has strong evidence of, and the religious conviction that what the bible tells us is irrefutable. When questioned most religious denominations will provide answers from their interpretation of the bible even though it is becoming increasingly difficult to support beliefs that are being constantly bombarded with revelations that tell a much different story. To support the literal version of our origins is akin to still believing the world is flat. The idea that God created the world and all that inhabits it in six twenty-four hour days poses numerous questions that can no longer be realistically defended. Something I often wondered about myself while still a church member was why God performed all those incredible miracles in the span of one short week and then for thousands of years since had done nothing or at least very little. It struck me as rather odd that God was only active a way back in obscurity but refused to demonstrate his almighty power in the present.

The fact that man has evolved through various stages is all but indisputable and for me personally is fact. When I went on a search for my own enlightenment I gradually began to understand why the physical realm came into existence and that understanding conflicts with most traditional religious beliefs. For me it is a knowingness that is beyond doubt. Nothing outside of myself influenced these revelations. I arrived at them through a personal meditative process that probed the deepest recesses of my being until I was finally able to access wisdom that transcends empirical awareness. It was revealed to me that lower levels of the creator are evolving through and as creation. Evolution that has long been a source of dispute and misunderstanding is a process peculiar to all that exists. Material things ultimately decay or deteriorate and reappear in different form but the net result of this process is evolution to higher or more advanced states.

The eternal substance that animates the physical realm is evolving through the actions of material forms which is the basic reason for the existence of materiality.

It is extremely important to grasp this fact Adam for it defines our fundamental purpose as human beings and which purpose is *spiritual evolution.*

We've chosen an endless variety of life experiences evidenced by the wide range of activities we indulge in but everything we do is essentially some part of the creator having experiences through and as us.

The process exists ensuring that the physical could and would evolve but the nature of the process is such that the *future cannot be known.* This can be scientifically demonstrated and it's called innate indeterminacy or chaos theory.

At one point it was even thought that if enough data were fed into a computer it would eventually be able to predict our future. After several failed attempts it had to be conceded that it wouldn't happen and it never will.

Humanity is constantly reconstructing its future by the choices it makes in the present and unless we consistently make predictable choices, which we don't, then our future is unknown. A foreseen future would be pointless, much like knowing the outcome of some game before the game was played. Always keep in mind the process, not the results, is the purpose and precisely why our planet exists."

"Jenny you've made some confusing statements. What do you mean by 'lower levels and some part' of the creator? I thought God was one whole and complete entity."

"It is Adam and will forever be. There are complex features about the nature of God that must be taken in small bites, otherwise it can sound like fantasy. But we're getting off track. Remember I was going to elaborate on the vast amount of work that storks had to do to get the whole process started."

"Since we've detoured, let's stay on the detour. I'm sure the storks will follow us."

"Adam this might not be practical right now."

"Why not?"

"I don't want to throw some curves that might turn you away before you've had time to connect all the dots that form the big picture."

"Jenny," he answered laughing. "If I've made it this far without running away in terror, I'm certain anything else you can serve up won't do it."

She tapped the tabletop with her fingers for a few seconds and said, "okay Adam. But we'll only go so far with it for now."

After another short silence and deep breath she began. "It is readily obvious that evolution will finally take us up and beyond the need to reincarnate into physicality. A few highly advanced souls have graduated, so to speak, to the spiritual realm where they continue their evolution in ways that may not be readily understood or accepted by most of us remaining on earth. Since they have moved beyond the need for physical experience, their evolutionary process takes on some different characteristics and right here is where it can get a little dicey." She stopped talking and stared straight at him for a moment.

"Don't stop now. I'm having no difficulties."

"Many of these advanced souls," she continued speaking slowly. "Provide the between life counsel to those of us who must still reincarnate to finish our agendas on earth. But there is always a minority who evolved to higher levels. Now let's back up a bit and review what happens to us as we evolve." She stopped talking again and gazed at him in silence.

"Meaning what?" he finally said.

"I thought maybe you'd like to tell me."

Shrugging he said, "as we evolve we become more enlightened."

"Besides that?"

He stared back at her for a moment then shook his head. "You've lost me."

"What is the underlying reality of our being?"

"We are spiritual beings."

"Which also means we are?"

"Okay. We are expressions of God."

"And at that point we have all the qualities of God in potential form."

"So you've told me."

"Then the process of enlightenment must mean we are uncovering more of our god truth."

"I guess so."

"Where do you think these revelations will ultimately take us?"

"As you said we can become counselors."

"Yes, but remember evolution is always happening. We wouldn't remain counselors indefinitely. So what comes next?"

"Well we would uncover more of our god truth, I guess."

"Right, but what activities would we then engage in to continue our evolution?"

"Okay," he answered nodding slowly. "I see what you mean by the nature of God becoming complex."

"Let's leave it right there for now and give you some time to mull it over. At some future point we can take a few more bites.

Getting back to the birth of the physical universe. This is a highly controversial topic both in the fields of science and theology. The big bang is the popular theory but it contains many flaws. Another theory claims that the universe never had a beginning. It has always existed and therefore always will. This much I know for certain. The universe and specifically earth exists to further the creators need to evolve. To support this belief, divine laws also exist that ensured the evolution of the physical realm but the specific direction it would take was left open to the unpredictable nature of physicality.

This was a deliberate act on the part of the creator that contradicts the biblical idea that our destiny is already programmed in. Maximum benefit from the experience of the physical realm can only be gained if it is left to the whims of evolution. All that was certain, in our distant past, was that a sentient being worthy of soul inhabitation would ultimately appear on the scene. This was guaranteed by what is known as the four basic laws of physics that have always presided over the evolution of the material universe. Contrary to the rest of the universe which is in constant flux the values or mathematical properties of these forces has remained unchanged and are exactly the same everywhere in the universe."

"Jenny how do you—how does science know this? Do they have any way of proving it?"

"Yes. They have done comparisons in labs proving that the current values of these forces are exactly the same as they were as far back in time as they can reach. This suggests that there is "intention" back of the process. Science even has to admit that they cannot explain it in any other way but stops short of speculating on the nature and purpose of that intention.

Accordingly every particle and the more complex structures that they evolve to is, in some way, God appearing as those entities. This understanding answered my question about the apparent absence of God in modern times. In truth God is constantly active in It's creation because God is outpicturing as creation.

Fundamentalists are often dismayed because they can't understand why God does not intervene and prevent the horrendous atrocities that often take place. But not wanting to rock a boat that has taken them thousands of years to build, they chalk it up to the usual explanations most of us have heard; 'It is God's will. God works in mysterious ways or God is presenting another challenge for us to overcome.

Any way the process moved along more or less as Charles Darwin postulated, although his theory has since found to be flawed in many ways. Natural selection was partly responsible for screening out those species that could not adapt to the pathway evolution was taking bringing us to the point we are at today. There was no divine finale already built in because the Divine Itself is also the process. That is why we really do not know what the future holds for us. There are those such as Nostradamous and Edgar Cayce who could more directly access the spiritual realm or akashic record as it is sometimes called and they made some remarkably accurate prophecies but they too have frequently been wrong. It was never a foregone conclusion that what they predicted would happen. In fact Nostradamus was known to have said his negative prophecies would only come true if we made no attempt to avert them. These two seers were observing, in part, a possible outcome based on the trend humanity was taking at any given point in history. We had and will always have complete freedom and authority to make whatever changes we decide to make. This is not opposing some divinely inspired outcome for the planet because there is no such plan. The creator avoids manipulating our destiny to ensure maximum benefit from the process of reaching toward it. Many will strongly oppose this idea because they have been taught to believe that God is all knowing and all powerful and we humans, by comparison, are little more than pawns. If there was separation between us and God then this could be true but there is only *one* mind, one being, one life and we humans are integral components of that one existence. Therefore we are each playing specific roles essential to the overall function of the one life and cannot be separate from it."

"Whoa," he said. "You've lost me a half a dozen words ago. What do you mean by just *one* life? There are well over six billion persons on earth."

"Let me explain it in another way. The creator needs various methods through which it can fully express itself. This is easily understood because we have the same needs. The fact that we involve ourselves in a wide range of activities means the creator is gaining its desired experience in proportion to the experiences we have. Earth is a realm of opposites that enables us to be aware of variety. The more variety we encounter in life, the broader our horizons become and the more experienced we are.

We, being expressions of God simply means God is also having those experiences which it utilizes in ways we have yet to understand. Still with me Adam?"

"I think so."

"It should become more clear as we move along. Our freedom of choice ensures that the ultimate fate of humanity cannot be predetermined. If it was predestined, it would immediately negate the benefits of experience on the physical plane by knowing the outcome of things before they happen. We freely wrote our agenda for any one lifetime before entering, which is one more example of free will but seldom do we remember exactly what we wrote. If we did remember, it would further reduce the value of the physical experience since we could, if we chose, simply perform according to a schedule. We gain immeasurably by having only certain clues to our agenda since the effort we invest in identifying those clues is extremely beneficial. For that reason God cannot intervene in human affairs because God participates in those affairs as each and every one of us. If any apparent miracles or interventions do take place, it is attributable to those highly enlightened humans who can express more of their god truth than the rest of us. Understand that God is not evolving in the sense that we perceive evolution. God is using the human evolutionary process as a means of gaining a fuller awareness of its own nature.

As humans advanced the human ego became dominant camouflaging the underlying spiritual reality or purpose in the human experience. Ironically this aspect is beneficial because it gives rise to a certain degree of internal conflict which is an essential facet of evolution but this must be kept in perspective. Conflict is only beneficial because of the challenge it presents us with when one embarks on their journey to enlightenment. You must fix firmly in mind that you are not your ego. We so often identify ourselves with such things as our status in life. My brother we might say is a plumber and his wife a school teacher. The neighbor next door is a lawyer and the man down the street is a movie producer. We are none of these things, Adam. At the true level of our existence we are spiritual beings having this temporary human experience and those various careers I just mentioned are the ways in which we express ourselves on behalf of God."

"That could leave the Pope, Cardinals, Bishops, Priests and Deacons all out of the equation."

"It would leave their titles out, not them as individuals. As I've already said Churches and theologians can be a benefit to society if they finally dispense with the arrogant belief that they are somehow an exclusive channel to God. If you do accept what I've just related then obviously we are all channels to God.

Anyway," she said getting up from her chair. "I must do some ironing." Gazing down at him for a moment she added. "You might want to review what we've just discussed. It is a major departure from tradition and not something that the neophyte can readily grasp and in some cases doesn't want to grasp."

"I hear you," he said watching her lower the hinged ironing board from its upright position in a wall recess and lock the two folding legs in place.

He tried visualizing the response of his friends and acquaintances if they suddenly had to relinquish their station in life. Status and achievement was very important and for some all consuming. If her philosophy was to make even a dent in society she had a massive challenge ahead. On the other hand she was no crusader. She would only disseminate her belief to those who were ready to listen. "But then," he thought grinning wryly to himself, "if she could sway him, anything was possible."

He never ceased to be amazed at her self sufficiency in this antiquated old house and ironing clothes was no exception. After the two metal boat shaped irons had been heated on top of the cookstove she snapped a detachable handle onto one of them and began pressing a pair of trousers stretched over the board. When the iron cooled beyond effectiveness she returned it to the stovetop and resumed her work with the other one. Occasionally she sprinkled water on the clothing which he guessed was the mountaineer version of a steam iron. She was proficient at the job and soon had the huge basket emptied and all items hung neatly in closets.

A few minutes earlier she had started a pot of coffee brewing and now filled two cups and sat down at the table again.

"I'm played out just watching you," he said with a grin.

"Nothing that years of practice won't achieve."

He sipped the hot coffee in silence and watched her do the same. She was without doubt the most unique person he had ever met. Although living in conditions rivaling that of earlier settlers, she did everything with a feminine flare. She had even managed to keep her fingernails daintily manicured despite the fact that she tackled every job from carrying in armloads of wood to sewing buttons on shirts.

"Well Adam," she broke into his thoughts. "Shall we continue?"

"Actually I'm still reeling from that last lecture. But I'm likely beyond the point of no return so let's go."

"What were we talking about?"

"The nature of God and if what you're saying is true, then I've wasted forty years attending church."

"No you haven't, Adam."

"Okay, nothing is wasted. Actually you have clarified some things and one is the statement that God is within us. I never before quite caught the gist of that one."

"It would really be more accurate to say that we are within God. 'Born again' Christians frequently make the statement that they've been saved and are now doing God's work which is amusing because they've always been doing God's work and so has everyone else. We cannot avoid doing God's work because everything we do is some part of God doing that thing.

Accordingly then it becomes obvious that *all* events that take place on earth are experiences that God is having which includes, as it must, everything from the horrendous to the beautiful and sublime. Now don't be lulled into thinking that heinous atrocities are okay or will go unpunished. Nothing escapes the law of cause and effect, or karma. Human justice systems often fail miserably but the law of cause and effect has no such imperfections.

Appropriate justice will always be meted in the great infinite scheme and we will all, in one life or another, have to balance our own scales. We will expand much more on this later but for right now it is important to understand that all actions have their origins in the one creative source and for that reason they are not necessarily positive or negative, harmful or beneficial. They just are. We, as individual expressions of God, freely make the decision to behave as we do and therefore must take responsibility for the consequences. This points up how absolute our free will is and it is not something that God gave us but something we inherited. We cannot avoid having free will simply because the creator has free will.

The literal understanding of the Bible paints a much different picture. The bible reveals that our fate is already known which means we have little choice in the matter. Free will becomes conditional because our ultimate destiny has been decided for us."

She stopped talking and smiled gently at him for a moment. This gentle smile was always disarming and at such times he found it difficult to focus on the topic. Turning away to maintain his composure he asked, "was all that information revealed to you during your mountain sojourn? I think a lot of it could be found in a library or bookstore."

"Perhaps it can Adam. I read constantly and certainly have encountered material that resonates with my beliefs but my basic source is the God truth that inhabits us all. It is well to corroborate our beliefs as much as we can and if we're looking to find support for the existence of God one substantial piece of evidence is the perfect order built into the process of evolution. I don't mean perfect creation because in this physical realm there is no such thing. Everything is constantly evolving and will never reach a state of so called perfection firstly because we don't even know what perfection is and secondly if 'perfection' was somehow attained the earth would lose its reason for being. The system launched by the creator is a measure of perfection insofar as it is perfectly suited to support the evolutionary process that is constantly happening.

For scientists to ascribe the process to divine intelligence violates the tenets of science so until demonstrable proof is forthcoming, it remains the sphere of mysticism. That proof is not far in our future Adam. Many scientists who now debunk the idea of divine creation will soon reach a point whereby they cannot explain our beginnings in any other way and will then actively seek to prove, rather than disprove the existence of God. They will find, too, that although man is the pinnacle of physical evolution he is not the only reason for it as most have always believed.

Man was a logical product of evolution and being imbued with conscious awareness many believe he automatically fell heir to stewardship of his environment. Not conquerors Adam. Stewards. But man has arrogantly twisted this responsibility so completely out of context that he is now facing annihilation by his own hand. Therefore we do well to explore our beginnings and the original purposes attached to them and for this we can turn to science once again. Life and consciousness, as we can now observe it, were implicit in the very beginning and the stable laws I mentioned earlier guaranteed that evolution would take a direction in which a sentient being would finally emerge. This entity would be, and is, ideally suited to soul inhabitation. It possesses human ego giving it the potential for conflict even within itself and as already noted conflict is an integral part of the process.

The development of man could be likened to the construction of a shopping mall. During the various building stages it is nothing more than an assortment of empty spaces or lifeless shells. As construction progresses each compartment is gradually developed or 'evolved' to a point where it is ready for occupancy. Soon some business operation moves in which then gives the space a certain character defined by the nature of the business. It now expresses various features that identifies it as a separate functioning entity but it is still an integral part of the one larger whole."

"You do have a way with analogies, but if your concept of our beginnings is right, what are we to make of the biblical Adam and Eve?"

"The story of Adam and Eve is a metaphor that has the potential for many meanings. Taken literally it is valueless."

"Now just a minute Jenny you are talking about one of the cornerstones of Christianity. You don't just casually wave off something like that."

"If you recall I said Christianity would have to undergo some fundamental changes to survive and literalism is a major one. But aren't we straying from the topic?"

"Okay but this is something I want to return to. Perhaps traditional Christianity will have to make some changes but if we start tampering with its very foundation, it will collapse completely."

She stared at him in silence for a few moments, then turned away and fastened her gaze on the old cookstove that was crackling noisily from blocks of wood she had added in earlier. She looked back at him again and started to say something but quickly turned away once more and shook her head slightly.

"Uh...Jenny..."

"I'm sorry Adam," she said looking back again. "What were we talking about?"

Now it was his turn to stare. What happened to her at these times when her thoughts seemed to be transported away so completely that she became oblivious to everything else? Where did she go. What consumed her so thoroughly that she almost had to be reoriented once again. Apologizing for the second time she said, "I guess I got carried away in my thoughts. Now what were we talking about?"

"Our origins," he answered slowly. "But you had also mentioned a previous life which obviously means reincarnation. Prior to my near death experience I believed that reincarnation was, at best, ridiculous nonsense and at worst, the workings of Satan. I'm still skeptical but I guess now I'm ...curious."

"Well you should be," she said smiling now. "According to a message I'm getting you were a terrible fire breathing dragon in a previous life."

Grateful that she had returned to her normal self he responded quickly. "And I can still breathe fire in this life. Now before I burn your house down…"

"Okay. Okay. Control your emotions. We can't afford to build a new one."

"You have five seconds."

"Dreadful person. Anyway at a certain point in the development of the universe and in particular planet earth, millions of souls chose to expand out into the material realm to fulfill the creators objective of material experience. Note that they 'expanded' out. They did not separate from the parent body simply because they can't. This could be considered the birth of souls since they now had a separate identity and a primary theme for their excursion through the physical plane. As young souls they were playful and carefree inhabiting, for short periods, the only forms of life in existence. This provided a certain elementary exposure to the material world but was limiting because plants and animals have a very narrow focus in the grand evolutionary scheme.

As the young souls matured they became aware of the need for a much broader range of experience and so they began their search instinctively knowing a suitable and more permanent vessel was awaiting them. At the same time primitive man had developed to a point where he was ready to serve this purpose and so souls began inhabiting physical bodies. This was a gigantic evolutionary leap for mankind since he was now transformed from a purely instinctive entity into one that included compassion, self-awareness, and all the attributes that make us fully human.

Free will is our single most important trait. It enables us to make choices resulting in the diverse panorama of events and activities constantly happening all around us. As I've already explained many of these events we perceive as negative and in some cases horribly evil but they are, in fact, a measure by which the positive can be recognized and fully appreciated. Diversity is necessary for the creator to experience the fullness of physicality. Therefore a minority of souls even chose dark pathways that would contribute to this end.

Since any one human lifetime is relatively short the amount of experience available is proportionately restricted and so souls, very early, recognized the need to occupy numerous human forms over thousands of years to complete their mission in the physical realm. This is the basis of reincarnation and it shouldn't be difficult to understand. Even in this modern age do we seldom participate in more than two or three primary activities in one lifetime which means we need many lives to complete the entire program. Some even spend numerous lives perfecting only one ability which explains the so call 'genius' of a Mozart.

He entered the life most of us have heard about bringing with him expertise developed in earlier lives and this applies to us all. We're not all Mozarts but most of us will find that at the very least we are strongly motivated to do certain things or are naturally talented in some area. If this was traced back, we would find that this ability had its origin in a previous life."

She stopped talking and got up to refill their coffee cups. What he had just heard opposed almost everything he had been taught to believe but in an unsettling way it readily explained many things that had always puzzled him. He felt caught in a squeeze because here was a spiritual philosophy that would be labeled heresy by his church, but answered questions that the church wouldn't even address.

"Jenny," he said after she had seated herself once again. "Don't you think the Bible version of our beginning contains any validity? After all you are opposing firmly established tradition that influences a large portion of the human race. I know it has its controversies but to totally ignore it?"

"I am not ignoring anything Adam. I'm relating what is true for me. I've said before that everything, including religious beliefs, plays a certain role in the function of evolution and Christianity a very significant one. I've already indicated that I can no longer agree with it which exemplifies the complete freedom of choice we have and we do ourselves a disservice if we fail to exercise that freedom. The fact that there is controversy amongst various religions or anywhere else controversy exists is an essential aspect of the human journey. This may sound counterproductive in a world where the emphasis is usually on achieving peace and harmony but that, in fact, will never be attained. We settle one dispute and another one flares up. As we advance technologically the conflicts simply become more sophisticated. Conflict will always be with us but paradoxically we must never resign ourselves to the 'inevitability of conflict'. The effort expended in overcoming contentious issues is precisely why we are here. I'm going to repeat that because it is important. The effort itself or the manner in which we deal with controversy is, or should be our objective. We can facilitate this endeavor by following spiritual principles in everything we do or we can impede it by ignoring them. Ironically being faced with negativity is beneficial because it points up the benefits of playing by the rules.

Getting back to your concern about excluding Bible based religions I can only point out that ultimate reality is very much broader than the narrow focus of organized religion and what I've just said would be shunned by most of them but I am going to say it again. If something can exist at all then it has been sanctioned by the creator because it is a part of the creator showing up as that thing. This includes, as it must, all the evil that most religions claim to be fighting. If we are to accept that God is all and everything then we cannot exclude any part of God's creation and everything that happens in it. Those things appearing to be so grossly wrong are nothing more than negativism playing its part in the experiential process."

"Well you're right about one thing, it would be shunned by almost every traditional Christian religion on earth. Tell me this, if, as you say, God set the universe in motion for the purpose of evolving it would mean He is not the epitome of perfection that most of Christianity claims."

"She is absolute perfection but requires a means of expression to fully exercise that perfection. Practically everything on earth is in opposition to something else therefore that need is readily met."

"I notice you often refer to God as she."

"Yes Adam, just as much as 'He'. Actually God is gender neutral but for various chauvinistic reasons it has been assigned male orientation."

"Now that's a tough one to concede," he said with a grin. "Anyway Christianity claims that creation in its present form is sufficient evidence of God's perfection which is a pretty strong argument. Producing a flower, a frog, a horse or a human is quite an achievement."

"I repeat God did not create anything directly but simply set the process in motion and it is still in motion or evolving. Therefore creation cannot be labeled perfect because creation is incomplete. If we were to go backward in time the process obviously reverses. The quality of everything would diminish in direct proportion to the distance we traveled back. This refutes the claim that God created everything all at once and pretty much as we see it today. When we look back on the primitive lifestyle of Moses, for example, living standards appear to be very crude as our present lifestyle will be seen a hundred years in the future. Evolution is not conditional. It applies equally to every aspect of the physical realm. We cannot accept the phenomenal progress that man has made without accepting that man and therefore God is a part of it. Nothing is static Adam and this fact tradition seems to ignore. To say that something is perfect is to say it has reached a state of completion but every aspect of creation is still evolving. Completion will never be reached which means the creator is incomplete in certain respects and is continuing to evolve through Its creation. Not imperfect Adam; incomplete. It took we humans right up to Darwin's time before we realized that evolution was a natural phenomenon and to this day we still have dissidents trying to oppose something that is happening right before their eyes. The evolution of creation."

"Almost everything you say attacks Christianity. If we were to go with your belief, Christianity as we know it could cease to exist."

"I'm quite aware of that. I know that this is a major departure from tradition so let's take a look at it from a different angle. Completion is not the final objective of this physical experience for if completion was attained it would mean a state of perfection has been reached and earth would lose its reason for being. Perfection is a pointless state of existence because it negates further need for purpose. To dwell in the realm of perfection would result in stagnation, even madness rendering that state of existence both undesirable and forever unattainable. The perfection of God, then, is measured not in terms of some euphoric destiny but by Its capacity to eternally reach into the infinite unknown and gain gratification through the process of reaching. Granted God functions in a manner we as humans have yet to comprehend but that does not mean we are denied understanding as much of God as we are capable of.

God outpictures as the innate facets of Itself. In other words we can see the nature of God in the behavior of Its creation and since this behavior is evolutionary the source of it must also be. If this wasn't so it would be God contradicting Itself which is an impossibility."

"So prior to creation, as you define it, there was only God."

"There may not have been any such thing as a before creation existence but this much I know, a large part of it's make-up is pure intelligence containing the potential for all that exists. It even lies outside of measurable energy that is the basis of physicality. If we probe beyond all energy we find there is nothing at all, at least nothing we can perceive. There seems to be only a void in which all properties are absent. Time and space as we understand them do not exist. Space is both nowhere and everywhere and time is just one eternal now. This is about all that science knows of God and it bears no resemblance to the white robed, bearded old man that traditional Christianity created. However we refer to the realm of God as nothingness only because we lack the means to understand or describe that nothingness. It is even incorrect to call it the realm of God because God is the realm. There is only one supreme being and everything else is an outpicturing of that one. We know it has intention or purpose because we have. We know it has emotions because we have them. We know it is on an evolutionary pathway because we are. We know it is seeking diversity of experience because that's what we seek. We know it is having experience through and as us in order to know itself better because we are constantly learning more about ourselves."

"Phew. That will take some digesting."

"I wasn't trying to complicate it."

"Of course not. I'll just chew on it for awhile. You've mentioned karma several times and I've often heard the word used prior to coming here. What does it really mean?"

"There are numerous misconceptions of karma which is unfortunate because in order to resonate with karma we must properly understand it. Karma is frequently called the law of cause and effect and in one respect it is. But in this context it is often misconstrued as a rigid inflexible law which it isn't. Many have this mistaken idea that karmic function is direct and specific. If we commit a misdemeanor in this life, karma ensures an appropriate payback in the next and misfortunes experienced in this life is karmic restitution for misconduct in the last one. Another erroneous belief held by some is the inevitability of karmic punishment. If we constantly experience some hardship it is karma they tell us and must not be tampered with. Suffering throughout one's entire lifetime is the only way to work off the karmic debt. We certainly might experience difficulties as a result of opposing karmic law but we do not, and in fact should not, resign ourselves to the inevitability of our plight. We start working it off the moment we start on the pathway of recovery and this is anytime that we simply make the decision to do so. Karma has only one purpose and that is to maintain harmony in the universe and for that reason is also called the law of balance. Karmic law is an impartial law inclining toward harmony in our personal lives as well as all other functions in the manifest universe.

If we've gotten off course karma exerts a pressure to draw us back but it is not necessarily aiming specifically at us. It is simply functioning as it must and that is to pull imbalance back into balance. We may even live a number of lives in violation of karmic law with little adverse effect. Eventually however karmic pressure increases to a point whereby we find that in order to restore harmony to our life we must do an about face and conform to the law once again. Now here is where karma can seem complicated. We'll return to it later. But right now I'm going to give you one example. If, as I've just said, we've strayed a long way off course for a number of lives we've then created a strong momentum in that direction. Ultimately, we will find that the hardships created by constantly opposing karma becomes intolerable prompting us to finally change our ways and commence living once again according to spiritual principles. Even though we've now made the right decision, the inertial force we've set in motion by going against the flow for so long still exerts a strong pull in that direction creating an internal conflict that may take one or several lives to balance. These transitional lives are usually difficult because we are struggling with two opposing forces both competing for control of our life. This can be one reason why we often see persons constantly experiencing hardships even though they appear to be trying their best to live a good moral life.

Our soul purpose or the agenda we've set in place for any one lifetime also plays a major role in karmic function. In the example just cited it may appear on the surface that karma is unjust when in fact the individual experiencing the hardship was conforming to karmic law by drafting an agenda prior to incarnating which included those hardships. It's important to understand that karma is not making us do this as some persons believe. Nothing is making us do anything. It is us, ourselves finally realizing we must conform to karmic law in order to bring harmony into our life once again.

Between physical lives we are able to view our journey in a much broader perspective and can see how our behavior, during previous lives, has created who and what we are in the present. It is also important to understand that we do not change character when we return to the spiritual realm. Some still believe that if we've made it to 'heaven' we are automatically 'sainted' and can no longer do wrong. The only difference is once we've left the physical body we can view our overall existence in a much broader perspective enabling us to choose from a greatly expanded view. We also have the assistance of older souls or counselors, mentioned earlier, who will offer us guidance in choosing a future life but the final decision is ours alone. This fact exemplifies the total freedom of choice that we have but for some it is not what they want to accept. Many still feel that much of what happens to them is beyond their control and therefore they cannot be held responsible. In the final analysis, Adam, each and every one of us is totally and completely responsible for who and what we now are and will be in our future. The manner in which you live this life will determine, in part, the nature of your next physical life. When you return to the spiritual realm you will review your own performance which could be considered judgment if we want to view it that way. But it is us judging ourselves or more accurately assessing ourselves. There is no god to pass judgment on us as traditional Christianity would have us believe. That God was a man made divinity created to conform to the needs of ancient man when he was still incapable of understanding the nature of his being as we now do. Karma, then, functions as an impartial law the same as any other spiritual law. Violate it and we will, sooner or later, experience adverse effects."

She stopped talking as she frequently did and he knew it was to allow him time to digest what she had just presented. He was grateful for these interludes because it was the only way he could keep pace with the massive volume of new ideas that at times inundated him.

Musing over her explanation of karma, he suddenly became aware of something he hadn't noticed before. She seldom wore slacks. This was in contrast to most other contemporary women who seldom wore dresses. Probing his memory he could only recall her wearing slacks when she had to be outdoors for any length of time and upon re-entering the house would immediately duck into her bedroom and change into a dress. Thinking about it now, he was very much in approval. To him a dress seemed to accentuate a woman's femininity. Her full bodied figure was especially well suited to any frock she donned which included the polka dot one she was presently wearing. She had gotten up from her chair a few seconds earlier and with her back to him was washing Trina's food dish as she did everyday. He stared in admiration at her impeccably kept auburn hair and well proportioned body that seemed to fill out the dress just right.

"Adam," she said without looking up. "You are supposed to be reviewing karma and its implications."

"How do you know I'm not?"

"Females have this sixth sense," she answered turning to face him. "It lets us know when a man's thoughts have strayed into areas that could get him into trouble."

"I see. Well would you mind telling me what I was thinking on May 3, 1996 at 2:19PM."

"Oh you really don't want me to utter that out loud do you. I blush just thinking about it. We'd better get back to discussing karma. You seem to have more than your share of it. Bad karma that is."

"You do have a way of taking the joy out of life."

"I think you mean lust. Now what were we talking about?"

"You said karma was an impartial law, so why should it be partial to my thoughts no matter what they are?"

"Even karma has its limits of tolerance. But more importantly I think I've just figured out what your primary theme is."

"My primary theme?"

"Right."

"Okay. What is meant by primary theme?"

"Fundamental to our purpose for every physical life is a primary theme that we selected at the beginning of our expression as individual souls. This central theme is something we carry with us until we've completed our journey through the physical realm and ideally the soul purpose we choose for any one physical life should contribute, in some way to that central theme. As we've already seen karma will tend to nudge us back in the direction of our chosen purpose if we stray and most of us have, some more so than others.

This is us exercising our free will but if it is in violation of karmic law we will ultimately realize we must also choose to get back on course. Obviously the more we are aware of what our soul purpose is and the more we choose to follow it, the more harmonious life will be. This doesn't mean there will be no challenges, for that is what earth school is all about. It does mean we are progressing according to our soul agenda and we will experience a purposeful sense of satisfaction each time we've overcome another hurdle.

Clearly delineating our soul purpose can often be challenging but the more we do so the greater our progress. Using a process of elimination helps since we can more often readily identify what we don't like than what we do. As a starting point we can strike off the major violations in life that shouldn't need repeating but a large portion of the human race still acts as though they haven't learned them so here they are again. If we lie, cheat, steal, injure or kill we are breaking the laws and amends will be required. We may or may not be subject to human restitution but we will not escape karmic law. Crimes against our fellow man are the most tragic and karma will ultimately cause us to face right up to the suffering and sorrow we have inflicted on others. Crimes against our environment are equally disastrous. Wanton destruction of forests, lakes, birds, animals and the atmosphere carries with it karmic repercussions that are even now being felt all over the world.

The law of karma is flawless. It will eventually bring about balance in any situation where imbalance prevails. For us personally, it may take numerous physical lives depending on how resistant we are to enlightenment but we must sooner or later correct all errors before we can once again move forward on our chosen pathway.

We will deal with specifics later Adam which, among other things, should help more clearly identify your purpose for this lifetime but I think we've gone far enough for today and besides I must start supper."

CHAPTER 17

He was eagerly looking forward to resuming the discussions after breakfast the next morning but the junior Henry Meade had other ideas. The youngster had been up on several earlier occasions just to check on them and then report back to his parents, but this time he came loaded down with preserves and pastries that Beatrice Meade seemed to be famous for in the valley.

It was obvious that the fourteen year old adored Jenny. He practically begged her to allow him to do a few chores around the place before leaving which she graciously complied with. Today as was often the case he washed windows that needed no washing but he tackled the job with relish because it allowed him to stay in her presence a little longer.

Adam retired to the living room when the boy announced he was also going to fill the huge wood box in the kitchen.

"Thank you Henry," Jenny said "and you must stay and have dinner with us. It's the least we can do for our hard working man."

Beaming at her compliment he practically ran out to gather his first armload of wood. When the box would hold no more he spent the rest of the forenoon out in the barnyard with Andy. Just before the midday meal he returned to the house to clean out the fireplace that had been cleaned the day before.

He had given Adam several quizzical looks on earlier visits but this time he openly stared. Feeling slightly annoyed Adam lowered the book he was reading and glared back.

"Oh...s'cuse me sir," he stammered. "I was just wonderin..."

"Wondering what?"

"Well if maybe you was related to that Mr. Saunders Miss Jenny was goin to marry. It was a long time ago, but you kinda look like him from some pictures I saw."

Adams curiosity was instantly piqued and for a moment he was tempted to carry out a full fledged interrogation. It would have been easy, Jenny had stepped outside and the boy apparently didn't realize it was a taboo subject. Remembering his promise to Jenny not to pursue the incident further he declined by answering "no I'm not Henry. I'm only here because of my broken leg. I live over in Alberta and I'll be returning as soon as the leg heals a bit more."

"Oh. I'm sorry sir. I was just wonderin, I know taint none of my business."

"No need to apologize Henry. No harm done."

Wanting to change the subject he said, "I'll bet you're starving and whatever Miss Jenny has cooking out there on the stove smells darn good doesn't it?"

The boy nodded in agreement and left to dispose of the few ashes he had been able to scrape out of the fireplace.

"He's a very sweet boy," Jenny said seating herself after Henry had left and the dinner dishes were washed once again.

"And he has a king sized crush on Miss Jenny."

"Oh nonsense. He's just a fine young man who likes to help people much like his father does. Now where did we leave off yesterday?"

For a moment he was tempted to ask about 'Mr. Saunders', but the temptation finally gave way to discretion and he answered. "We were talking about the dreadful blasphemy of reincarnation and karma which probably means we've finally succumbed to one of Satan's most devious ploys."

"Exciting isn't it?"

"Indeed. There's no thrill like doing time in the toaster. Anyway since we are now incorrigible we might as well go whole hog and maybe if we beg for forgiveness later there might still be some possibility of salvation."

"I doubt it. I think we're doomed."

"Right and in that regard the only reference the church ever made to reincarnation was to steer clear of it because it was evil."

"Did they explain why?"

"They said reincarnation was the work of the devil and he used it to lull unsuspecting humans into complacency thereby relaxing their vigil on sin."

"That's interesting. How does reincarnation do that?"

By getting us to believe we have as many lifetimes as we need to correct our erring ways. We can indulge in philandering until we've had our fill and then just take a life time or two to set the record straight and all is forgiven. He tempts the unwary with this lie and if they swallow it they run the terrible risk of dying in sin and becoming one of his captives. Then, too late, they realize the error in their thinking, but there is no turning back. They now face eternity in Satan's clutches and subject to whatever morbid punishment he has in store for them."

"My, my. He is a nasty fellow isn't he?"

"That's what the church tells us."

"Sounds like he invented reincarnation just to trap sinners."

"The church tells us that too."

"Who invented the confessional Adam?"

"The confessional?"

"Yes. It serves a similar purpose doesn't it? I mean you can sin as much as you want and then have the slate wiped clean by occasionally confessing those sins to a priest. Of course you have to be careful not to die between visits, but even then, a qualified priest, if you can find one fast enough, can administer last rites and still get you off the hook, right?"

"Well...yes."

"And even if you miss out at that point one need only do a stint in purgatory to erase any remaining sin."

"More or less."

"A nice convenient arrangement."

"So is reincarnation."

"Oh but there is a world of difference."

"In what ways?"

"Basically this. You believe your sins are absolved through confession because some priest said so. Whereas the reincarnationist believes you can only restore balance by experiencing difficulties proportionate to those you doled out. Hence the need for many lifetimes. Reincarnation does not provide any easy shortcuts for writing off sin. That is something one can only accomplish by taking the long road. We can shorten the negative karmic period by working diligently on our violations but that is about the only deal we can make with reincarnation."

What she was revealing kept filling in gaps that had been open questions earlier in his life but, he wondered, was he resonating with her philosophy because of his feelings for her? Fearing his emotions might be clouding his logic he reaffirmed his conviction to ensure every nook and cranny was explored. He still had an endless list of questions and now felt challenged to pose one she couldn't answer satisfactorily.

Speaking slowly he said, "If we've had many past lives why is it we don't remember anything about them in this present life?"

"The truth is we do and we'll expand on that later. But right now I want you to think of unpleasant events that have happened earlier in your life which weigh heavily on you in the present. The loss of your son is one example but I'm sure there have been others that add to the load."

"Indeed there has."

"Depending on their severity some stresses can become quite debilitating. In fact you poignantly expressed how shattered you were after Jeffery's death. Your capacity to do anything, you said, was reduced to near zero and hasn't improved very much."

"Right."

"That's only one incident. As we go through life more difficulties are piled on top of the heap until sometimes we feel we just can't go on."

"I know the feeling well."

"Most of us eventually pick up the pieces and resume our journey but a minority choose not to. I know of a young married man in his early thirties who had developed a serious drinking problem that was a constant source of dispute between him and his wife. One day after an exceptionally vicious confrontation this man, who was already quite drunk, stormed out of the house and got into his car. Driving wildly he spun the car around in the yard and sped off down the road to his favorite bar where he consumed liquor until he passed out. Some time later he awakened in a jail cell and was told that, without realizing it, he had backed over and killed his three year old daughter who had been out playing in the yard when he drove away. His life was essentially over with at that point. He deteriorated rapidly over the next few months and finally committed suicide.

Fortunately most of us never have to contend with a tragedy as terrible as that one but the point is if difficulties encountered in this one life can drag us down to the extent that we can no longer function effectively, think how much worse it would be if all the trauma of previous lives was added to the load. We probably couldn't function at all so the universe mercifully blocks out most of those memories enabling us to start out fresh in any new incarnation without the burden of previous ones to inhibit our progress. You see Adam, over the centuries most of us now alive have been everything from a horrendous villain to an adorable hero.

We have murdered, raped, pillaged, plundered, saved, soothed, healed and loved all for the purpose of evolution and although that was all necessary we could not now continue on our pathway if negative memories weighed us down. Even positive achievements in the past are better left in the subconscious since they could lead to complacency in the present. Resting on our laurels for noble acts of compassion does us little good. The objective is always to evolve and anything that opposes that thrust will cause tension in our life. Now as I said earlier not all memory is blotted out. In truth what we really have is selective memory which appears in life as likes, dislikes, strong abilities in certain areas and a complete lack of ability in others. We are also drawn toward certain people, repelled by others and often remain neutral toward the rest. This is the infallible nature of the universe selecting from out of our past only those memories of events and activities that can contribute effectively to the program we've designed for this present life. We may not remember specific events but if, for example, we seem to be constantly plagued with financial hardship it is possible that we caused that very problem for someone else in a past life. Ultimately we realize that we must make amends that we include in our agenda and then the universe selects only those portions of our history that will be useful to us in this endeavor. These are usually camouflaged as instincts, intuition, skills and abilities but they direct us toward our purpose if we pay attention to them."

"Wouldn't a more clear memory of those events be helpful though?"

"The universe supplies what is right for us at any given time. Only a minority knows from childhood onward exactly what their destiny is for this life and even at that, they just simply 'know'. They still don't have specific memories. The rest of us have to grope around, often for many years, before we connect with our purpose and still others appear to wander through life with no purpose at all. The truth is there is purpose in every life style even for those who seem not to have one. Their purpose could be to have a certain experience from aimless dabbling in a variety of activities. What is paramount is the benefit we gain from the effort we expend determining what our purpose is.

Perhaps the most reliable indicator of our primary purpose is to recognize issues that constantly create distress in our life. For example if we are always giving to others, to the extent that we impose hardship on ourselves, we should then start to look suspiciously at that compulsion as something out of control with roots buried in our past. We may have brought it forward because we were guilty of taking from other vulnerable persons causing them hardship. When I say giving I am referring to all aspects of our life which includes much more than material goods. Are we giving kindness, caring, support, understanding and encouragement to a point that we are finally drained and depressed ourselves because there has been little or no reciprocation. It is one thing to give unconditionally but it's quite another to feed into a masochistic addiction.

Hank and Beattie Meade are two of the most caring, giving persons I've ever known in my life but they also ensure their own needs are met. If they gave beyond a realistic limit it would create harmful stress in their life resulting in an imbalance that transcends love for our fellow man and enters the realm of karmic addiction. As I frequently said we do not have to resign ourselves to the inevitability of some life long karmic punishment for errors in the past. The very moment we recognize an abnormality for what it is, is the very moment we are free to start turning it around. The process of reversing a destructive trend is how we gain freedom from past life infractions. It is not accomplished by subjecting ourselves to suffering and hardship in our present life from which nobody gains.

Keep in mind I am referring to behavior that brings stress into one's life. If it doesn't, then a lifestyle, although appearing stressful to others, is actually right for the person living it.

Another example of destructive behavior is greed and this may be more common and disastrous than its opposite. I've known persons who became physically ill if they had to spend money for anything beyond the bare essentials and we've all heard of persons who have committed suicide because of heavy financial losses. This is stress taken to extreme. There are numerous milder forms of greed related stress. Depression, isolation, paranoia and relationship problems are a few. The only time these persons appear to be happy is when they've saved a lot of money or avoided spending any at all and incredibly they often seem gleeful if their gain has come at someone else's loss.

There is no true happiness in a life like this simply because the lust for money diverts their focus away from their true purpose of soul evolution.

These are only two examples. There are many more. Staying in a bad relationship, allowing someone to dictate our life, a constant urge to dictate to others, child and animal abuse, gambling, alcoholism. The list goes on and on Adam and in every case, happiness is forfeited because the destructive behavior relegates our true purpose to the background.

Remember the process of reaching toward a goal, not the goal itself, contributes directly to our evolution. Therefore having only vague direction forces us to work much harder at finding our niche than if the whole plan was laid out for us right at the starting gate."

"How does this square with freedom of choice? It seems to me as though it is compromised if we can't bring at least some specific memories from past lives with us."

"Oh we can if we choose to. Some have actually tried that and found that, like the man who ran over his daughter and killed her they were hopelessly devastated. The only thing they gained from physical life was to realize they must leave most of the previous one buried. When we do choose to reincarnate the counselors I mentioned earlier will assist us with the choices we make for the upcoming life and they will strongly advise against retaining past life memories but the final decision is ours alone.

Vicious and brutal dictators who have imposed horrendous suffering on millions will require numerous physical lives to correct their misdemeanors because of the sheer magnitude and volume of evil they've commited."

"But you said we can all make a turn around the minute we decide to do so."

"Yes we can Adam. The very instant we sincerely decide to do an about face and actively direct our efforts down the right pathway is the same for all of us. How rapidly we achieve desired results is in direct proportion to the volume of negative karma we've built up. The Saddam Hussein's, Idi Amin's, Adolf Hitler's, Benito Mussolini's and Joseph Stalin's of the world will not achieve a complete disposal of all their negative karma in one lifetime or in many. Once they recognize the error of their ways, they have the same freedom as we do."

"I'm getting mixed messages here. If I understand you correctly we included those counterproductive activities in our agenda in order to correct past misdemeanors which means they are our purpose for this lifetime."

"They are our purpose only to the degree that we benefit through our efforts to turn them around. We do not have to suffer an entire lifetime of hardship just to comply with some negative condition that we included in our pre-incarnation agenda. To do that opposes spiritual evolution that is the fundamental purpose for every human being. We begin the process of correcting karmically induced difficulties when we take the necessary steps to do so. There are some such as those persons I've just named who will sooner or later do a turnaround. But remember they must start by chipping away at the base of a mountain whereas many of the rest of us may only have to level off a small hill.

Now there is a minority—a very small one who do remember as much of past lives as they need to in order to carry out their purpose in this present life. These are highly enlightened persons who have returned not to gain further experience but to assist the rest of us in some special way. This is a topic for more detailed study so we'll leave it at that."

"You sound like you are one of them."

"Why?"

"Your knowledge of the other side."

"I gained that knowledge on this side because of a karmic obligation to do so."

"Yes but you are claiming a far greater insight than most

others. How is that possible?"

"That insight is available to every one of us when we are ready for it Adam. The path to enlightenment requires total unwavering faith in one's conviction to truth. The slightest doubt will cloud your ability to see truth."

"I still have a problem with so called 'truth'. The world is overflowing with persons and groups claiming that their truth is *the only* truth and I believe this includes Jenny Ingram. Doesn't it?"

"If you think so then you're missing my point entirely. I am giving you what you asked for which is ultimate reality as I experience it. To discover truth one must dig deep within oneselves until they route out their own unblemished and unvarnished truth and then apply it to every aspect of their life.

If at some later date, we have evolved to a point where we find we must redefine our truth so be it. The lie enters in when we refuse to do this because we're so committed to our earlier belief that we cling to it even though evolution has revealed something different. Evolution is a divine process. To oppose it opposes God in action.

The challenge Adam is to clearly see your truth and integrate it into your life. Truth is being true to oneself. If you cannot accept something that I advocate then for goodness sake don't try. I offer my philosophy only as a guide. If it rings true for you that's great. If it doesn't that's equally great, for now you are starting to analyze rather than blindly accept ideas conceived by someone else. It is sheer and utter nonsense to subscribe to a philosophy designed by another source which may have nothing to do with the script you've written for yourself."

"I can see why analyzing beliefs is so demanding."

"If it isn't demanding Adam then you haven't dug down to the very root tips of your current beliefs. Numerous challenges will start to appear when you resume your journey and among them is knowing when your true inner self is speaking to you. We've become so conditioned by the dictates of society that the distinction between our God self and our ego is blurred to the point that we often don't know which one is speaking. It takes practice to distinguish between the two but it can be done and indeed *will* be done before we leave earth experience behind for good.

In the meantime you may, occasionally, find yourself inclined toward things that are labeled as wrong which you might find puzzling. However it could be something you wrote into your script before reincarnating and the reason for it being there is to deal with the challenge of overcoming it.

Universal laws, like human laws, can be violated but sooner or later you will comply with the laws simply because you will eventually tire of the hardships that opposing them brings.

By now it is probably obvious that being true to ourselves may frequently be in opposition to society's concept of good. Good is a relative term defined by the culture that spawned it and although most of us know this we still act as though our particular version of good is the right and only one. For example we practice monogamy in our marital relationships and frown on the polygamy that is considered normal in certain other cultures but for them this polygamous behavior is seen as good, or normal.

Obviously they don't consider that having more than one spouse is wrong and in fact they feel they are being true to the dictates of their culture if they have several.

I'm not suggesting you should go out and engage three or four wives just to oppose the establishment but rather to help you see it is more important to be real than to be good because so called good is always subject to the whims of society.

Expect to violate social norms if you persist on your own pathway to enlightenment. That's unavoidable but the value in knowing you are being true to yourself soon relegates social standards to the background."

"If we really have established soul purpose before entering this life, then knowing what that purpose is should very beneficial."

"Learning your purpose and living in alignment with it is the most beneficial thing you can do for yourself Adam."

"What about all of those books and self help programs on the market. Many of them claim to provide peace, joy, happiness, harmony, prosperity and a whole raft of other benefits if you faithfully follow their directions. I could see some conflict here if, for example, your soul agenda included the need to actually experience hardships."

"You will only benefit from any outside assistance in direct proportion to the degree that that assistance harmonizes with your soul purpose. Claims are frequently made by profit oriented groups promising you every thing from genius abilities to lavish wealth but only a minuscule portion of the participants ever gain very much at all. I'm not suggesting that those groups are frauds because some impressive results have been achieved but these results are in the minority and if the facts were known you would find that the self help process resonated strongly with the individuals personal script.

The most valuable self help program you can ever embark on is clearly defining your own pathway. You might then want to engage some outside assistance if that assistance appears to support your direction.

"So how do we identify that direction? It seems like an impossible challenge since we can't remember why we set it up."

"It's not as difficult as you may think but it does require discriminating analysis. So often many believe that finding a guide, guru or shaman will supply the answers to life's mysteries and indeed these persons can contribute something of value but bear in mind they frequently take you down their own pathway which may contain very little that applies directly to yours.

There are a number of actions necessary when attempting to more clearly define our purpose. As a starting point a balanced mixture of isolation plus interaction with other persons is essential. We learn much about ourselves in relationship to others but excessiveness of either situation will distort results. Constant socializing can be confusing if we don't give ourselves sufficient alone time to evaluate the feedback we receive and too much isolation can similarly distort our conclusions because they haven't been tested in the school of life. Everyone you meet along the way, Adam, has something to offer although neither you nor that other person may realize it at the time. The trick is to be observant enough to spot the lesson contained in the meeting.

Finding one's life purpose is a huge endeavor that can occupy much time so I'm only going to present it in general terms and then if you wish we can explore it in more depth at another time. Perhaps the single best indicator of your purpose for this life is just this: What activity really excites you and gets your juices flowing? Now before you answer think about it for a while because there could be several such activities vying for that spot. If so then try to recognize which one would be of the greatest benefit to your fellow man? How does it fit with what you feel is your responsibility to the world at large?"

"Well I know now that assisting with a slow down of environmental destruction is likely my primary purpose. But is it possible to have a secondary purpose?"

"Oh indeed it is Adam and most of us do. Now let's leave it right here for today. Give it some thought until tomorrow and see what you come up with. But keep this much in mind, select the activity or activities that causes butterflies of excitement when you think about them, even though they may seem impractical, impossible or ridiculous. Assume, for the purpose of this exercise that there is no restriction of any kind, that money is no object, that you have direct access to everything you need to proceed; that nothing is inhibiting your efforts. The sky's the limit here so pull out all stops and give free reign to your most outlandish dreams."

CHAPTER 18

"Okay Mr. Finlay," she said as she seated herself across the table from him the next morning after completing her usual household chores. "Were you able to choose something that excites you more than anything else?"

"Oh indeed I did," he said cupping his chin in his hands and giving her his best evil grin.

"Adam I said the sky is the limit. You've obviously gone in the wrong direction."

"But you said I should give free reign to my wildest dreams so I did."

"You have a broken leg and a heart condition. Try fantasizing something more attainable."

"Yes but they'll both heal."

"Well in the meantime…"

"Okay. But I hope you realize you've just shattered my primary life purpose."

"Then let's talk about your secondary purpose."

"I'm too distraught."

"Adam for goodness sake," she said collapsing into laughter.

He joined her and once again just for a moment everything about that scene felt familiar, as though he had always been here with her and this was where he belonged.

"Honestly," she said after their laughter subsided, "you are impossible sometimes."

"I pride myself on it."

"That's obvious. Perhaps that's your soul purpose."

He smiled at her in silence and had to suppress the strong urge to cradle her in his arms and tell her that he loved her more than he had ever loved another woman. That sounded so corny, he thought, and he was glad he hadn't uttered the words but it was exactly how he felt.

It certainly wasn't the dramatic impulse of a teenager expressing his undying love to his first girlfriend. It was a mature love that had its roots somewhere in the depths of his being that up to now had never surfaced. He was at a loss to understand why but the why no longer mattered. He could have taken his leave weeks earlier but was still here and he knew it was for two reasons. The strong attraction he felt toward this enigmatic woman and an ever increasing respect for the wisdom contained in her spiritual philosophies.

This time she smiled back at him with that sweet smile he had come to know so very well and one, he was certain, could melt a block of ice.

Suddenly she stood up and walked around to where he was sitting and gazed down at him. Then she leaned forward and wrapping both arms around his neck pulled him tight against her. She held him close for a few seconds and then quickly released him and turned away.

Staring at her back in shock he was certain she brushed away tears. This seemed strange but his surprise at her unexpected move left those few seconds vague.

"Jenny," he began but she quickly turned back to face him and place a hand gently over his mouth.

"This cannot happen Adam," she said in a soft voice.

"But why? I don't understand…"

"Please bear with me Adam. You will understand at some point in the future but for now it is very important that we continue with…our discussions on spirituality."

He stared at her in silence, frustration replacing the excitement he felt when she had embraced him.

Appearing to sense this she spoke again quickly this time.

"Adam there are times when certain facets of this life can only be revealed in the same manner as a jigsaw puzzle coming together. We will see the whole picture when all the pieces are in place. I'm sorry… I'm just very sorry it has to be this way but it cannot be otherwise. I take all the blame. I should have kept my feelings in check."

He looked up at her in sober silence and then shaking his head slightly turned to look out a window.

"Hey look," she said picking up both his hands. "The weather is beautiful out there today and I think you've been cooped up in the house long enough. Let's take a day off and go for a sleigh ride. I'll get Andy to hook Sampson up to the cutter and we can go sight seeing. Hank has opened up a number of trails now so there's lots to explore. What do you say?"

He brought his eyes back to meet hers again and then smiling faintly nodded in agreement. He knew he would have agreed to almost anything she proposed but not wanting to be too obvious, he muted any display of enthusiasm as best he could.

After requesting her brother to hook the horse to the cutter she said, "I'll pop our supper into the oven before we leave. We'll likely be starving by the time we get back and passing out in the forest once in a winter is enough for you."

"Right," he said now struggling with his parka as she deposited a large roaster into the oven and then added in several blocks of wood to cook whatever the roaster contained.

The tinkling of harness bells and the dog barking outside signaled the arrival of the horse and cutter. Andy opened the door and nodded to his sister, then departed to do whatever it was that he always seemed to be busy at.

"Alright Mr. Finlay. The acid test. If you can make it to the cutter in an upright position you have graduated back to the outdoors once again."

With her assistance he hobbled without incidence to the antique sleigh and was soon seated on the wooden bench.

"I have to run back in and get my gloves," she said after rummaging through her coat pockets. "I'll only be a few seconds."

He sat back and took in a deep breath realizing this was his first time outside the house since they had dragged his half dead body in some three months earlier. "Where had the time gone?" he wondered and what changes had taken place. His other life seemed so far away and foreign now that he wondered if he could ever face it again.

The loud barking of the dog broke into his thoughts and he turned his head in time to see the gray animal charging toward the cutter at full gallop.

"Dusty," Jenny called loudly as she emerged from the house. But the dog was already circling the cutter growling and barking at Adam and causing the horse to prance nervously.

"Dusty down!" she yelled again. But he ignored her and continued expressing his objection to Adam's presence. Suddenly he stopped and began wagging his tail in a sign of friendship. Shrinking back as the animal hesitantly moved closer, Adam was grateful when Jenny grabbed his collar and pulled him back.

"I'm sorry," she said, "I know he is wary of strangers but I thought he was gone with Andy. Are you okay?"

"I'm fine. He had me worried for a moment though."

"He'll be alright now," she said releasing the animal after a few soothing words.

Rather than keep his distance from Adam, the big dog moved in closer and whimpering slightly began licking Adam's hand.

"I don't believe that!" Jenny exclaimed staring wide eyed at the scene. "He never makes friends that quickly with anybody. That is ... strange."

"Oh he just knows good people when he sees them," Adam answered now petting the dog that was acting as though Adam was a long lost friend.

"You've probably been spying on me over the years and secretly made friends with Dusty so you could move in and ravage me with no resistance."

"You've got it but I didn't think Dusty would give our secret away."

"Your plan really went up in smoke didn't it? You broke your leg trying to sneak in the back way and when you did get here you had a heart attack. Was that really the best you could do Adam?"

"They will both heal at which time appropriate restitution will be made."

"Oh I see. Well in the meantime you'll have to settle for a sleigh ride in the forest," she said flicking the reins to spur the horse into motion.

His association with horses was limited to what he had seen on television or at a movie which was scant preparation for the actual experience of this invigorating ride. Accustomed to the luxury of the plush seat in his Mercedes he could only wonder at the fact that some people actually enjoyed this activity.

Jenny had obviously mastered handling the huge animal because he responded readily to her every command even though her words were almost inaudible at times.

The day was crisp and clear and soon he found himself beginning to enjoy the ride.

This, he knew, was due partly to the narrow seat that forced them close together. The scent of the perfume she always wore, the warmth of her body against his and her cheerful chatter caused him to relax into a peaceful state of mind.

The beauty of this backwoods country was undeniable. He had

always been a city dweller but it would have been impossible for anyone not to appreciate the constantly changing vistas of nature awaiting them around every corner. Jenny named every bird, plant and animal that came into view easier than he could have identified the streets of Edmonton. This, he knew was due, in part, to her training but it was obviously accentuated by her love of the wilderness. She fit into this environment as readily as the wildlife she identified.

After what seemed like only minutes he checked his watch and was amazed to find they had been out nearly three hours. Right then Jenny reigned the horse in and pointed to a huge fallen spruce tree only a few feet off the trail.

"Recognize that spot?" she asked.

"How could I," he shrugged. "I've never been outside your door?"

"That was before you ever entered our door. However it was dark and you were unconscious. I guess you can be excused," she said laughing.

"Is that the tree?" he asked looking closer.

"That's the one. If you must get clobbered by a spruce tree, that was the best place to do it. We only had to drag you a short distance to the house."

Able to get his bearings now he sat upright and took in as much of the surrounding scene as he could. Something prodded his memory for a few moments and then popped to the surface.

"I was going in the wrong direction after all," he blurted.

"Adam?"

"My directions, that night in the storm, I had forgotten to bring my compass and was totally confused. I remember coming this way because I thought the wind was blowing out of the northwest but feeling as though I should be going that way," he said pointing east. "The wind must have changed direction and I didn't realize it."

"Did you really go the wrong way Adam?" she said looking at

him soberly.

"Yes I did. You see in order to rejoin my group I should've…"

"Really Adam?" she interrupted.

He stared at her for a few moments, then smiling faintly he nodded. "I wasn't was I?"

"What do you think?"

"Obviously my guardian angel was on the job that night. I'm still in God's good book."

"You were never out of God's good book. Anyway we've come full circle. The yard is just around that corner ahead and I bet you're starved."

"I could eat Sampson."

"And leave us without transportation? How about the chicken and vegetables I put in the oven before we left? They should be ready by now."

"Sampson's safe then," he said smiling at her as they re-entered the yard and came to a stop at the back door of the house.

CHAPTER 19

When he awakened the next morning the sun streaming in through the window caused him to sit upright quickly and rub his eyes.

"My god," he thought, checking his watch, "that fresh air is a great tranquilizer." He had slept without stirring for nine hours.

"Well, well, well," Jenny said when he hobbled out into the kitchen, "who do we have here? You're not related to Rip Van Winkle are you?"

"Be quiet and besides it's your fault. You insisted on the sleigh ride."

"Oh I see. Well my apologies then. Anyway here's breakfast," she said bringing a plate of scrambled eggs and pancakes out of the stove warming oven and pouring coffee for them both.

"How do you feel today?" she asked seating herself across the table from him.

"Very good," he said chewing on his first bite of breakfast. He was constantly amazed at her cooking ability in this old fashioned kitchen which was completely devoid of modern appliances. He had once suggested she could make a fortune if she was to open a café in some town or city and serve her special style of home cooked food.

"But where would I get wood to burn in the stove?" she had answered laughing. "Cooking with anything else would ruin the food."

He smiled at her again happy for the light hearted talk that frequently entered their discussions.

"Laughter," she had often said, "was as essential to one's well being as food."

His suggestion that there was another equally important activity was met with a mock expression of shock and a comment that his sinful mind was incorrigible.

He had ceased thinking beyond any one day. He knew a time of reckoning lie ahead but he was no longer able to perceive of his future without her in it but right now their worlds were light years apart. He had even toyed with the idea of selling his business and moving closer to her. This, however, was still fantasizing because a thousand hurdles would have to be negotiated before that might be possible. Besides could he adapt to this country? To her lifestyle? And taking her to a large city, even if she did agree, would be the classic square peg in a round hole. She had also insisted that a relationship between them must not happen but he viewed this as nothing more than an impulsive outburst of emotions she had temporarily lost control of and was indirectly reprimanding herself.

Little did he then know that the dilemma would soon be resolved in a manner that transcended the boundaries of credibility.

"Adam," her laughing voice broke into his thoughts. "Where were you just now?"

"A place I want to take you to."

"Oh dear me. I'm sure I wouldn't be safe."

"That is the whole idea."

"Lately you've had a one track mind. Perhaps we should get back to discussing soul purpose before it is too late."

"We have been discussing mine."

"Adam Finlay."

"Oh all right. Soul purpose it is. Where did we leave off?"

"Attempting to plumb the frightful depths of your primary purpose and so far all you've come up with are desires that shouldn't even be uttered in front of Trina."

"That's why I can't seem to conclude what mine is."

"Try anyway."

"Well number one on my list now is the environment and likely will be for the rest of my life, but there is one other thing and this seems to be out in left field."

"Well," she said when he didn't continue.

"It's…music."

"Music."

"Yeah." He looked at her sheepishly for a moment, then turned his eyes away."

"Adam Finlay you are embarrassed about that when you should be proud. I love music but more importantly you have admitted to something you love. Have you ever told anyone else?"

"No."

"Why haven't you?"

"Well it always seemed to be so…whimpish…for a man."

"Shame on you Adam Finlay. You have suppressed a life long desire just because it didn't seem manly. Have you any idea how many wonderful male musicians that are out there?"

"I know but I just couldn't bring myself to…"

"To indulge in an activity that seems so benign. After all what would everyone else think if the tough, hard-nosed Adam Finlay was caught enjoying something that counteracted his aggressive image. Why it's even possible he might even appear just the slightest bit gentle and heaven knows he couldn't allow that."

"You've just mortally wounded me."

"Well I'm just getting started. Now before I beat the daylights out of you tell me which musical activity appeals to you the most."

"Playing...piano."

"Oh that is really whimpish. Do you have any idea of the number of male pianists there are all over this planet? Why the organist who plays in the valley church is a big strong weather beaten farmer who even works part time in the coal mine to help support his family. Yes Adam you should really be ashamed of yourself for such a feminine desire."

"You're cruel."

"And you've racked up a karmic accumulation that will likely take the next five lives to correct. If you weren't so incapacitated, I'd cart you down to Mrs. Hartz to start music lessons right today."

"Actually I did take lessons."

"And I'll bet no one else ever knew about it."

"Uh...right."

"You did have a piano at home?"

"Yes."

"Now let's see. I suspect you bought it for the kids but the real reason was so you could play it yourself when no one else was around."

"Well..."

"And when you moved to your apartment?"

"I bought another one."

"And you probably kept it hidden."

"Well...kinda."

Tapping her fingers lightly on the table, she looked at him; a faint smile playing at the corners of her mouth. He glanced at her, then turned away quickly to hide his own smile. After a moments silence she said, "well?"

"Well what?"

"You know what. I think it's time to get started with that beating. Adam yours is a classic example of someone ignoring a true purpose in favor of society's demands. You may not necessarily have made your living from music although you could have, but at least you should've freely expressed your love for it. Can you not see the joy that it would have brought into your life as well as pleasure to others? Music is among the most divinely inspired activities that there is. How did you feel when you did play the piano?"

"Well I felt…"

"Fulfilled, gratified and happy right? And what sort of fantasies did you have about music when you thought about it?"

"I always admired concert pianists."

"And somewhere deep inside, you fancied yourself being one."

"I guess so."

"Well I know so. Do you realize what you've deprived yourself of?"

"I'm starting to."

"Adam," she said in a gentle tone. "I'm not trying to make you feel guilty, but rather use this example to illustrate how we so often cheat ourselves. The need to express yourself through music has had its origin in previous lives. But for reasons buried deep within, you still resisted doing so in this life and society was right there to support that choice. Let's take a look at your career and your life with music now in the equation.

Firstly you would never apologize for involving yourself in your property development business because you see it as something commendable, something ethical and respectable because it is providing a service, employing other people and making money and indeed it is doing all those things. Besides you inherited it making it an even more binding obligation. Once again to what extent are you doing it just because it does fall into the foregoing categories and to what extent because you have a strong passion for it? Your passion for music on the other hand, comes straight from the heart because your desire for it is unfettered by external influences. But society is still in control because you are concerned about how it will be viewed so you keep it hidden.

Let's hypothesize for a few minutes. Let's assume you had always openly admitted your love of music, that you had even become a fairly accomplished pianist and finally one day decided to turn it into a full time occupation. On that day it is immediately cast into a different role. For starters how would society view it? 'Poor Adam Finlay', they might say, 'has lost his grip on common sense. He sold his highly successful business and opened up a music store, of all things.'

Besides you would likely have been concerned about making enough money to provide a decent living for your family if you had one. Why you might even have to relinquish your membership at the country club, sell your mansion for something more modest and drive a less expensive car. Horror of horrors and all this just to play the piano? Unthinkable. So you continue along doing what the culture keepers have decided you will do and relegate your passion to the back burner. The desire for music is still there smoldering away in your heart but you now have it so under control that if it makes even a brief appearance you can smack it back into its place once again. Is that fairly accurate?"

He grinned at her for a moment then said, "actually many of those very thoughts had crossed my mind on the rare occasion I did consider music seriously. So what should I have done?"

"You are probably asking the wrong person because I follow my heart first and then adjust every other aspect of my life to fit that direction."

"What is that direction?"

"I live it every day Adam. Everything I do is in some way connected to my purpose, which basically is spiritual development, but it wasn't always that way. As a younger person I too followed the trends. I was immersed in church activities, was preparing myself for a career in accounting, expecting to be married at the appropriate age, have a family, maybe live in a large house in Vancouver, all those things that, in retrospect I thought I should want. Then one day after a series of tragic events and a lot of soul searching I came to my senses and realized that what I really *did* want had little to do with what I believed I wanted."

"You might have a certain advantage over me though. You've got me thinking about the importance of making a more direct contribution to the good of humanity. You are a living role model of what is required to help put the human race back on track. But if I would have opened up a music store, it might have satisfied my own desires but what does it do for others?"

"Firstly do not lose sight of your desire to assist with environmental problems because that is your primary purpose. But music, not property development, is likely your secondary purpose.

There are many, many ways of serving our fellow man but first consider this, your strong passion for music is in some way connected to your soul agenda and in order to fulfill that agenda you must conform to your passion. Remember you wrote your script which means it is critically important to your spiritual progress. There may seem to be no relevancy at all when viewing it through human eyes but here you must trust the inner voice that tries to propel you toward an activity that in some way corresponds to your purpose. This, alone, contributes something to your fellow humans because you are now on track, which means we now have a happier, contented and more fulfilled Adam Finlay. But beyond that there is always some way we can apply our passion in service to others. It is nothing more than simply deciding to do so. Artists donate expensive paintings to charity, professional musicians do charity concerts and if Adam Finlay had chosen to be a concert pianist so could he. Writers tell the sad stories about persons in third world countries and photographers take the pictures that create public awareness of their depraved conditions. There is no such thing as not being able to mesh one's passion with service to others. We need only to choose to turn our focus away from profit and on to assisting our fellow man. This does not mean we must live below poverty level ourselves. If we are constantly struggling for every morsel of food we cannot effectively help others. However, know this, the very act of unconditional giving activates a basic universal law ensuring that our own needs will always be met. This must be *unconditional* giving born of love for all mankind. There must be no expectations of some future pay back for our contribution and it must never be done with the object of elevating our own status. It must be done for one single solitary reason and that is because we truly care. Giving in this manner opens up a channel that makes way for an inflow of all we need to fill the vacuum created when we gave. The saying that nature abhors a vacuum is true but if we create that vacuum for purely selfish reasons we may discover that nature has also plugged the entrance. Another well known saying that addresses this law is 'as you give so shall you receive' but once again analyze the words carefully. *As you give.* In other words what was your intention when you gave. If it was for the right reason, you will receive in like manner. It did not say that because you gave, riches will come flooding back and in fact they may only be a trickle if the giving was done with the idea of eventually getting something in return. Give, Adam, knowing the universe will take care of you if you gave out of love for all of God's creation."

"Whew," he said exhaling slowly. "I can see now what you meant when you said the spiritual pathway could be a difficult one to travel."

"But it can also be a wonderful experience and in fact eventually will be. I, too, had to go through an adjustment period. But I now have a sense of peace and contentment that is not attainable in any other way. I still have challenges. That's an innate aspect of physical life. But I meet and deal with those challenges knowing that I am on purpose and every time I overcome another hurdle I have moved up a rung on the ladder of evolution and with every rung the challenges become less drudgery.

To achieve something that is in alignment with my soul purpose is now an exciting accomplishment that motivates me to do even better the next time. This is not just to attain perfection in this life but to increase my spiritual development through the effort expended in the process of doing something better every time I do it. We should always strive to improve on our previous efforts for in so doing, we honor the inner spiritual reality that is the source and reason for our very being. Evolution is God's purpose and therefore ours. We fulfill this purpose each time we do the very best we can no matter what it is we are doing"

"It's obvious that knowing our soul purpose is important but equally obvious it can be difficult to find," he said. "You mentioned earlier that there are a number of ways that can assist us. What are they?"

"In your case play the piano—with pride."

"Okay," he grinned. "Besides that."

"There are various considerations that one can take into account when identifying one's soul purpose. For starters observe your health relative to your current work. Your body can give you signals as to whether or not you are on purpose. Some persons have actually experienced illness because they were striving to achieve something that was contrary to their mission."

"Once those persons embarked on activities that contributed to their purpose rather than oppose it the illness cleared up."

"Another thing one can do is analyze one's fears. Fear can be experienced when dealing with a conflict brought on by suppressing the desire to work on purpose. Conversely, however, both of the foregoing conditions can occur when you *do* embark on your purpose because your ego might still insist you should be doing something 'more practical'.

This conflict will gradually disappear if you persist in your new direction. You will likely be faced with challenges at the outset because few if any of your current circle of friends and acquaintances will be strongly supportive."

"How does one cope with that?"

"Those who abandon you simply because you changed direction Adam, were dubious friends anyway, but you may actually find yourself abandoning them because you can no longer identify with their principles. This does not mean you become enemies but it does mean you will align yourself with other persons of like mind because of the mutual support available.

People still controlled by the dictates of society have little to offer spiritual travelers and will gain even less in return because they are not yet ready to look reality in the eye. Don't waste time on these people not because they are unworthy of your time, but because it would be far better spent interacting with those who are prepared to resume their spiritual journey.

Is there some activity that you have a desire to learn more about? Something you are willing to study in detail? Even returning to a school or training program that specializes in the activity? In your case you've already done that in secret. I've known persons who hated school but readily returned to a program of concentrated studies in the area of their passion when they discovered what that passion was.

Is the work you are presently involved in a constant struggle? It has often been found that people working at something other than what their true passion is will constantly have an uphill battle on the job. They are never ahead with their work and in fact often behind. They do just enough to hang on and dread even doing that much but they struggle along from one day to the next usually because 'the money is good'. It is both astonishing and shameful what we are willing to sacrifice for money.

And here's another downside: if we are constantly failing, as in the foregoing example, we begin identifying with failure. We start seeing ourselves as a failure in everything we do which can stick around to haunt us even after we've immersed ourselves in our true purpose.

Do you have role models? I'm referring to persons you look up to or admire for their achievements. These individuals can reveal things about yourself that you alone cannot see but can become aware of by observing their performance.

These are a few of the observations we can make to help identify our soul purpose Adam and I've presented them only in general terms. A detailed study would be time well spent for anyone ready to get onto their spiritual pathway."

CHAPTER 20

"You've often mentioned spiritual laws," he said when they resumed the discussion the next day. "Wouldn't these play an important role when defining one's purpose?"

"They play an important role no matter what pathway we're on and they're more apt to be violated by persons who are off purpose. An integral aspect of anyone's mission is abide by the laws no matter what that mission is."

"What about persons who have actually chosen some very negative experiences such as spending time in prison? They would've had to break laws, both human and spiritual to comply with their agenda."

"They may have chosen experiences that necessitated violating laws but only insofar as those experiences contributed to their rehabilitation. The ultimate objective for our human existence is to transcend any desire to oppose spiritual laws which can only be achieved by first having negative experiences in which we did oppose them. I've repeatedly said that the purpose for planet earth is to provide a curriculum through which we are exposed to all possibilities from the most horrendous to the most beautiful. We can't know what is good if we've never experienced something bad to compare it to. Imagine living in a world that supplied only joy, happiness, harmony, peace, contentment and prosperity. We would actually be *unable to know it was all of these things because we had never experienced their opposites.* As harsh as it may seem the unpleasant aspects of life are as beneficial to our evolution as are the pleasant ones. The attainment of happiness is really nothing more than a measure of our progress. Always reach for happiness Adam, for in the reaching lies the only true joy we can know in this life and that joy will be maximized to the degree that our efforts are aligned with our soul purpose.

In the example you provided, the individual who broke the law had to do so in order to finally appreciate the benefits of obeying laws which in his case could take several lifetimes.

As this person evolves, however, he will realize that conforming to spiritual laws will bring him a measure of satisfaction he couldn't otherwise know.

Human laws, on the other hand, are often obeyed simply because of the negative consequences of disobeying them. For example, the only reason that most persons don't speed when driving their car is due to their fear of being caught and paying a penalty. They don't necessarily feel a sense of achievement because they obeyed the law and in fact many consider it an achievement if they did speed and weren't apprehended.

As we develop spiritually, obedience to universal laws becomes a preference not an obligation. When, for example, we give unconditionally to a fellow human who is less fortunate than ourselves we engage the law of cause and effect. The giving, in this case, is the cause that produces a highly rewarding effect because we've mitigated his hardship. For those of us who are sincerely traversing the spiritual pathway we will feel pure joy in this act for no other reason than the love we have for all of God's creation. There are still many who have not yet reached this point on their journey. They place more emphasis on getting for themselves than giving to someone more needy. They are usually easy to spot. They seldom give anything voluntarily and if they do they expect something in return. Persons in this category still need considerable experience in this physical realm or in a similar dimension."

"I think it's time for me to learn those laws."

"You don't have to learn them you simply have to remember

them because they are already etched deep within your intuitive being. All I can do is help you along in the process.

We've already dealt with cause and effect so let's go next to freedom of choice because it is often controversial. It is fact, or law, that we have chosen every thing in our life no matter how much we feel we are victims of chance or fate. This can be a difficult one to accept. Many so called burdens, we believe, were imposed on us by some outside force beyond our control when in fact those burdens are the result of choices we made at some earlier point in our journey.

If we have a physical or mental handicap, for example, we bemoan the unfairness of this condition which we believe was inflicted on us against our will. We certainly would not have done this to ourselves if we would've had any choice in the matter or so we believe. Acceptance of reincarnation, however, paints a very different and comprehensive picture. Since we've had numerous earlier lives we have also had unlimited opportunity to participate in everything that the human condition allows for. Traditional beliefs can never satisfactorily explain the reason for our handicap but if we subscribe to esoteric wisdom it immediately makes sense.

We chose the defect because, for reasons buried deep in our past, we needed that particular experience to assist us on our journey. Will we now try to understand what lesson the adversity is presenting or will we disclaim any responsibility for it and spend our life mourning our misfortune?

Everything we now have, do and are is the result of choices we've made during previous lives and we will always be making those choices whether or not we want to accept that responsibility. To rebuke this truth is nothing more than us making a choice to rebuke this truth. To say it is God's will is us choosing to blame the creator. The man who hates his job can choose to change it. If he isn't qualified to do something else he can choose to retrain in another field of work and maybe this time it will be the right one.

The woman who feels stuck in a rotten marriage is choosing to stay in it until she chooses to get out. It is sheer and utter nonsense to feel locked into a relationship because of the kids, the church, money, work, friends, relatives and a hundred other reasons we can dredge up to avoid taking responsibility for breaking out.

Freedom of choice is a law that sets us free and this truth is readily demonstrated by those persons moving forward on their spiritual pathway. They exercise that freedom by picking and choosing from life's menu, those situations and activities that best facilitate their journey. They are not constrained by any traditional belief that might impede their progress.

Casting off the constraints that we've allowed society to impose on us is something we must do if we are to conform to another law. This one says we must embrace the light of our own truth because our spiritual growth will be inhibited until we do. It is law that we will experience frustrations and distress as long as we subscribe to a lifestyle not of our own making and it is law that when we do start to conform to our own truth our life will start to change for the better. The law can be stated in different ways but boils down to the law of attuning to your own reality. Remember life won't become a blissful bowl of cherries just because we've started to harmonize with our soul purpose but it will give us a sense of satisfaction because the challenges we'll now encounter are integral to that purpose.

Another important law is one that tells us there is an appropriate time for almost anything we undertake. We usually abide by this law, because it is a natural response to our environment. The majority of us, for example, sleep during the night or the dark portion of the day and this is for more reasons than the fact that daylight enables us to more easily do things. The soothing quiet of night tends to condition our mood and bodies so that we are more receptive to sleep. Granted shiftwork is a fact of life for many nowadays, but that does not change the natural urges built into our physiology.

This fact extends to every aspect of our life. There is a time to be careless and a time to be cautious, a time to love unconditionally and a time to guard our emotions. A time to buy and a time to sell and with a little effort we can learn to recognize these times.

The coming and going of the seasons and the manner in which

nature conforms to these constant changes also illustrates this truth. Birds and animals respond in an appropriate manner to the approaching winter, by storing food, migrating or preparing to hibernate. They instinctively know that change will soon occur and they resonate with it. We don't see birds building nests in September or squirrels storing nuts in April. This trend is even evident at the level of soil organisms that can only be seen through a microscope. In the spring and early summer these tiny bugs are present in large numbers which stimulate vigorous plant growth. In the late summer and fall their numbers decline significantly accompanied by a corresponding drop off in the growth rate of plants. Other factors such as available moisture and nutrients also influence plant growth but in general terms the whole process conforms to the influence of the seasons. Try as hard as you might you cannot force plants into lush growth in October just as we shouldn't try to force something to happen in our life if the time isn't right.

This law could be termed the law of appropriate timing that tells us to patiently wait until the time is right.

This next law has to do with compassion and is often grossly misunderstood. We readily feel compassion toward something we think is deserving of our compassion when in fact all of creation is.

What we really have is selective compassion that extends to those persons or things that are easy to feel compassionate about: a neglected child, an abused animal or battered wife. And, well we should, but in order to fully comply with the law we should feel compassion for all because all is some part of the creator."

"That's a tall order Jenny. It is pretty damned hard to feel anything but revulsion toward the scumbags who destroyed the towers in New York. They certainly weren't demonstrating compassion."

"Adam I'm not saying we should blithely accept their destructive behavior but to fight hatred with hatred results in a dominant atmosphere of hatred when we should be striving for one of love. We must isolate those types in some way for the protection of the rest of humanity but remember they are still many rungs down on the evolutionary ladder. We were all once down at that point and if we are unwilling to express compassion for those persons still there then we haven't risen much above them. To the extent that we can feel compassion for all is the extent to which we have cast off the dominance of ego. I know I'm repeating myself when I say we are all some part of the almighty one but it needs to be repeated until our acceptance of that truth prompts us to treat all persons as we would want to be treated ourselves. In the final analysis how we treat anyone extends to everyone including ourselves. By that same measure mistreatment and ill thoughts about ourselves inhibits our capacity to feel compassion for others.

You must forgive yourself first for only then can you completely forgive someone else. We cannot escape the ripple effect built into the fabric of the universe. It is an inevitable consequence of our behavior which means the degree to which we accept full responsibility for our own thoughts and actions is the degree to which harmony is restored to our life.

This law of compassion extends as well to the treatment of our environment and indeed the entire planet. Many of us can demonstrate genuine compassion for one another but have little concern for this earth we inhabit. We pollute, deface, destroy and generally exploit the natural resources of our earthly home with mindless disregard for the future until one day soon our world will backfire with deadly consequences.

We were born out of the love of God and given the opportunity to gain greater understanding of the depth of that love through experience on this physical plane. Causing irreparable damage to our earthly domain clearly indicates we still have much to learn but of greater concern is the possibility we might completely destroy ourselves before we've learned enough to prevent that destruction. 'Learned' is not even the correct term. We need only be willing to implement the corrective measures that we are already aware of.

I'm sure by now you are thinking that these so called laws are nothing more than good common sense ethics that most of us have heard repeated time and again since childhood. But I also expect that you probably never viewed them as laws. Most persons see them as those 'good' things we should do and occasionally we do. But if at times we are lax, we shrug it off blaming it on the fallibility of human nature and promising ourselves we will do better in the future. Seldom do we realize, or would even be willing to believe, we are breaking a divine law. The consequences are not always catastrophic and may not even be noticeable. Since life usually goes on pretty much as it always has we cannot accept that we've actually done anything very wrong because there would be some sort of negative result if we had wouldn't there?

Well no not necessarily, at least not something obvious and right here is where we cheat ourselves. The fact that one's life is still going along as usual is the negative result.

We are here to move forward not maintain the status quo. Our purpose is to grow and we inhibit that growth by disobeying the rules. You won't be hauled up in front of some heavenly jury to answer for your misdemeanor but you will be sentenced to a continuation of the struggles you've always had and come to accept as the way life is. We are opposing our fundamental purpose of spiritual evolution and opposing our own soul agenda regardless of what it is, when we break the laws. It doesn't matter if someone came into life with suffering, sorrow and misery written into their script. Their objective should be to overcome those adversities and this will never be accomplished as long as they refuse to play by the rules. For some it takes many lifetimes to acknowledge this fact which is one reason why we see so much hardship and struggle among human beings."

Shaking his head slightly he said, "sometimes I feel that the more I learn the less I really know."

Laughing she said, "at some secluded spot in your being Adam you know the whole story. All that is required is for you to let that awareness come through but more importantly to act on that awareness once it is revealed. Our problem is partly one of not knowing but also an unwillingness to implement what we do know. I mentioned earlier the mindless consumption and destruction of our planet and if it continues unchecked will result in disaster that is unthinkable. The gravity of that situation far exceeds what many either truly do not understand or more often do not want to. As the health of our earth goes, so goes the fate of the human race."

"We've certainly taken the long road to get to the link between spirituality and the environment, but I'm starting to see the connection between the two."

"It was necessary to understand the basics of spirituality so that the connection made sense Adam.

However I've been neglecting some housework. I must do our laundry which will take the rest of the day. Let's pick up on this subject tomorrow."

Grinning crookedly at her he said, "I'm beginning to think your primary motive is to drive me insane. Just when we really get into something you have to gather eggs, peel potatoes, do the laundry or go out and talk to birds. Do you realize how close to a nervous breakdown I've come?"

"We wouldn't want you to lose interest."

"I may lose my mind."

"Okay if it's that serious I'll assign some homework which you must have completed for tomorrow's class. What are the various direct connections between spirituality, our physical environment and the way we treat it. If it's not completed to my satisfaction then tomorrow you peel the potatoes. Deal?"

CHAPTER 21

"Are you all set to peel potatoes Adam?" she asked with an impish smile as they resumed discussions the next day.

"Oh no. I'm way ahead of you I thought about it half the night but first getting back to the environmental group I told you about sometime ago now, I've developed a few different views as a result of our discussions this winter. God created earth for man's use or for man to develop spiritually and admittedly we may not be taking real good care of earth at the present time but we've also developed technologies that I believe will correct environmental problems before they reach the serious proportions you mentioned. If, as you say, we are expressions of God then somewhere within ourselves that God-like wisdom will out pace any mistakes we've made and set us back on track. After all the creator is not going to allow the destruction of a realm he designed for the purpose of helping us attain spiritual maturity on his behalf."

"My, my. You did do your homework."

"Of course Miss Ingram. Now about my reward…"

"You don't have to peel the potatoes today."

"That's not what I had in mind."

"What you had in mind would've overpopulated the earth years ago. It's no accident that your name is Adam. But tell me this.

Do you really think technology can keep pace with our destructive practices?"

"I think it already is. Certainly we will have to become much more environmentally conscious but I do not see the whole human race going down the tube by its own hand. That would seem to violate God's agenda. He might finally lose patience with our behavior and inflict a few disasters to whip us back in line but He would not allow us to pull our own abode down around our ears."

"So you think that God will intervene in our affairs and salvage us at the last minute?"

"Yes if it should come to that. I don't believe He is going to sit back and allow us to destroy ourselves anymore than a parent seeing their child playing out on a busy street is going to sit back and just watch."

"Adam…"

"I know you've said that our total freedom of choice precludes any intervention by the creator but it seems to me that there would be limits to that idea. If we are faced with complete annihilation He will step in and save us from ourselves."

"Didn't we agree that the creator is already active in everything that happens on earth by manifesting as each and every one of us."

"Perhaps, but I still think he will somehow move in and avert the ultimate disaster."

"You then obviously believe that the earth was created exclusively for man."

"I feel that man was God's ultimate objective as I believe does most of Christianity and I recall you saying that spirit only reached full expression when It was finally able to inhabit human bodies."

"Actually I referred to them as sentient beings. But tell me what you think is the purpose in all the rest of physicality if the ultimate reason for earth is for man's use."

"It's a support system. If man is to live and thrive he must have all that constitutes his environment in order to do so."

"If that is true it would seem that man never grasped that fact himself since he's already destroyed a large portion of the environment."

"I can't deny that."

"But you still believe the final objective of creation was reached with the appearance of man on the scene."

"Yes I believe it was."

"Everything else on earth is just for the purpose of man's existence."

"I think so."

"Elephants, aphids, magpies and dandelions are here only to ensure man's survival."

"Yes."

"Then evolution would have stopped with the arrival of man?"

"No. Why should it?"

"If man was the final objective why would it continue?"

"It's a natural process Jenny. We wouldn't even want it to stop would we?"

"So you agree it is still happening?"

"Yes I do."

"Then through the process of evolution species have come and gone, dinosaurs disappeared, entire civilizations rose and fell but man in his present form is somehow exempt from that fate."

"As I said God will prevent it from happening."

"She didn't seem to think it necessary to save earlier civilizations, why do you think she would bend the rules now and salvage this current crop?"

"What other civilizations?"

"The Mayan, Incan, Ancient Greeks, Romans, Inhabitants of Easter Island all vanished leaving nothing more than a few relics to let us know they were once here on earth. In fact all early man right up to the Cro-Magnon became extinct. We are evolved descendants of Cro-Magnon man and so far are still here to tell our story. But we too are now skating on thin ice and unless we change our ways and change them drastically I don't think God is going to play favorites and save us. We simply must do what our earlier relatives didn't; take the necessary steps to ensure our own survival."

"The advent of Christianity changed the whole scheme of things Jenny. Jesus came to earth and by offering himself up for sacrifice ensured the survival of man from that time on."

"So man prior to the time of Jesus wasn't worthy of salvation."

"According to the Bible, no he wasn't."

"And we are to accept the Bible as the ultimate authority on this issue?"

"Well a large portion of the human race does."

"What about the millions who have been killed in wars and all manner of disaster since the advent of Christianity. God still seems to be rather biased."

"Okay what is your version of our environmental situation."

"The mistaken belief that the earth was created solely for man's use, or misuse, is probably a good place to start. I saw very clearly during my spiritual sabbatical that earth as a whole is a living, breathing organism with all the various components such as plants, birds, animals, insects, air, water, microscopic organisms and sunlight making their respective contributions to the healthy function of the planet. This could be compared to our physical body with its various organs that work cooperatively to ensure the proper function of the whole entity. If any organ becomes diseased or injured the body malfunctions or become ill. If the disease is severe and prolonged, such as cancer, the body might die. The body, however, like our earth has a remarkable capacity to resist and recover from many ailments. Once an alien organism is detected both the body and the earth go to work in their respective fashions to deal with the invader and restore conditions to normal. In situations of prolonged and excessive abuse of our physical bodies the damage may be irreversible and the results tragic. Examples are the cirrhosed liver of the alcoholic and damaged lungs of a smoker whose life spans are often shortened simply because they abused those organs beyond their limits of tolerance. The planet responds to the way it is treated in much the same manner. Over consumption, abuse and misuse of various resources will result in a sick world and that is precisely what we have right now, a world that is very sick. The difference, however, between the planet and our body is the planet will not die at least not from this present scourge. Earth has survived every disaster, invasion and abuse imaginable during its four billion years of existence and it is certainly not going to capitulate to this current threat. Make no mistake, Adam, planet earth will survive and it will do so by eradicating the offending organism which presently is man. We may make a terrible mess of it before our demise but with man out of the way and after a few thousand years of healing time earth will return to it's original condition."

"Boy you don't hold out much hope for our survival. I've heard more optimistic views from fundamentalist Christians. They believe, as I still do, that God will step in at the last minute and at least salvage the faithful."

"I can only repeat what I've said before. During my sojourn alone in the wilderness I was privy to divine information that, among other things, revealed the potentially disastrous results to humanity if we continue on our destructive pathway.

This doesn't have to happen Adam. We can still reverse these trends and salvage not only the so called faithful but the entire human race. It is critical, however, to take immediate and decisive steps. We must act now and in a positive manner because every day we delay, the solutions to our problems become more difficult to resolve."

"Don't you think the remedial work already being done will

turn the tide?"

"Let's back up and analyze the role that man has played versus the role he should have played in shaping conditions on earth. The arrogance of man is a principle factor in the devastation we've wreaked on the planet. Contrary to what many believe, including Adam Finlay, Earth was not created for the exclusive use of man. Man is a very recent appearance on the scene but instead of taking his place as a polite newcomer he moved right in believing that this world was his for the taking and his primary objective was to conquer it. The human ego became dominant early in man's history and the lust for money and power soon pushed his spiritual side almost out of sight. This condition dominates right to the present day and although many realize we've dangerously exceeded certain limits very few genuine counter measures are being implemented."

"You seem to be contradicting yourself. You have said that man or a sentient being would eventually emerge because our spirit required that kind of vessel for maximum expression and further this being would, and does, have complete freedom of choice. To me that seems to indicate that the world evolved to its present form in preparation for man."

"Some form of being with the potential for sentience was the inevitable result of evolution, but the creator's scheme was not to engender an environment for that being to pollute and destroy. The intention was to create conditions in which man could take his rightful place. Earth evolved the various features of itself with man forming only one component of those features. Souls ultimately inhabited man because man contained the greatest potential for soul evolution, but the objective in this process was for all organisms to live in harmony with one another. All, except man, have been successful in this effort."

"It seems, though, that the environment has always been under attack. Numerous disasters prior to man have wreaked all manner of destruction on the planet. Volcanoes, fires, floods, droughts have constantly reshaped the face of our world."

"Those were natural events Adam, the process of natural selection at work bringing our world to the state it was in prior to the appearance of man. Since man has entered the picture, the process has gradually become more and more *unnatural*. Forest fires that razed hundreds of acres in the past were actually beneficial because they cleared away diseased, decaying and dead old growth to make way for the introduction of new healthy stands, but this happened selectively ensuring that the ecological chain was left intact. When man entered the picture, this changed. Many forest fires now happen because of man's carelessness. Others are deliberate to provide farmland in countries that are constantly battling starvation and the most tragic of all, clearcutting to satisfy man's greed.

Man did not fall heir to stewardship of the planet as many believe. The planet needed no stewardship before the arrival of man. Man fell heir to assuming his rightful place in nature and since man was imbued with conscious awareness his role should have been to ensure his presence made a beneficial contribution. Every organism has a role to play in the ecological chain of events that sustains our planet. This whole process was in place and working perfectly when man made his appearance. That alone should have told him something, but he obviously didn't get the message or didn't want to."

"Don't you think that having total freedom of choice was a guarantee that a certain segment of mankind would be prone to greed and power mongering."

"If it had been a guarantee Adam, then we never did have freedom of choice. It was an option that allowed us to make the decision to either interact responsibly with our environment or make a mess of it as we've done. We could have long ago chosen to take steps to avert the disaster we are now facing."

"You seem to place a lot of emphasis on forest destruction. Would you explain, in uncomplicated terms please, why forests are so important. What goes on in there that maintains ecological balance?"

"This can get rather detailed. Are you sure you want to explore it?"

Shrugging he answered, "If I'm to accept that clear cutting is detrimental I'll have to learn why."

Exhaling slowly she began. "Old growth forest is linked together by plants and animals, above ground and an underground network of root systems. Taken as a whole it functions as one organism or an ecosystem.

Biodiversity plays an important part in an ecosystem because all species in the system have a certain function. To mention a few they capture and store energy, produce organic material, decompose organic material, help to cycle water and nutrients throughout the system, control erosion or pests, fix atmospheric gases or help to regulate the climate.

Entities active in this process are large old trees, snags, fallen trees, saplings and a myriad of microscopic and macroscopic plants. Damage to one or two from disease or insects can be harmful, but the diversity in the forest exercises a natural self regulating control system that keeps invaders in check. Clear cutting, by contrast, permanently ruins any potential for recovery to natural forest status and seriously damages the environment in many other ways. In an undisturbed forest, trees, undergrowth and a mat of decaying plant materials on the forest floor soak up rainfall slowing both its surface and underground flow and releasing it back into the atmosphere through transpiration."

"What is transpiration?"

"Moisture in the soil is collected by plant roots and moved up through the plant to be ultimately discharged or transpired through leaves into the atmosphere."

"I don't understand. I thought the plant needs all the moisture it takes up. Why does it get rid of it?"

"It does use a certain amount primarily for photosynthesis but aren't we getting off topic?"

"Just keeping you on your toes."

"How nice of you. Now getting back to clearcutting and soil erosion. Flooding readily occurs when rain impacts bare soil. Unrestrained runoff carries a certain amount of the soil away and leaches nutrients out of the remainder. The whole devastating process disturbs microorganisms which could help replenish the lost nutrients. Clear cutting causes another equally serious problem due to increased amounts of carbon dioxide released into the atmosphere which in turn contributes to the greenhouse effect."

"How does clear cutting increase carbon dioxide levels?"

"Because there are fewer trees left to use it up."

"Trees use carbon dioxide?"

"Yes in the process of photosynthesis. Adam do you really not know this or are you just giving me a hard time?"

Grinning at her he said, "a little of both. I know that trees are a primary source of oxygen and I know photosynthesis is the process but I can't recall the details. Remember my degree is in commerce."

"That's elementary biology that you should have learned before high school."

"I vaguely remember some of it. Guess I was preoccupied at the time."

"Flirting with girls I presume."

"That's a biological process."

"It doesn't include photosynthesis."

"Well there's your answer, I thought it did."

"Right Adam. Okay. Very simply trees, in fact all green plants require carbon dioxide for photosynthesis to take place. The carbon dioxide combines with moisture in the leaf and in the presence of sunlight produces food for plant growth. Oxygen is given off as a byproduct."

"That doesn't happen in women?"

"No Adam it doesn't."

"Now I'm upset. All these years I thought it did."

"Sorry to burst your bubble. I know women are far superior to men, but even we have our limits. We have to leave oxygen production to trees."

"Let's get back to the topic."

"I think we should expand on the superiority of women."

"Jennifer!"

"Well if you insist," she said feigning wide eyed innocence. But are you really sure…"

"*Jennifer!*" he repeated struggling to suppress his laughter.

"Oh all right now where were we?"

"Somewhere between carbon dioxide and the arrogance of the female gender."

"Actually I used the word superior. Anyway in the past a balance between carbon dioxide and oxygen was maintained even though some European countries have long ago denuded most of their land.

The largest remaining boreal forest in the world spans portions of Canada, Scandanavia and Siberia. This, in combination with huge tropical rainforests in the southern hemisphere has always used up carbon dioxide at rates optimum for normal atmospheric functions. This has changed drastically. These forests are being clear cut at unprecedented rates and the associated problems are no longer something that even the industrialists can renounce. They still try but scientific proof is now so plentiful and irrefutable that they simply ignore the evidence and keep on with their destructive practices. They hope that environmental control measures will continue to lag behind allowing them to rack up very huge short term profits at the expense of the long term stability of our planet. With government emphasis on the economy there is little chance that this will change in the near future."

"From what you are saying, humanity many not have a distant future."

"That is a very distinct possibility Adam."

"Isn't that rather unjust? The large majority of the population is sincerely trying to do nothing more than make an honest living. We have little control over the disruption of the environment and yet we will suffer the same fate as those persons and corporations who perpetuate the problem."

"If our physical death was the end of our existence, then it would be terribly unjust. Don't think for a second that those greed motivated destroyers of the environment will not experience harsh negative consequences as a result of their wanton self serving behavior during this life. Karma will bring about balance imposing many unpleasant future lives on those individuals. In the present they may be powerful moguls believing they are above all laws and superior to the average person. But in the grand scheme of things they will ultimately be reduced to nothing more than groveling paupers grateful for even a smattering of recognition from persons they once looked down on.

If extinction does happen it won't be total. There will remain pockets of humans who have chosen to be responsible for re-establishing the race. The rest of us, the greater majority, will simply return home to the spiritual dimension to evaluate experiences we had on earth and ultimately decide our next venture. This might even include coming back to earth to assist with its restoration. Planet earth has offered us a great opportunity for spiritual progress. Many of us have developed a deep affection for the planet and may want to return to resume a process of enlightenment. Those who were instrumental in the initial breakdown of the planet's biosphere will find they must return to repair the damage they've done."

"Well I'm sure they are in the minority. I for one would not want to return if the near death experience I had was a true picture of the other side."

"You've just had a small sample, Adam. Once you've spent time over there you will realize what you must do to continue your journey which will include a return to earth."

"Do you think I've wracked up that much negative karma?"

"Your one track mind alone has done that," she smiled.

"I've heard that reforestation should counteract the excessive logging."

"Don't change the subject."

"Just trying to keep intelligent dialogue going."

"You're trying to escape the dreadful consequences of a depraved mind."

"Reforestation Jenny. That will rescue the human race, including me."

"Is that so. Well if ever there was a ridiculous farce, reforestation is one of them. The insane greed that justifies the so-called management of forests defies any kind of common sense. They initially violate the ecosystem to ensure the availability of trees for harvesting. This is done by suppressing fire, the natural cleanser of the forest. Nature has a reason for forest fires which should occur according to nature's schedule, not man's. No matter what lengths we go to sooner or later a fire will start, perhaps by a lightning strike, and if the area hasn't already been clear cut, an abnormal amount of fuel or dead wood will have accumulated. The fire then becomes an inferno destroying trees far in excess of what would have occurred had nature not been interfered with. This delays forest recovery primarily because of damage to the soil. Intense heat causes crusting that resists water infiltration leading to erosion. Now they add another cost when they finally realize they've broken natural laws. They try to reintroduce some balance by conducting remedial and very expensive control burns. This is one example, Adam. Another takes the form of greed motivated indifference by timber company operations when they clear cut. Everything is removed including underbrush, downed wood and standing dead trees. These materials provide habitat for beneficial insects, mammals and birds that keep forest diseases and infestations from reaching epidemic proportions which is a natural process Adam: a natural process. Then to finish this destructive job and really mess up the system, they apply herbicides to get rid of any remaining materials that stand in the way of a profitable timber harvest. Now they replace the natural multivaried species with single age, single species stands of commercial timber which leaves the forest completely defenseless against ravenous plagues of insects and disease. Then comes the final insult, the final act of insanity, all under the spurious veil of progress. In order to combat the abnormal outbreak of disease and insect attack, they make massive applications of pesticides. These are toxic chemicals that kill non-target species and dangerously affect the quality of water in nearby ponds and streams which in turn is detrimental to the myriad of life that inhabits these areas and…well I'm sure by now you get the picture.

Let's assume we continue on this same path of destruction debating a lot about what should be done but actually doing very little and in some cases nothing at all. We continue to pollute and destroy our environment, even at an accelerated rate since no agreements are reached about what, if any, control measures should be implemented. Then of course there is the large segment who, for various reasons, don't believe we even have a problem. At least they don't want to so we trundle along our merry way doing more or less just what we've always done until suddenly one day we find we can go no farther. We have finally stepped over the limits of environmental tolerance and the planet retaliates with all manner of disasters and catastrophes. Make no mistake we won't take the planet down with us, we may beat it up but it will emerge the winner and the human race the loser in this insane battle that never had to be fought. As we, the few remaining humans, lay beaten and battered, we might then, right at that point finally concede that 'yeah, we would have done it differently if we had known it would actually turn out like this.'

Is that what must happen Adam? Must we bring ourselves to the point of no return before we will finally admit that we could have been doing everything the right way all along if we would have actually believed that the planet wasn't going to tolerate our childish actions forever? We were warned over and over but we chose to ignore what was staring us right in the face. Then on that last day we'll look out across a barren, blistered and antagonistic landscape if there is anyone left to look and finally admit when it's too late that we always knew which path was the right one. Why in God's name didn't we take it?"

"It's rather strange to hear all this pessimism from such a positive person. Do you not see any light at the end of the tunnel at all?"

"I am not pessimistic by nature, but a strong reality check is overdue and that is what I'm trying to do. The time has long since passed whereby we can ignore what amounts to a vicious attack on the very entity that sustains us and we will be the losers because we are violating the laws of nature. Abject greed and lust for power entered the picture a long time ago. We broke the laws with senseless abandon until we pushed ourselves to the brink of catastrophe. This could be compared to the kind of insanity that motivated Adolf Hitler and Nazi government prior to, and during, World War II. They embarked on a heinous endeavor that they were destined to lose the very moment the mad mind of Hitler conceived the idea. Likewise the whole human race has been at war with a benevolent mother earth and as with the Nazi's in World War II, we will lose. We were lost the very first time we chose to break the laws.

We've reached a point where all the counter arguments are simply attempts to stave off any interruption of profiteering. All the fancy rhetoric coming from politicians, bankers and corporate presidents will soon no longer matter. If we push ourselves to ground zero, well informed Ph.D's will be no better off than the high school dropout other than the fact the Ph.D can give us a highly technical explanation as to why we hit rock bottom but at that point it really won't matter.

We will change our habits immediately and dramatically or nature will do it for us and in fact that has already begun."

Nodding he stared out a window at a lush forest that still stood on their property. Curious he asked, "have you ever been approached by lumber companies to sell your land?"

"Ingram Mountain will forever remain in its natural state," she replied in a firm voice.

"How can you be so sure though Jenny? You can't control what happens after you're gone."

"For as long as there is a planet, there will be this mountain covered with forest. My father on his deathbed said 'Jenny don't ever let outsiders come in who would mess up Ingram Mountain. Always keep it in the pure state that God intended.'

That will be done Adam. Make no mistake."

For the first time since meeting her, there was a hint of belligerence in her voice. He didn't understand why, but right then felt it prudent not to ask. Wanting to change the subject he casually inquired, "how much land do you have Jenny?"

"Seven hundred acres."

"Seven hundred ...my God you could be a millionaire."

"Many times over which would immediately violate every spiritual principle I stand for."

"What about Andy?"

"Andy stated years ago that no harm would come to the mountain as long as he was alive and right here is where he would die."

Somehow he knew that everything she was saying would be fact. There was an unfamiliar icy tone to her voice that caused him to shudder slightly.

"Jen," he finally spoke after a few moments of awkward silence. "I didn't mean to pry into something that is none of my business."

"Yes it is, Adam."

Surprised he turned to look straight at her again. "What do you mean?"

She didn't answer, just stared back with the penetrating gaze that had shaken him up on earlier occasions. After a few moments he looked away feeling once again the strange sensations that always accompanied these weird interludes.

The heavy silence in the room was finally broken by the gentle pitter patter of Trina's paws on the floor as she came out of the living room and stretching in mid stride, walked slowly toward Jenny.

"Uh...if you'll excuse me," he said reaching for his cane. "I must go to the washroom."

"Oh I'm sorry Adam," she said placing the back of her hand across her forehead. "Can you manage or should I call Andy in?"

"I'll make out. I'm getting pretty handy with this cane now."

"Yes indeed and please forgive me. I guess I got carried off in my thoughts."

She sounded like herself again and for that he was grateful.

CHAPTER 22

"I think a large portion of the problem can be attributed to overpopulation," he said when they resumed discussions the next morning. After all the planet has a limit to the number of persons it can sustain."

"The deplorable conditions in third world countries is not sustenance, Adam?"

"No I know it's not, but if their birth rates were curbed, it would at least be a step in the right direction."

"Which is saying they don't have the same rights as we do in the west."

"Meaning?"

"Meaning that we can have as many offspring as we choose and generally with little concern about their well being because of the wealth of our countries."

"We have poverty in North America too."

"Adam, the most poverty stricken person in North America is living in luxury compared to many persons in Africa. But to answer your question, we don't really know whether we are having an overpopulation problem or not. Some experts believe that the planet could support ten billion with ease. The real problem lies with the behavior of the population. It is a proven fact that if all resources were evenly distributed, every inhabitant on earth would be moderately wealthy. In affluent countries such as North America there's over consumption and waste on a scale that is almost incomprehensible. For starters, if we could somehow donate all the food we waste to third world countries, starvation would be largely eliminated. That is only one example. We are over consumers of almost everything. Ours is a disposal society. This runs the gamut from baby diapers to automobiles. Computers, camera's, video players, television sets are often obsolete a year or so after purchase prompting us to frequently buy new ones. Think about cell phones. Within a few years they have developed from the cumbersome devices they once were to tiny palm sized instruments that will fit neatly into your shirt pocket. Naturally we all, or most of us, keep pace. As soon as newer, smaller and more efficient models are on the market, they are gobbled up with complete abandon. This would all be quite acceptable if every other person on earth could live at that same standard but our planet could not even begin to support that kind of energy consumption. Until such time as those of us in affluent countries are prepared to reduce our standard of living to realistic levels, then over population will be targeted as the culprit."

"Yes but millions of dollars are already donated to underprivileged countries by large corporations as well as by thousands of individuals. Don't you think they deserve any credit at all? There are generous persons among us. I donate fairly large sums myself."

"Often that can be camouflaged greed. Large corporations and wealthy individuals can contribute millions without denting their pocket book and their pay back is a more favorable public opinion of them as well as a major tax write off. Granted some do give out of the goodness of their heart, but to what extent are they willing to give? We still have unbelievable poverty on earth and in some instances right next door to a fifty room mansion owned by a biilionaire. The real test of generosity is how willing would we be to donate to a point at which our own standard of living is reduced? Using yourself as an example. You have made significant contributions to charity and that's commendable. But how far are you really willing to go with this endeavor Adam? Would you sacrifice your lavish lifestyle in order to mitigate starvation in some part of the world. Are you willing to part with your Mercedes which you probably trade up every year or two and settle for a plain Ford so you can give even more? Are you willing to convert your six bedroom mansion to a shelter for the homeless while you live in a modest apartment? Would you sell the cottage at the lake and turn the proceeds over to charity while you settle for an occasional weekend picnic. Even take a dozen poverty stricken kids with you? Would you sell that holiday trailer that is far more luxurious than the ramshackle house that millions of others call home and donate the proceeds to a housing project for the underprivileged. Would you reduce your six figure annual salary to forty or fifty thousand a year and donate the rest to feed and clothe a dozen families in a third world country?

Maybe you would go to these limits yourself, but you can be certain that very few others would. The measure of true unselfish generosity is how willing are we to bring our own lifestyle down to a modest level so that our impoverished fellow man may one day have some hope of moving his lifestyle up near that level.

The disparity between rich and poor is already obscene and is increasing almost daily. The extreme wealth on one hand and the unbelievable poverty on the other creates a tension that counteracts the laws of the universe. We have emperors, sultans and monarchs who wallow in unbelievable wealth while their countrymen go hungry. It is difficult to understand the ethics of such persons when they could, with a wave of their hand, eliminate so much suffering. But most remain completely indifferent to it. A sovereign person may, for example, own a fleet of the most expensive cars on the market simply because he or she doesn't want to ride in the same one two days in a row. The price of any one of these cars would provide a living for three families for a year and yet just outside the palace gates people starve to death. This is greed in its lowest, most repulsive form and one that will help bring humanity to its knees.

It is certainly prudent to keep the size of one's family in proportion to their ability to support that family but the issue of over population has numerous complexities that must be subjected to a lot of diverse analysis before it can be labeled one of the true villains in our environmental breakdown.

His leg was healed to a point where he now walked without assistance, although he still had to limit the amount of time he spent on his feet. Doc Greer had suggested that, weather permitting, a short daily stroll would benefit both his leg and heart since both were healing quite favorably.

Several weeks earlier a plan had started to take shape in his mind. Selling his business and returning to Ingram Mountain was no longer a fantasy but a very real possibility. Although he hadn't talked to Jenny about the idea he intuitively felt that she would be receptive when she realized how sincere he was. He knew it would be a monumental shift of lifestyle for him—one he had never before even casually considered, but he also felt it was no longer an option. It was something he must do. From now on he would divide his life into two distinct phases: the time before meeting Jenny and the time after with the former being something he could no longer identify with.

He still had a few spiritual issues to debate before disclosing his plan and he needed answers that were completely satisfactory. He grinned wryly to himself. A very small part of his competitive nature was still evident as reflected on his attempt to present her with an argument she couldn't counter.

He had gradually come to a point where he was unable to understand why competition was so important. It had been effective in the dialogue with Jenny because it dug to the very roots of her philosophy. But to compete just for the sake of competition no longer contained any appeal and in retrospect he wondered why it ever had.

CHAPTER 23

"If we were to make all the adjustments and cutbacks you are suggesting it would seriously undermine the economy at least in most of the western world. I think that would be nearly as disastrous as environmental problems."

"Well now just what is it we want to be left with Adam? A struggling economy which we created ourselves or a world that will be barely habitable in the future. We brought ourselves to a point where we will very soon be forced to make such a decision. We are certainly between a rock and a hard spot but who do we blame for it? If we continue spiraling down the tube, we will undoubtedly have various factions pointing fingers at one another and everyone else which will only prove we've learned nothing. We're still engaging in activities that helped bring us to this point. If we do choose to reduce the planet to rubble, then the economy won't matter. Basic survival will be our only concern.

When talks aimed at controlling environmental devastation do occasionally get underway, one of the first issues to be raised is the negative impact on the economy. Huge corporations battle tooth and nail to minimize any proposed control measures because such measures would seriously interfere with their profit margins and they swing a very big axe.

A handful of sincere, dedicated environmentalists have worked themselves to a point of exhaustion trying to make government and industry understand the gravity of our situation and most of the time with only marginal success. We are at a point where the majority will start pulling in the same direction or we will all suffer the consequences.

Yes Adam there will be economic downturns, jobs will be lost and we'll suffer numerous hardships, sacrifices and radical changes if we are still intelligent enough to reverse our destructive trends. If we don't then none of it will matter. There will be few left to experience unemployment, financial loss or any other hardship.

We have a choice that must be made very soon; knuckle down and bite the bullet or it will bite us."

Shaking his head slightly he said, "I realize it's bad, but surely to god there are still people in positions of power with enough foresight to avert complete annihilation of the human race. I know you feel strongly about this issue which may be causing you to overreact."

"Well would you like us to find out the hard way? Should we be willing to gamble with the future of humanity just to find out if the environmentalists were right or wrong?"

"Of course not and I don't think anybody else would be. I know we've created problems and we must tread cautiously from now on, but I just can't accept we are right on the very brink of destruction."

She drew in a deep breath and leaned her head back against the chair's headrest to stare at the ceiling.

Sipping his coffee he watched her intently. It was not his objective to try to win this debate with her because he knew he couldn't. He was bringing up rebuttals only to ensure he clearly grasped the message she was trying to impart.

After a few moments of silent reflection, she lowered her head and looking at him soberly said, "let me take another approach to it. Our economic system had its origins back in times when both industrial development and populations were small. The environment then seemed infinite. It yielded endless resources and absorbed waste with no noticeable effects. Obviously if we would've remained at those population and industrial levels, resources would have, in effect, been infinite.

Today's economic system far exceeds what the environment can continue to supply leaving only one viable choice; the system must be refitted to function within the boundaries of our planet's biosphere. We are presently exceeding those boundaries and to continue doing so will lead to disaster. It's a redundant statement to say the earth's resources are finite and this is what's baffling. Primary violators keep behaving as though they are unaware of that fact. Unless we take immediate and stringent measures to work well within the limits of environmental tolerance, we are in serious trouble. Every conceivable approach has been taken by environmentalists, scientists and others to convince government and industry of the seriousness of our problem with success ranging from mediocre to none.

Aggressive tactics such as laying down in front of logging trucks have done little more than antagonize logging operators causing them to become more defensive of their rights. All that is really left is to dump the mess right on their lap and say, "okay you're in the driver's seat, where are you going to take us? You may be the pilots but just remember when the plane crashes you will be killed as surely as any other passenger on board. Owning the airplane was never a guarantee that you would be the only survivor."

"I could see strong resistance to that one. I think they would retaliate by saying it's the responsibility of every one of us since we all benefit from their products."

"Adam the time for arguing trivialities has long since past. This has already gone on for far too long seriously reducing the amount of time left to do something tangible. It reminds me of a story I once read about a well heeled gentlemen sentenced to the electric chair for murdering his wife. His major concern as he walked out to the execution chamber was that he wasn't wearing appropriate attire for the occasion. It was later revealed he had lost most of his mental faculties which accounted for his bizarre attitude, but a large segment of the human race acts the same way and they supposedly still have all their wits about them.

Of course we all have a certain responsibility toward the environment but where does the major responsibility lie? I can, for example, guarantee that this seven hundred acres will never be touched and it won't. But that's a mere pittance compared to the millions of acres clear cut every year. I repeat it's time to get real and stop the childish bickering about who is to blame for what. If we hope to have a future on planet earth, then the major responsibility for ensuring that we do lies squarely on the shoulders of those persons who created the bulk of the problem in the first place and who are now in the best position to change it. It's just that simple no matter how else you try to read it."

"I agree with what you're saying, but I see this as a massive challenge. You're not talking about a few minor adjustments to the system, you're talking a complete overhaul. I can't even begin to conceive of the chaos that this would engender."

"Well then consider the alternative. The truth really boils down to a strong desire to change our ways. Human ingenuity will find a way if a firm commitment to do so is in place. Once again it is nothing more than choosing what we know we must choose and dispense with all the reasons why it can't be done. Persons in wealthy nations have become very attached to their lifestyle and although most will acknowledge we do have environmental problems, most are reluctant to give up the good life with all its attendant toys. To emphasize this mentality a columnist wrote an article that appeared in major newspapers about a year ago. It was entitled 'Canadians Reject Environmental Scare Mongering'. Notice he used the term *Scare Mongering*. The fact that anybody takes that stance, let alone writes about it in major newspapers is frightening."

He went on to point up that an annual poll had asked the question, 'what was the most important problem facing Canada to which the respondents ranked various concerns starting with unemployment, health care, national unity, taxes, poverty, education and crime. Tragically concerns about the environment were on the bottom of the list. This, coming at a time, when the only possible way to ignore the overwhelming evidence of the pathetic decimation of our planet would have been to take up residence on a space station.

Mass consciousness must make a shift if the human species is to survive and if that shift occurs we will find a way. We will establish a new economic order; a way of engendering an economy based on cooperative sustainability rather than industrial driven profiteering. We will always come up with answers, will always achieve goals even though seeming to be insurmountable if the motivation to do so is strong enough. Evidence of this fact is everywhere. We need only look back at the statement made by the American President Kennedy in the early sixties when he committed the United States to be first to land a man on the moon. At the time he made the announcement, very little of the necessary technology to achieve this monumental feat was in existence. They had to come up with a way, in fact many ways which they did and the rest is history.

When and if we collectively and passionately throw ourselves headlong into anything, when we experience a shift in consciousness, when we've redefined our philosophies, adopted a different story about our existence as humans, we will find a way. That is not the issue at all. It's a simple matter of choosing between our present short sighted destructive lifestyle or developing a long term philosophy of living in sustainable harmony with all of creation. I repeat *we will find a way*. It's a simple matter of deciding we want to."

"You sure don't leave much room for argument. I'm starting to feel guilty because I haven't done more myself."

"You mustn't do that Adam. You've been following a pathway that you had to travel because it was included in your agenda. But you are now free to choose a new direction, one that enables you to contribute as much as you want to the betterment of your fellow man. And there are many more ways to do this than just by donating large sums of money. Changing the consciousness of humanity through teaching spiritual truths is, I believe, the top priority. As man becomes aware of his true purpose, both individually and collectively and acts on that purpose we will find that abnormal poverty and hardship will self regulate."

"Abnormal? Is there such a thing as normal hardship?"

"Think about earlier discussions Adam. Indeed there is normal hardship. The connective thread of challenge runs through every phase of life. We will always have challenge in everything we do, but by the same token gain in proportion to our conquest of the challenge. The one facing us now, the entire human race, is the ultimate challenge which is survival of the species. This could be considered abnormal because we violated universal laws beyond their limits of tolerance creating an unnatural tension that can only be released by abiding once again by the laws in everything we do. We become much more capable of this in proportion to our degree of understanding and acceptance of those laws."

She stopped talking, stood up and walked over to gaze out a window onto the barnyard behind the house.

He had been dreading this moment.

Somehow he knew it signaled the end of their discussions.

"This is as far as we go isn't it Jen."

"Only for now Adam. Learning which translates into evolution will never end for as long as we stay on the evolutionary pathway. At some point when we've gained all the experience we can on this physical level we will move to the next higher place of existence and continue with the never ending process of evolution.

Spring is soon upon us and I sense your need to return to your home which will enable you to put into practice what we've discussed this past winter. This is important, for without the opportunity to relate once again to your earlier life, some doubts would always be left in the back of your mind and should you choose a new pathway, you must not be inhibited by any restrictions. If you choose to continue…"

"If? There is no if about it Jen. I will back as soon as I put my business up for sale and take care of the details."

"You are selling your business?"

"Yes I am."

"Adam be very certain about that. Please do not make a final decision for a month or so after you've been back there."

"I'll do that but Edmonton is no longer my home. I know where I belong and that's here with you. The next question, are you in agreement with that?"

"You know I am."

"And I'm under the impression that there's more to your esoteric teachings."

"We've only scratched the surface."

"I want to continue learning for as long as you will teach Jen. I know what I must do for the remainder of this life and I hope you will travel that road with me."

Smiling she answered, "I'll be right there Adam."

"Your knowledge, I believe, must be taken out and presented to all who are ready to hear. Together we can commence assisting the human race with every resource at our disposal. Hey I will even be able to openly play the piano anytime I want to."

"Of course you will and that's wonderful Adam."

"Jen since the spiritual counseling is over let's talk about our future. There is obviously many exciting but necessary activities we can engage in to help put this old world back on its feet."

"Indeed there is," she said walking over to where he was sitting.

"And Jen, I've uh…that is I am…" he stopped talking and avoiding her eyes, nervously tugged at an earlobe.

"I love you too Adam," she said mercifully putting him at ease. We've both been aware of that for a long time and I know I kept it in check because your spiritual transition was first and foremost."

"But now that's over with," he said taking her arm and pulling her gently down on his knee, "we are going to talk about us."

"Careful of that leg Mr. Finlay."

"To hell with the leg," he said wrapping both arms around her and planting a firm kiss on her warm lips. She responded with a gentle passion that left no doubt in his mind how she felt.

The love that had been bottled up during the long winter months now erupted without bounds.

CHAPTER 24

"Hank made connections with your friend in Edmonton," she said struggling to remove her parka after returning from the Meade farm. "He will meet you at their place around noon tomorrow. I can take you down in the cutter. No point in having him attempt the drive up here. He may have problems with our road."

"Oh god Jen I don't want to be away from you even for an hour."

"And I don't want you to be Adam. But we both know what you have to do. You must be very certain of your resolve to traverse a new pathway. I believe you are ready to do so, but please explore every nook and cranny of your consciousness to ensure that no doubts remain. Your commitment to your new direction must be absolute because you still have one very huge challenge to face. This may be the most difficult challenge of your entire life, but if you can overcome it, then your transition to your new direction is complete."

"What kind of challenge?"

"You must experience it for your self when it is presented. Revealing it prematurely might undo all that you've gained."

"Not even a clue."

She answered by walking over and planting a gentle kiss on his lips. Then cradling his face in her hands said, "that will have to serve as a substitute."

"No complaints there," he said giving her a wide grin. Then pulling her close to him added, "since you're not going to tell me anything more, perhaps we could indulge…"

"Adam Finlay wasn't last night enough?"

"Yeah, but that was last night."

"Honestly you are incorrigible. Remember we still have one more night together."

"I'm not sure I can wait until then."

"Come and dry the dishes for me. Maybe that'll get your mind back where it belongs."

"Only temporarily."

If there was such a thing as a soul mate he knew he had found his. Never before in his life had he experienced love for a woman that equaled what he felt for her and he knew the feeling was mutual. One thing did trouble him and he wanted to get to the root of it. He felt at times that he detected a sadness in her demeanor that was puzzling. Maybe he was just getting a wrong impression. But if there was even the tiniest blip in their relationship, it must be cleared up because what they had between them was too precious to compromise.

After the dishes were washed and put away, he took her by the hand and seated her at the table across from him.

"Jen," he began. "I may just be imagining this, but recently I feel at times that you seem rather sad. Am I wrong or is there something I still don't know about?"

"Well you are running away on me," she said in a teasing voice.

"We both know it isn't that. All hell couldn't keep me away. Is it a carryover from that tragedy in your past?"

"In a certain way I guess it is."

"Promise me that someday you will tell me that whole story."

"When you return, Adam."

"The whole story? Nothing left out?"

"All of it. Every last detail.

"Is that to be the major challenge you mentioned?"

"It's an integral part of it. My darling Adam please understand, I'm not being deliberately evasive. In order for everything to unfold as it should some things can only be revealed when the time is right. Please bear with me for a while longer."

"This is going to be an exciting time for both of us," he said. "We are embarking on a wonderful new venture that I know can keep us happy for the rest of our lives. We're still both young enough to be able to do much good for this ailing world. Hey we've got a lot of work ahead of us if we are going to help conditions improve. There will be no time for sadness."

"That's wonderful Adam," she said squeezing his hand tightly. "It's good to see you so excited about life once again. I remember when we dragged your half dead body into the house last fall. That Adam Finlay bears little resemblance to the one sitting here now."

Pausing for a moment she added, "it has been so wonderful…this time we've had together."

"Jen, we're just getting started. I'm going to ensure you never have another unhappy day for as long as we live. Now cheer up. I'll only be gone for a few weeks, maybe a month and when I get back we can start making plans for…well you name it. You once said the sky's the limit. Money will be no problem, I do have lots of it. We'll preserve every tree, flower and blade of grass on Ingram mountain and.."

"Adam," she interrupted with a laugh. "Of course we will. You don't have to convince me. I know you are sincere. Perhaps right now we should pause and reflect on all that has transpired during this past winter and just enjoy each other until you're gone."

"You've got a deal sweet lady."

CHAPTER 25

Dark clouds were starting to loom over the treetops when he deposited his backpack and rifle in the cutter for the ride down to the Meade farm the next morning so it was decided that Andy should be the driver.

"Could be a bad one coming in," the old mountaineer said as Adam turned to re-enter the house. "Might wanna hurry."

Something in Andy's tone of voice made him turn and look back. He was staring straight at Adam with a look that seemed to be expressing more than just concern about the weather.

Other than quick glances Andy seldom looked directly at any-one but now he was making unblinking eye contact that was puzzling. Adam stared back for a moment searching for some meaning to this uncharacteristic behavior. But other than a hint of concern, he detected nothing.

The threatening storm caused him to quickly forget Andy and re-enter the house to say his goodbye to Jenny. She was standing by the kitchen table with one hand resting on the back of the chair that he had sat on for countless hours while she guided him through spiritual revelations that had completely changed his life.

Without hesitation he walked over and took her in his arms and pulled her close to him. She wrapped both arms around him in return and for a few moments they stood in silent embrace.

"Jenny," he started to speak but she pulled his head down and pressed her lips firmly against his. Emotions came flooding to the surface once again and they kissed each other repeatedly. Suddenly tears began streaming down her cheeks causing her to pull away and turn her back to him. Her body shook from the intensity of her crying so he put his arms around her, this time from behind and kissed her several more times on a wet cheek.

Bewildered by her behavior but with no time left to try for an explanation he said, "Jenny, my sweet Jenny there's no reason for tears. I will be back. You do believe that don't you."

"Yes I do Adam," she answered wiping her eyes with a handkerchief pulled from a sleeve.

"Hey as I've said before I'll only be gone long enough to get the sale of my company underway and then we can be together for the rest of our lives. Nothing else matters to me now. I truly mean that Jenny."

On impulse he removed a signet ring his mother had given him for his thirtieth birthday and placed it on her ring finger.

"There," he said kissing her again. "That will have to do until I come back with the real thing."

The ring dangled loosely so she closed her hand to keep it in place and pressed it to her lips.

Outside the wind was gaining its strength and he knew he would have to leave immediately if he was to connect up with Willis Clarke for the trip back to Edmonton.

She turned to face him once again and for a moment gazed deep into his eyes. "I love you Adam Finlay for many more reasons than you now know and when you return these will all be revealed to you. Now it is essential that you leave right away to avoid the storm that is coming. Do not let it detain you because you must return to your home even if only for a short time."

With that she kissed him once again and then gently nudged him toward the door.

"I'll be back Jenny," he repeated stepping outside once again. "Nothing on earth can keep me away. You know that so please just keep a watch out for me."

Once seated in the cutter Andy spurred Samson into a fast trot. The wind was roaring through the cedar trees and heavy snowfall had reduced visibility to a few yards. He turned and looked back and although only barely visible through the blowing snow he could still see Jenny's outline in the doorway. He waved as they rounded a corner that took the house out of sight then drew in his parka hood ties to protect his face from the pelting snow.

The storm was rapidly becoming more intense and the old horse was laboring to keep up the pace that Andy was demanding of him. Although Hank Meade had recently plowed the road new fallen snow combined with the force of the storm slowed them down considerably. Samson was trying to respond to Andy's demand for more speed but at times reached his limit and slowed to a walk.

Adam breathed a sigh of relief when Andy finally said they were nearing the Meade's gate. At the same time he caught a glimpse of car head lights through a break in the driving snow coming from the south and guessed it would likely be Willis Clarke. "We'll have to get out of here fast," he thought otherwise we'll be buried until May.

Andy raced the cutter through the gate and came to a stop in front of the Meade house. In a surprise move he reached over and clasped Adam's hand. "Take care of yourself," he said. "Now git goin'. You don't wanna be trapped somewhere out on the road in this kinda weather."

"I'll see you soon Andy," he yelled reaching for his belongings.

"Never mind those. I'll drop them off at the gate fer you."

With that he turned the cutter around and was quickly out of sight.

Hank Meade appeared in the doorway and hollered at Adam to get his friend and come back to the house and wait out the storm.

"I'm not sure if it's him Hank," Adam yelled back. "I'll have to go right to the road. I can't see from here."

"I'll get dressed and come with you."

"No, no Hank. No point in us both struggling through the snow."

The farmer shouted something more, but his words were gobbled up by the wild blizzard.

After a few moments of struggle, Willis Clarke's big blue cadillac came into view. He had managed to get the car turned around and was yelling at Adam through a partially opened window to 'get in'.

"You're gear's in the trunk."

As soon as Adam was seated Willis said, "let's get the hell out of here while we still can."

"It might be dangerous out there Will. We can stay with these folks until the storm passes."

"The road isn't that bad yet Adam. I had no trouble getting here, but it's gonna be bad pretty damn fast and if we do stay god knows how long it will be before we can get out."

With that he accelerated the big sedan and they sped away. Visibility was limited to a few yards, but Willis seemed determined to get them out of the valley as fast as the car would take them.

They drove in silence for ten or fifteen minutes, the car swerving dangerously when they encountered heavy snowdrifts. Finally the storm started to let up. The visibility increased and Willis slowed the car to a more comfortable speed.

"I think we're out of it Adam," he said. "That was a weird one. On my way in the heaviest, blackest cloud bank I've ever seen in my life had started to build and was centered over that valley. But look up ahead now. There are traces of blue sky."

Gradually they emerged from the storm center completely and Willis pulled over and brought the car to a stop.

"Don't know about you," he said drawing a metal flask from a jacket pocket. "But I need a drink after that one."

Adam smiled at his old friend. "You haven't changed Will. Still drink Canadian Club?"

"Is there anything else?" he answered with a grin handing Adam a small plastic glass filled to the top. Then he took several large drinks from the flask and exhaled slowly.

"Now then Adam Finlay," he said screwing the lid back on the shiny container. "You've got some explaining to do. Just what the hell have you been up to all winter? We figured you were a goner last fall when we lost track of you in that storm. We organized a search party and kept looking until you called your mother on your cell saying you'd been found and aside from a broken leg were okay. I guess your phone played out before you could tell her very much but at least we knew we could call off the search and breathe a sigh of relief."

"How's my mother been doing."

"Not too well Adam. As you know she failed a lot after Jeff got killed and then when you went downhill yourself it added to her distress. She's been in and out of the hospital most of the winter. Far as I know she's at home now but has a live in nurse providing full time care. Seeing you again will likely give her a boost. Anyway let's hear about you and your little escapade. Understand you were rescued by some hillbillies. Is that right?"

Willis had put the big car in motion again and Adam not knowing where to start or how much to reveal remained silent. If he told the story in detail he knew his old friend would laugh most of it off as nothing more than fantasy. A year earlier he would've himself. But now? That part of Adam Finlay was completely erased. He chuckled faintly remembering a comment Jenny once made about the likelihood of losing old friends if he chose new spiritual directions. Was this to be the first test of a friendship dating back to childhood.

"Hey you haven't touched your drink," Willis broke into his thoughts. "Don't tell me those mountain dwellers have gone and reformed you."

"If only you knew Will," he thought. "If only you knew."

Outloud he said, "guess I'm not up to one right now. You want it or should I just toss it?"

"Oh my god, don't talk like that. Give it here. I think I read somewhere that wasting good rye is a criminal offense. Now then," he resumed after tossing back the drink. "I'm still waiting to hear about your stay up in the hills. Was there at least a woman or two up there to help keep you warm?"

Not wanting to indulge in the vulgarity that he knew Willis was prone to he said, "a broken leg and a heart attack kept me pretty honest Will. Spent most of my time recuperating."

"You had a heart attack? God I'm sorry Adam. I hadn't heard that. I knew you'd broken your leg but nothing more. How are you doing now?"

"Pretty well back to normal. Have to take it easy for a while, though."

"Hope it won't keep you off the golf course. I want a chance to win back at least some of that money you've taken off me over the past, what's it been, twenty years or so?"

Adam smiled wondering if he would ever swing a golf club again. His new lifestyle would include very little of what he once considered important. He also knew that few, if any, of his circle of friends would be able to make any sense out of what now motivated him.

"Got a little more out of you," Willis chided. "Think you can manage the whole story by the time we get back to Edmonton."

"Well after being found by Andy…by those folks and dragged into their house, I spent most of my time convalescing."

He had decided to reveal only what he knew would interest his long time friend and avoid the awkwardness of trying to explain anything else. There would be time enough for that if, in fact, he would ever talk about it to anyone besides Jenny.

The miles and hours flew by as he talked and after several

coffee breaks and a lunch stop, they decided to call it a day and find sleeping accommodation.

On the road again the next morning Adam asked, "heard how the Finlay Company's been doing?"

"Runnin' damn smooth Adam. That manager you hired a couple of years ago, Ike Horton has been doin' a real respectable job. When he found out you were going to be away for at least four months, he…"

"Wait a minute Will. Who said anything about four months?"

"Whoever placed those calls. The second one came directly to your office and Ike took it himself. They told him not to expect you back until March."

"Until March?"

"Yeah and I know that for a fact cause Ike told me himself."

"How many calls came out?"

"Five, maybe six. I'm not sure. But Ike told me they always seemed anxious to let everybody know you were doin' okay…almost as if they didn't want anybody to come looking for you. Fact is I was startin' to get suspicious myself and decided to do some investigating when we got that call the other day to come and get you."

"When did Ike get the second call?"

"December sometime. I know it was before Christmas. Because we were all disappointed you wouldn't be home for the holidays. But knowing all that you'd gone through, we thought maybe it was best to just leave you alone. I for one figured some quiet time in the boon docks might just be the medicine you needed. At least back then I did."

He knew he shouldn't be baffled by anything Jenny was a part of. Her uncanny psychic ability was, at times, frightening and this was one of those times. Regardless of who placed the extra phone calls, they would have been initiated by Jenny. Somehow she knew, even at a time when his only desire was to get off Ingram mountain, that he would be there until spring.

But six or more phone calls? He had only been aware of two besides the short conversation with his mother on the cell phone. Why would she keep that from him? One thing is for sure, he thought, life with her will never be boring. God I better not let anything cross my mind I don't want her to know about.

"Any idea how long it'll be before you're ready to get into the harness again?" Willis asked. "Ike's doin' a great job but you seem to be a hell of a lot better than you were back in November. I'm thinking now that maybe something you're familiar with might just be the right medicine to keep you on the recovery trail."

Adam stared in silence at the passing landscape. The Clarke and Finlay families had worked close together since before Adam was born. Willis being ten years Adam's senior began mentoring Adam in the business when his father was sidelined with a heart condition and had kept an eye on Adam's progress ever since. For those reasons he dreaded what he now had to tell his old friend. Willis might even feel betrayed, possibly their friendship would be endangered, even cease to exist, but that none of that mattered. Jenny was front and center in his life.

"You're what?" Willis exploded when Adam stated his intentions to sell the Finlay company. "Tell me you're not serious."

"Afraid I am Will."

"My god Adam. That company's been in our families forever. Are you forgetting your grandad and mine got it started away back in the twenties? They only formed two companies because the one got too big, but we've been working hand in glove ever since."

"Will I know and I've given it a lot of consideration. I haven't forgotten all that you've done for me—for my company when we expanded and I hope that someday you can see it my way. At the very least I hope it won't jeopardize our friendship. But Will this is something I must do."

"Well be careful how you tell your mother. News like this could do her in."

"I've considered that and I know I'll have to tread lightly. I realize it's going to be difficult for her, for anyone to understand."

"*Difficult!* Are you sure those hill hoppers weren't feeding you some strange mushrooms during the winter?"

"No they weren't," he laughed. "In fact I've got a clearer head now than ever before in my life. But Will, I'm not dropping off the planet, I'm just selling out."

After a moments silence he asked, "do you think Clarke and Co. would be interested in buying?"

Shaking his head lightly and puffing violently on a cigar he had just lit, his old friend muttered, "I might buy it just to keep it around handy until you come back to your senses. Look, do me this one favor Adam. Don't talk selling until you've been back for at least a month and if you're still hell bent on it at that time, then come and talk to me. Will you do that much?"

"You got it. But only a month," he said knowing his decision would still stand. He had agreed to Will's terms out of a sense of loyalty to a deep rooted relationship that he would not treat lightly. He would take his leave on solid ethical terms, but one month from now he knew, he would be on his way back to Ingram mountain.

Chapter 26

It was still an hour's drive but already he was feeling heady excitement as he steered his black Mercedes down the road that led back to Jenny.

The time had flown by at high speed since his return. True to his word Willis Clarke did buy the Finlay Company after the one month waiting period. However a thousand details had to be ironed out stretching the time to five weeks before he was freed of his obligations sufficiently to return.

Being busy was a blessing. He had little time to be lonesome for Jenny and knowing they would soon be reunited, kept his spirits up in the clouds. If only she had a phone he frequently thought. God I'd call every day. Sure gonna rectify that when I get back.

Most of his friends expressed their amazement at how much of a changed person he was. Good natured ribbing was everywhere. When asked if it was the mountain air, that mountain woman or mountain dew he coyly answered all three. His happiness knew few bounds. Willis Clarke even commented at lunch one day that he walked around as though he was floating on air. "Maybe you ought to have a rudder installed on your back so you don't crash into a wall," he added with a grin. Even his mother who had initially expressed shock over the sale of the Finlay Company later stated that if her son could find true happiness in this life, it didn't really matter what he had to do to hold onto it. She appeared to be on the mend herself, but he insisted that she obey her doctor and check back into the hospital again for a few tests.

"I'll call back everyday to see how things are going Mom," he assured her. "Doc Brady said it would only take two or three days, then you can go home again. You won't be alone because Aunt Harriet is going in too. Her asthma is acting up."

The takeover of his company by Willis Clarke had progressed to a point that finally allowed him to get away and he wasn't waiting any longer to see Jenny.

He was now on the gravel road that passed through the valley. Landmarks and buildings meant nothing to him since his only trip over the road had been in a blinding blizzard. He finally spotted a mailbox located at the entrance to a large farmyard bearing the name Meade. "Okay," he said to himself. The next left exit up the mountainside has got to be the one I take. Five more minutes of driving brought him to the narrow road and he cautiously swung the big car onto it. "Boy oh boy," he said to himself after going a short distance. "I'm going to get some equipment up here as soon as I can and make a decent road for them…for us," he added with a grin.

The road was deteriorating rapidly until finally it was little more than a wagon trail of ruts and mudholes. The tall cedars on either side would shade it for a good portion of the day which, he reasoned, probably caused it to stay wet longer than usual.

Snow had thawed away amazingly fast. There was no evidence of it anywhere. Driving was becoming increasingly difficult. He slowed the big car almost to a crawl, but at times had to accelerate forcefully to get through muddy spots. The slick surface also caused the car to swerve dangerously, twice narrowly missing huge trees close to the roadside.

"I knew it wasn't a four lane highway," he thought. "But this would challenge a bulldozer."

Slowly he crept forward, tires spinning out, then grabbing dry ground, then spinning out again.

At last an opening in the trees loomed some distance ahead and he breathed a sigh of relief as he caught a glimpse of a stone chimney.

"That's the house," he thought. "None of the other buildings are tall."

He felt his heart pounding wildly and he raced the car the last few hundred feet to the yard.

The sight that greeted him caused him to sit and stare in shocked silence.

"I must've taken a wrong turn somewhere," he thought. "This certainly isn't the place."

What lie before him was an abandoned old farm yard and house that no one had obviously lived in for a very long time. With the exception of the house the buildings were all in a dilapidated shambles and cattle were grazing everywhere in the yard.

"How could I have made a mistake," he wondered. "I didn't think there was any other road to take."

God if only they had a phone. The first damned thing I'm going to do when I do find them is have the line installed with a phone in every room."

He pondered his situation for a few more moments and finally decided to go back down to the Meade farm and get directions. He eased the car into gear and began turning around when a man on horseback trotted into the yard and stopped in front of him. Startled he slammed the brake pedal and stalled the engine.

The rider was an elderly man probably in his early seventies Adam guessed and judging by his attire was a farmer or rancher.

"Afternoon," he said as he dismounted. Saw you drivin' up this way so I thought I'd better check and see if you made it. Nobody's driven a car up here for years. The old road's in pretty bad shape. Funny you didn't get stuck."

Stepping out Adam said, "I guess I took the wrong road. I seem to be lost."

"Where was you headed?"

The Ingram farm. Jenny and Andy Ingram. I was…"

"You've found it."

"Pardon?"

"You've found it. This is the old Ingram home place. Nobody's lived here for over fifty years now. But this is it."

Stunned into silence Adam just stared at the old man for a moment. Finally finding his voice he blurted.

"There's got to be some mistake. I was here less than two months ago. I had an accident and stayed with them…"

"Couldn't've bin here. Maybe you mixed them up with somebody else. You from around these parts?"

Adam shook his head and slowly turned to take a look at the old house which up to now he had only glanced at. A closer inspection only added to his confusion. Even in its deteriorated state the old building was still recognizable.

"My god," he thought. "Am I losing my mind? What is going on here?"

"Don't believe I got yer name," the old man broke into his thoughts.

"Finlay," he said walking closer to the old building.

"Henry Meade here. Pleased to make yer acquaintance. He paused for a few seconds watching Adam inspect the house. Then said, "well I gotta be getting back. Hope you get things straightened out Mr. Finlay. Be careful comin' down on that road. If you get stuck, give me a call. I see you've got one of those cell phones. Here's our phone number. I can bring up a tractor and haul you out."

After handing Adam the slip of paper, the old man mounted the horse and started back across the year when the name suddenly registered on Adam's dazed brain.

"Wait a minute," he called after him. "Did you say your name is Henry Meade?"

He reigned the horse up and nodded.

"Do you have a grandson, some other relative with the same name? A young person?"

"Nope. Only had daughters myself. Three of 'em. They've long since married and moved away. No other relatives around here. My folks came from Victoria."

"Look Mr. Meade, do you remember who…"

He stopped and rubbed his forehead so shaken, he wasn't certain what next to ask.

The old man gave him a questioning look and said, "you okay Mr. Finlay?"

"Yeah…no…look do you remember who last lived in this house?"

"As I said Miss Jenny and her brother Andy. This place belonged to the Ingram family far back as anyone remembers. That is until my Pa bought it back in about forty-eight. Bin usin' if fer pasture ever since. Wouldn't use it fer anything else."

"What happened to Jenny and Andy?"

"Jenny left shortly after Pa bought it and where she went, no one ever seemed to know for sure. She'd told my ma and pa she was thinkin about headin back east cause she had relatives there, but she didn't seem to be real certain about that either. Andy'd passed away about a year before from some kind of cancer and Miss Jenny said it was now time for her to move on."

Adam shook his head and took another long deep breath. Then pulled a handkerchief from a pocket and despite the coolness of the day, mopped perspiration from his forehead.

"What the hell has happened?" he thought. "I know I didn't just imagine last winter."

Finding his voice once again he asked, "did you notice anything unusual up here last winter? Was there a bad blizzard in November and again in March?"

The old man stared at Adam without answering. He appeared to be trying to decide whether or not it was safe to say anything more. He scratched his whiskered chin several times and spoke slowly. "Didn't come up here much last winter. Was no reason to. Winter was pretty mild. I just turned the cows back in about two weeks ago."

After a short pause he said, "look Mr. Finlay how be we give the wife a call and I'll get her to put on a pot of coffee and we could talk about it some more down at my place."

"No…thanks anyway," Adam managed a weak smile and exhaled slowly.

"Did you…" he resumed, "that is you must've known Jenny and Andy when you were a youngster. Is there…well anything, anything at all you could tell me about them?"

"Be glad to. But mind tellin me why yer so interested?"

"Well it's rather personal. But I'd really appreciate whatever you can remember."

Henry shrugged his shoulders and said, "Miss Jenny was thought of as a saint around these parts. Rode up here quite often as a kid. They never did have a telephone so Ma sent me up regularly to check on 'em and see if they needed anything. Winters was a lot worse back then and they'd get snowed in at least until Pa came up and plowed 'em out. Never seemed to bother either one of them though. They was never short on food either. Miss Jenny always grew the best garden around and Andy kept cows, pigs and chickens. I do remember a real bad blizzard back in the early forties. We all got snowed in that time. Soon as it slacked off Ma sent me up with a bag of preserves and stuff. They had this fellow stayin' with 'em which seemed odd cause there was no way anybody could've got up here. Turns out he'd broke his leg out huntin 'fore the storm started and Miss Jenny was nursin him back to health.

"Do you remember his name?"

"Fraid not. Was a long time ago."

"Or where he was from?"

"Never did know exactly. Somewhere in Alberta I think. Seems a tree fell on him. Andy found him and dragged him into the house. Said the feller would've died if he'd bin out there much longer."

"My god," Adam thought. "What is going on?"

Becoming more distraught by the second he surveyed the barnyard he had often watched Andy trudge across in his efforts to care for the animals he loved so dearly. He was only vaguely aware of the old farmer taking his leave and repeating his offer of any assistance he might be able to provide.

Feeling as though his legs would no longer support him, he sat down on the doorstep and cradled his head in his hands. This was the stuff science fiction was made of not the real world that Adam Finlay lived in. There had to be a logical explanation. Things like this just couldn't happen and somehow he would get to the bottom of it.

Realizing he was not up to the long journey home he drove into the small town Jenny had often mentioned and found a motel. Unable to think clearly he just shook his head in response to the desk clerks question about how long he planned to stay. He was only vaguely aware of the short, bald elderly man escorting him down a hallway and placing his suitcase on a chair when they entered the room. He dropped some loose change in the man's hand and then without removing his overcoat sat down on the edge of the bed and stared through a picture window at the sparse traffic out on the street. He didn't know how long he had remained in this position but was suddenly aware of the descending darkness that prompted him to get up and search out a light switch. After laying on the bed for a while longer he finally checked his watch and was surprised to find it was ten thirty.

He considered going out to find a restaurant but realizing he probably couldn't eat anything, he chose to go to bed. Knowing that sleep would likely be impossible he took two tranquilizers from a bottle he always carried with him and washed them down with several gulps of water.

He arose the next morning after a fitful nights' sleep and although not hungry was able to get a poached egg and some toast into his shriveled stomach.

Feeling slightly better after the meal he decided to call Henry Meade and see if they could meet up at the Ingram house once again. He had no idea what another meeting would achieve but maybe the old farmer might mention something more that could shed some light on this weird situation. Henry readily agreed to Adam's request and also provided specific directions when Adam, on impulse, asked where the community grave-yard was located.

"T'aint nothin fancy Mr. Finlay," he had said, "but then I expect it doesn't matter much to them that's buried there."

Smiling faintly he thanked the old gent and started out in the direction he had been given.

The cemetery was located adjacent to a small, very old white wooden church which Adam assumed must be the one that had once played a central role in the lives of valley residents.

The graveyard, although plain as Henry Meade said, was well cared for. The grass had been recently mowed and numerous small tidy flower beds dotted the area.

He didn't recognize names on the first few headstones, but finally he came across two side by side with the name Benjamin Larkins on one and Edna Larkins on the other. That rang a bell. Jenny had mentioned the widow Larkins and this was likely her grave beside her husbands. A quick check of the dates they had deceased confirmed his assumption. Ben Larkins had died nine years before his wife making her a widow for that nine year period.

A little further along he finally encountered the one he knew would have to be here if this whole uncanny situation was to make any sense at all. "Andrew Wallace Ingram" the inscription read. "Born 1886 Died 1947. Gone but never forgotten." He stared at it in silence for a long time. This just couldn't be happening and yet the proof was right there in front of him.

He moved slowly among the remaining stones catching sight of several more names he recalled hearing. Rafferty, Barlow and Chomsky were among them and off in a corner by itself was one with only a flat, moss covered concrete slab on it. The inscribed words looked as though they had been etched in with a thin stick while the cement was still wet. It stated simply, "Hiram Dodds 1889-1938." This person Adam knew had been tied in with the tragedy that had befallen the valley at some point in the past and had played a very negative part in Jenny's life. She had promised to tell the whole story when he returned. But now, would he ever find out anything more?

If it was at all possible then Henry Meade would likely be the only person able to tell it.

The old farmer was already sitting on the back doorstep when Adam arrived at the Ingram place once again. After a brief greeting Adam mentioned his visit to the cemetery and immediately asked Henry if he could tell him about a tragic incident in the valley involving Hiram Dodds and Jenny. The old man rubbed his chin and stared at Adam in silence for a moment. Then turning to look off in the distance he asked. "Sure you want to hear it Mr. Finlay? T'aint a pretty story."

"Mr. Meade, it is very important to me to find out every-thing… anything I can. Please tell me the whole story and don't leave anything out. Please."

The old man stared at the house for a few moments as if hoping anything he might say wouldn't offend the old building, then nodded in agreement. He reached into the pocket of his faded plaid shirt and pulled out a pipe. Stuffing it full of tobacco, he lit it and seated himself on a large nearby tree stump. After several long drags on the knurled old smoking instrument he began an amazing story that supplied a few more missing links in a chain of events that had changed Adam's life so dramatically.

"T'was the talk of the whole country back then and it carried on for a number of years. It made the headlines in the news-paper every week. Matter of fact we still got a whole mess of clippins ourselves. Ma cut out everything she saw written about it and kept them all in a scrapbook. We have to be careful handlin them now. They's gotten to be pretty brittle.

Anyway Miss Jenny belonged to the church, the one you saw today next the cemetery. Dodds was the preacher and he put the fear of the devil, damnation and hellfire into everybody who went. Most folks in the valley did belong cause they was too scared not to. But after listenin' to one of his bible poundin' sermons on a Sunday they was even more scared. I often heard Pa say he didn't know which damnation was worse, goin' to church or to hell. I was a youngster at the time but I can remember comin home on Sundays and bein so sick to my stomach from fright that I couldn't eat. I figured for sure I couldn't escape hell because I had done just about everything Dodds said was a terrible sin. In fact it seemed that almost anything anybody did had somethin' wrong about it. I recall hearin about some of the young men around who was getting up to the marryin' age makin' sure they kept their courtin all hushed up for fear Dodds would find out about it and lay a tongue lashin on 'em about the evil temptation of the flesh. When they finally did make it to the alter he give em another talkin to about marriage being only for the rearin of young uns and if they took any pleasure out of mating they'd have a lot to answer for come judgement day. They all got the same lecture cause at the time there was no other church around.

Now Miss Jenny was more tangled up in the church works than the rest of us. She was a real strong believer back then and spent all her spare time takin care of church affairs except for three or four winters when she was over to Vancouver to take some extra schoolin of some kind.

Anyway one of the things Dodds was real good at was convincin people that God might look on them a little more favorable if they gave every cent they could spare to the runnin of the church. There was two others, elders they called em, and they'd go out and collect offerins from anybody who hadn't bin in church on Sunday. If folks didn't have the money to give em right on the spot, they'd make em sign a paper sayin they'd pay up soon as they could. This went on for quite a few years and caused a lot of hardship in the valley, cause no one had much money, but they was all so afraid of fallin out of favor with God they'd go short themselves just so's they could put more on the offerin plate.

Then came the big blow up. Pa said rumors was flying around weeks before the true story came out. It all started when Miss Jenny just stopped going to church all of a sudden like. Dodds said she'd taken sick with somethin and needed time off to get her health back, but not everybody swallowed that story because a few other suspicious things about Dodds had started showin up, money gone missing and the like. Everyone thought a lot of Miss Jenny and so most folks at one time or another made a run up here to see how she was doin, but few of em ever saw her. Her ma always said she was feelin quite poorly and wasn't up to visitin anybody and maybe they could come back another time. That was real strange cause there was no more hospitable folks around than the Ingrams. Why if any of em saw you within hollerin distance of their yard, you didn't get away without comin in and at least havin a chunk of Granny Ingrams blackberry pie.

Anyway this went on for quite some time and then finally Miss Jenny spilled the whole story. It caused the biggest ruckus there'd ever bin in the valley. Miss Jenny had gotten in the family way and she said Dodds was the father cause he'd raped her. She said he'd had the help of his two cronies which wasn't hard to believe cause the wisened up little skunk couldn't've did it by himself. Seems she'd stayed late at the church that night to finish up some of the bookkeepin when Dodds and them other fellers drove up with the horse and buggy. They was talkin and laughin quite noisy like and when they came down into the basement where she was workin, she smelled liquor on em. That was a shock to Miss Jenny right off cause Dodds had always preached that even takin a sniff of the stuff was a deadly sin. Anyway he did it to her right there. Those other two held her still as best they could, but she put up a terrible fight and through it all she got pretty bruised up. That was the big reason, least at the start, why she didn't want to see anyone. She had black and blue all over herself even a few on her neck and face. She never would tell any of the details of that part of it, but she told the rest to everybody in the valley and folks took it real serious cause they all had a lot of respect for Miss Jenny."

Adam could sit still no longer. Rage and revulsion began

tearing at his insides causing him to get up and pace around in front of the house.

Henry Meade watched him in silence for a few seconds and then said, "you want me to go on Mr. Finlay? If not you better say so right now cause it gets worse. It bothers me just tellin it."

Taking several deep breaths Adam nodded and seated himself again.

"You be real certain," the old man repeated. "It's a black story."

"Please go on," Adam said. "I'll be okay."

"Well when Miss Jenny found out she was pregnant seems she faced Dodds with it tellin him she wasn't keepin quiet any longer. She was tellin the whole story and didn't care what folks thought or what happened to her.

Guess Dodds had figured on that ahead of time so he warned her that if she breathed a word to anybody he would cause a lot of harm to her Ma and Pa. Even threatened to set the house on fire. Also told her she was going to have the unborn aborted so as no one would ever know anything about it. I guess Miss Jenny was in such an upset state that she finally agreed and so Dodds set the whole thing up. Story has it she nearly died back then cause Dodds had dug up some back road butcher to do the job. Seems he only did it to get the hundred dollars Dodds paid im and he messed it up so bad that Miss Jenny had to stay in bed for weeks afterward to get her health back again. She musta had a real change of heart during the time she was bedridden cause soon as she was up and around she started spoutin the story all over the valley. Guess she figured telling the truth was more important than the threats Dodds was makin. Pretty soon it comes to light that this hadn't bin the first happenin of this kind. Seems Dodds and them elders might've fathered a few other young uns around the valley, but nothing was ever proved cause the young women who was said to be victims either married right away or left to keep from being disgraced.

Now bein' as Miss Jenny was in such close touch with the workins of the church, she'd noticed a few other things that didn't look quite right to her. For one thing Dodds was always usin money he wouldn't account for until Miss Jenny'd face im with it and then he'd write out a list of the things he'd done with the money and just keep addin' to the list till it tallied with the amount Miss Jenny said was short. My pa saw two or three of them lists when they was clearing up the whole mess afterwards and they showed hundreds and hundreds of dollars invested in companies that was later found to be just made up by Dodds. He told Miss Jenny this investin would soon pay back real good and then folks wouldn't have to give much to keep the church runnin. She said it did seem a little odd at the time, but back then she trusted Dodds completely and never once thought of im doin anything shady like. There was only the one newspaper around at the time and they printed everything Miss Jenny was willin to tell 'em and she spilled every last bean there was in the pot. Church members was all up in arms and they was finally able to haul Dodds and them other two into court. They couldn't make the rape charge stick cause it was her word agin theirs but they nailed 'em pretty good for the money skimmin. The judge said stealin the offerins of all them honest hard workin folks who had to struggle for every cent they got was a shameful crime and he laid the toughest sentence on 'em he could. They all got ten years each in jail and the valley breathed a sigh of relief thinkin the whole thing'd bin finally put to rest, but the worst was yet to come."

CHAPTER 27

"Miss Jenny never again set foot in the church even though they'd found a new minister who turned out to be a pretty good feller. Her folks passed away a few years later. Her ma went first and her pa lingered on a while longer. He was bedridden the last year or so but Jenny and Andy nursed 'im right here in this old house 'til he passed.

Miss Jenny wasn't seen much around the valley after that. All the neighbors was wantin to help them out anyway they could, but when they come up here the only one around was Andy and he'd never say a word more 'n he had to at anytime. For some reason, though, he was always willing to talk to my pa. Never could figure out why but he'd tell Pa things I swear he didn't tell the almighty which was how Pa found out about Miss Jenny's strange behavin. Andy said after their parents was both gone she'd pack up and head into the mountains and stay there for two and three days at a time. Said he never worried about her well bein cause she knew how to take care of herself out there, but he was worried about what had gone wrong with her. Andy'd never bin married and as far as anyone knew he'd only had one lady friend but she finally left the valley—something Andy couldn't do. Jenny was the only kin he had left and now she wasn't around much anymore. This went on fer two or three years even during winters when the weather was agreeable. But then one day early in the summer of '38 I believe it was, she came back after bin gone a couple days and had this feller with 'er. Seems he'd bin up huntin and got hisself lost but finally ran on to Miss Jenny who brought im back here to the Ingram house.

The gents name was Clement Saunders and it didn't take very long 'fore him and Miss Jenny got real chummy with each other. Turns out he worked for the railroad company and he'd bin sent out from Vancouver to these parts to take care of some sort of railway business. Anyway he started to courtin Miss Jenny real serious like and it wasn't long 'fore they was seen out together quite regular. I don't remember much about 'im but Pa said most folks around figured he was a decent respectable kind of feller which was what Miss Jenny deserved. As much as anything else they was all happy to see her out and comin around to her old self agin.

After about a year or so he popped the question to her and they set the weddin date. Now a few months before their weddin, Dodds got out of jail on good behavior and found 'imself an old house in town to live in. Seems the folks who owned it felt sorry for the old galoot and let 'im live there for next to nothin.

Nobody could figure out, right then, why he'd want to stay around these parts at all. He was about as welcome as a rattlesnake. He never tried to find work but then nobody'd hired 'im anyway. Suspicious thing was he had money enough to live on and it wasn't long 'fore trouble started brewin agin cause everyone was sure he was livin off the money he'd filched from the church 'fore going to jail. Anyway it was soon clear he was aimin to cause Miss Jenny more grief.

He musta still bin carryin a torch fer in a demented way cause when he found out she was engaged to Saunders he started goin on like he was crazy. In fact most folks around figured he was. He'd get hisself all liquored up and then start spoutin off about Miss Jenny bein his woman and if he couldn't have her nobody would. Most didn't pay much attention to 'im cause they was sure he'd gone off his rocker completely and there was a few around town who was tryin to get 'im put away into one of them mental hospitals so's he'd be out of everybody's hair fer good.

But he was getting more threatenin all the time to both Saunders and Miss Jenny. He'd written her a few letters sayin that if she went ahead and got married there'd be all hell to pay for it. She just ignored 'em but then he stopped Saunders on the road one day and actually threatened to kill 'im if he didn't get out of the country and leave Miss Jenny alone.

There was no police in the valley at the time. Never'd really had much need fer one so Saunders phoned his complaint to the nearest RCMP station but it took a fair length of time 'fore they was able to get out this way. Two of 'em finally did make it and they decided to stay around a few days and keep an eye on things.

About a week later Saunders'd gone huntin in the mountains south of the valley. Folks often said this was about the only thing him and Miss Jenny disagreed on. She couldn't stand to kill anything and he loved to hunt. Anyway he said it was just for the day and he'd be back 'for dark. When he didn't show up some folks got real concerned and they put together a search party that same night. They finally had to call it off cause all they had fer light was lanterns so they wasn't makin much headway.

I guess Miss Jenny was beside herself with worry cause when they started out agin the next mornin she was right there in the lead. T'wasn't long 'fore they found im, that is his body. He'd bin shot dead and police right off figured t'was likely old Dodds who'd did it. They made straight fer his place back in town and all of 'em expectin the old coot'd probably skiddad-dled but he wasn't going anywhere at all. They found his body in the basement and blood spattered against a wall. Seems he turned the rifle on himself cause he was still holdin it in one hand.

Miss Jenny seemed to go into shock. She came back up here and stayed in the house for most of a month after. Folks around was really worried about her this time, but they didn't know what to do. She wouldn't come out and talk to anyone when they came up. Just kept askin to be left alone. Finally she packed up and headed out into the mountains again and this time Andy was really worried about her. Told Pa she was actin like she had nothin left to live fer and he was afraid she might even put herself to death.

After three or four days of her bin gone Andy packed up hisself and went out to find 'er. He knew these mountains as well as she did so it didn't take 'im long to git to where he figured she'd be.

Now there is some real beautiful places up that way if you know where to find 'em and they's as pretty as any picture you'd ever see. The old Ingram folks'd built a small cabin next to a waterfall up there so's you could stay overnight cause it's a day's walkin either way. Miss Jenny used to tell that most wild animals had no fear of you cause they'd never seen enough of humans to know they should be afraid of 'em.

Anyway Andy found her all safe and sound sittin by the waterfall and seemin to be in pretty good spirits. Guess this kinda puzzled Andy cause he figured she might never git over losin Saunders and was expectin he may not be able to talk er into ever comin back home. Ma said she was so different after that you wouldn'ta thought she was the same person. She said sumthin to Ma about findin answers she'd bin searchin for most of her life and her stay up in the mountains had give 'em to her. Nobody ever quite understood what she meant but it didn't matter cause they was all happy to have 'er back and gittin on with 'er life agin.

Then came the blizzard of forty-one I believe it was when Andy found that stranger layin out in the snow pinned under a tree with his leg broke. That feller stayed up here with 'em a good four months or more which seemed kinda odd cause he'd likely done better if he'd gottin hisself out and into some hospital. Not that Miss Jenny hadn't done a good job of patchin him up. She was better at it than anyone else around but after the blizzard was over there was nuthin stoppin 'im from getting out to a regular doctor and makin sure his leg was healin proper like. I used to come up a lot as a kid. Saw the feller a few times myself. Anyway toward the end of March he did leave, but he must've been jinxed cause the day he left came another blizzard and it was the worst one anyone in the valley could ever recall. Didn't last long but while it was going on it near scared everyone to death. Funny thing was the day started out as nice as any we'd had that March and we was all lookin forward to getting the snow thawed down cause there'd bin a heap of it that winter. The Ingrams never did have a telephone so Miss Jenny'd been down the day before and got Pa to put in this long distance call fer the stranger. It was arranged that some friend of his would come all the way over from Alberta the next day to git 'im and that seemed kinda odd too cause it'd bin a sight easier if he'd just gone into town 'n took the train back. Anyway the arrangements was made so on that day Andy was bringing the stranger down to our place in the cutter cause nothin else could've ever travelled the Ingram road with all the snow on it. Just a short while ahead of 'em gittin to our place we knew something wasn't just right with the weather cause the animals all started actin up. The horses got real skitish and took to whinnyin' and runnin all over the corral as hard as they could go. Dogs was a growlin and barkin like they'd seen Satan hisself and cows ran bawlin into the barn.

Then the wind commenced to blowin and the blackest clouds I'd ever seen before or since started rollin in from the west. By the time Andy 'n the stranger made it to the yard the storm'd swung into high gear so Andy only stopped long enough to let the stranger out and then he headed back. Right about that same time we caught a glimpse of car lights coming from the other way which, musta been this feller from Alberta. The stranger just stepped inside the porch long enough to say he was goin back out to meet 'is friend at the gate cause he didn't want 'im to chance drivin in the yard and getting stuck. Pa yelled after 'im saying they should both get back here to the house and stay put till the storm passed cause it would be dangerous out on the roads. Never did catch sight of this other feller or his car 'cause by that time you couldn't see to the road, but one thing is sure cars back then wasn't near as good at buckin bad roads as they is nowadays and that caused us a worry. I guess they musta made it okay though cause we never did hear anymore about 'em.

"You're certain you can't remember any names?" Adam interrupted.

"Fraid not but if you want to stop by on yer way back we might be able to dig somethin up out of Ma's old scrapbooks."

"Perhaps I will. Sorry for interrupting, please go on."

"Well that storm was one never to be fergot. It was the talk of the whole country fer weeks afterwards and it did a fair bit of damage. They even wrote up a piece about it in the valley newspaper. Most everyone around cut out the clippin 'n kep it. We still got one ourselves. The real strange thing about it was thunder and lightnin. Far as anybody knew this'd never bin heard of in March and it sure hasn't since. The clouds was so black you'd thought it was nightfall and they covered the whole valley in a matter of a few minutes.

I remember our hen house getting covered right over with the blowin snow, cause the next day me and Pa had to go out and shovel a tunnel through so's we could get in and tend to the chickens. Anyway after it got goin good, the horses broke out of the corral and the dogs took cover in the barn along with the cows. Ma and my two sisters were huddled down next the woodbox and was a cryin 'n prayin all at the same time.

We always kept a long rope in the porch fer times like this and Pa yelled at me to get the end of it tied to sumthin strong. The cows 'n dogs was puttin up a terrible howl in the barn and he wanted to go out and shut the door and he'd need the rope to find his way back. I don't know how far he got before there came that thunder and lightnin. It was the loudest crash of thunder and brightest lightnin anybody'd ever hear of. Even durin' bad storms in mid summer there was never thunder and lightnin the like of that. This happened three or four times and I remember bein so scared I was down on my knees prayin and hangin on to the rope for dear life. I'd not had a chance to tie it to anything, so I just wrapped it around my wrists and held on. By this time I was dead sure this was either the end of the world that Dodds'd always preached about or at least Satan'd got loose and was out on a terrorizin spree. Right about then the rope jerked real hard and I flew head over heels out the door. I didn't know what happened but I hung on a fearing Pa'd be lost fer good if I let go. I remember the wind takin my breath away and the blowin snow stingin my eyes 'n face so bad it felt like sand peltin me. I kept trying to git up but the harder I tried the deeper I dug myself into the snow. I was screeching at the top of my lungs, but the wind was roarin so loud I couldn't even hear myself.

Somehow Pa managed to crawl back to where I was layin and fer a few minutes just covered me over with 'imself cause I had no outdoor clothes on. Soon's he caught his breath he got a good hold on me and we managed to drag ourselves back to the door and git inside.

Pa told me later he'd only made it partway to the barn when a heavy gust of wind hit him so hard it knocked 'im off his feet, but he'd held onto the rope and that's what dragged me outside. It wasn't long after that the storm started lettin up some so Pa lit two or three candles and set about pacifying Ma and my sisters.

In all the commotion we'd fergot about them other two fellers. Pa said they'd fer sure be there cause nothin coulda moved an inch in that storm and soon's it let up a little more we'd git out 'n see if they was all right. Ma'd got er wits back about 'er by now and was after my sisters to give 'er a hand and they'd start supper cause them fellers was bound to be hungry. I didn't feel like eatin anything myself but Ma always held that a good hot meal was the best way there was calmin everybody down from scare.

After about another half hour or so the storm'd dropped off some more so me 'n Pa got dressed agin and headed out towards the road. It was a dickens of a struggle gittin through the snow and we still couldn't see very far ahead so we had to get right up to where the car shoulda bin sittin, but it was nowhere in sight. That was a real shock. Pa said they mighta got away 'fore the worst of the storm caught 'em otherwise they was bound to be stranded out there somewhere.

Soonest we would get out agin was the next day. We checked all along the main valley road. Most of the neighbors was lookin too but they was nowhere to be found.

Pa even tried that long distance phone number agin to see if he could find out anything but the operator said she didn't even recognize the number. Didn't know what else to do, so we wished them the best and put it out of our minds.

Things settled down agin and we got on with livin about the way we always had here in the valley but fer someplace that'd never had anything more excitin than Mrs. Wilkes running off with young Chester Crabb that ten year spell was a real humdinger.

Andy's health started failin 'bout a year later and wasn't long 'fore he was gone. Miss Jenny only stayed around long enough after to settle up affairs and then she moved away. Everyone was saddened by her leavin. They threw the biggest going away party fer her that there'd ever bin in the valley and every one of 'em telling her they had a place fer her if ever she came back.

She'd bin born, raised and spent the first part of her life right here in this old house, but she's never bin heard tell of since. Rumor was going around town about a year ago that she'd passed away down east somewhere but no one knew if there was any truth to it. Some of the older folks was talking about it, but they tend to git things mixed up at times.

Everyone was really saddened by her leavin. There'd never bin anyone around these parts like Miss Jenny Ingram. A more carin, kinder helpful soul you couldn't find. She'd always gone out of her way to give a hand to those that needed it and'd never take a thing back in return."

The old man had become misty eyed and stood up with his back to Adam and tapped his pipe out on a tree trunk. After wiping his eyes with his shirt sleeve he turned around and said, "If Miss Jenny has passed on Mr. Finlay, I know the good lord has found a real special spot fer her up yonder."

Confused and heartsick, Adam could only nod in response. The pain of realizing he would never see Jenny again was equaled only by the bewildering and mysterious circumstances under which he had come to know her at all. "What had happened?" he wondered desperately again. Why? Nothing made sense. That four months with Jenny the past winter was as real to him as any other time in his life had been, but now he was being told it happened over sixty years ago.

"Fer some reason," the old man broke into his thoughts. "I

could never bring myself to use the house fer anythin else. Miss Jenny only wanted her personal belongins when she left so Pa paid her some extra money fer the furniture and it's still in there sittin about where it always has. I guess in the back of my head I'd always hoped she might come back someday so I've kept the house patched up over the years. I wanted it to be ready fer her to move right back in if she ever did show up."

He looked up at the old building for a few more moments then said, "Well I've gotta be goin Mr. Finlay. It's past chore time now but if you want to stop in on yer way back I'll get the wife to dig up them old scrapbooks."

"Thanks. Uh would you mind if I looked around inside the house before I leave?"

"Go right ahead. "T'ain't locked. Just a latch on the door."

The old man mounted his horse but continued to stare at the house. After a few moments he turned his attention back to Adam and spoke in a soft voice.

"There's many a thing I don't understand 'bout life Mr. Finlay. About the workins of the creator and such, but as anyone who ever knew her would tell you she seemed to have a big chunk of the divine in her and she gave it out real generous like to everyone she met. That's why she's remembered and many is fergotten. She left a mark in this valley no one else ever has nor likely ever will. What ever it is about Miss Jenny yer searchin fer now, I hope you find and pass along cause anything she had to offer would be a help to all folks everywhere."

With that he turned the horse and trotted away.

Adam surveyed the house with mixed emotions. He felt a pang of fear at facing the inside of the old building with the knowledge that Jenny would never again grace it. But overshadowing this was the urgent need to grab hold of any tangible threads that might help explain this incredible departure from reality that he seemed to be an integral part of.

His hand shook slightly as he grasped the antique knob and slowly pushed the door open. Shadowy silence and the musty odor of age oozed forth to greet him. The partially covered windows admitted only slender rays of sunlight limiting his first view of the interior to vague impressions.

He remained motionless for a few moments allowing his eyes to adapt until he was able to make out the scene before him and it sent shivers up his spine. He gasped slightly feeling like he was seeing ghosts. Everything was just as he remembered it even though age had taken a toll. The wooden table and chairs, the cookstove, the wood box, the cupboards, the water pail, now upside down on its stand, all seemed to be standing dutifully in their places as though awaiting Jenny's return.

He shuddered as he pushed the door fully open and gingerly walked in. Moving slowly around the kitchen he touched everything making sure it had solid substance to it. The door to the bedroom he'd occupied for four months was partially ajar and even before he entered he could see the home made cabinet that Jenny had kept spare blankets in. Once inside he stopped in front of the potbellied heater remembering the many times he'd watched Andy coax comforting warmth out of it by cranking and shaking several metal protrusions; the functions of which he never did understand. He looked over at the bed, remembering that night when he'd first regained consciousness and found himself lying on it. Jenny was looking down at him with concern and he recalled thinking, in those first few moments, that he had died and was now looking up into the eyes of an angel.

The bed no longer had a mattress on it, but otherwise nothing had been changed. He pushed the door to the washroom open and even in the poor light he could make out the porcelain jug still sitting on the small stand by the toilet.

Slowly he made his way back through the kitchen and into the living room. Protective covers had been draped over the furniture but by rolling back a few corners he recognized the easy chairs and the old sofa he had often dozed off to sleep on. The stone fireplace that under Andy's magic touch would quickly warm up the room now stood dark, cold and empty.

Henry Meade had obviously done much more than "just patch up the place." Nothing had been allowed to fall into disrepair. Doors all fit perfectly and hung solidly on their hinges. Even cupboard doors swung open and snapped shut with ease.

Nothing it seemed had been removed or changed. The dark picture moulding that had once suspended Jenny's favorite pictures was still in place. The high baseboards needed a paint job, but had not been tampered with. The plastered ceilings and walls showed evidence of repaired spots that had kept them intact.

Finally he arrived back at the door and stopped for a moment to take one last look around. "Would he ever understand what had happened?" he wondered, "or was this to forever remain some cruel mysterious joke the universe had played on him."

Suddenly he felt angry. Angry and cheated by this inexplicable series of events that had exposed him ever so briefly to the most beautiful person he had ever known and just as quickly, snatched her away again. If he was meant to learn some lesson from the experience, what was it? Was he being punished or rewarded? It seemed to be a mixture of both with neither one making any sense. His life had been permanently changed by Jenny's teachings and certainly for the better, but now what should he do? Where should he go? He had fallen more deeply in love with her than he ever had with any other woman and had planned that together they would continue the spiritual work they had started on this mountain. He had been relying completely on her to guide them in the right direction when he returned. In retrospect he realized she must have known all along that their encounter somehow transcended the barriers of time. She probably realized too, that the only way he would accept he had been transported back to another era was to come to that conclusion by himself. That would explain her occasional strange behavior, but it still left volumes of other questions unanswered. It felt much like leaving the theater before the movie was over. Without knowing the ending it would have been better not to have seen any of it.

He slowly pulled the door shut and made his way back to the car. Once behind the wheel, he sat motionless for a long time staring across the yard at the now dilapidated barns that had housed Andy's beloved animals. This was the stuff science fiction was made of. He had heard of such things but had always shrugged them off as nothing more than the wild rantings of tabloids hungry for the nonsense that kept them in business. Anything that did warrant serious investigation was sooner or later explained in logical terms and he had always been confident that if necessary everything could. But now? Now he himself seemed to be playing a central role in just such an event and even had he been a firm believer in the supernatural it would have been no less mystifying.

Reluctantly he eased the big sedan into gear to commence the long journey home. Pondering the situation was only complicating it. But his increasing despair that answers may never be found only fueled his already overworked brain.

Falling asleep at the wheel wouldn't be a problem he thought with a wry grin as he started the rough ride back down the narrow old trail.

CHAPTER 28

The telephone answering machine was flashing frantically when he entered his Edmonton apartment. The small pulsating red light seemed to contain an urgency that made him drop his briefcase on the spot and immediately activate the playback. The message was brief and chilling. "Mr. Finlay please contact the hospital at your very earliest convenience."

"Oh my god," he thought remembering his mother had gone in just before he left for what the Doctor described as a follow up routine examination. After several futile attempts to make the right connections, he quickly ran down the hallway to the elevator that would take him to the car parkade.

Within minutes he was standing at the nursing station trying frantically to get some information about his mother.

"She's been discharged Mr. Finlay," the nurse finally said after searching through some papers on the counter.

"Thank god," he said breathing a sigh of relief.

"But there is someone in room 307 who has been asking for you."

"Who is it?"

"I've just come on duty," she said. "I'll have to get the file…"

"Aunt Harriet," he thought remembering she too had been

admitted just before he left. Without waiting he charged down the hallway and entered the room. A very old woman hooked up to beeping monitors lay motionless on the bed. Her eyes were closed and she appeared to be asleep. He walked closer to get a better look, but she was no one he knew.

"Boy they've really got their wires crossed," he thought and turned to go back to the desk when the nurse entered the room carrying a handful of papers.

"My apologies Mr. Finlay. We've finally gotten it straightened out. I have the ladies name right here. It is Jennifer Ingram."

He just stared at the nurse in stunned silence. Finally able to speak he said in a trembling voice, "would you repeat that?"

Before the nurse could reply the old lady who's eyes were now open spoke in a weak raspy voice.

"Is that you Adam?"

Rooted to the spot and unable to reply he stared at the frail form on the bed. Chills engulfed his whole body and for a moment dizziness threatened to cause him to black out.

"Please come closer Adam. I'm sure you don't recognize me now. It has been over fifty years, but it's me Jenny."

He took several hesitant, unsteady steps that brought him to her bedside, but was still unable to find his voice. The once auburn hair was snow white and her body was little more than a skeleton.

"Dear, dear Adam," she said managing to raise her arm enough to clasp his hand and smile at him weakly.

Finding his voice he finally asked, "Jenny is it really you?"

Without answering she pulled the blanket down enough to reveal a gold chain hanging loosely around her neck on which hung a ring.

"Remember it was too large for any of my fingers Adam, so I put it on this necklace and I've never taken it off since."

He picked it up for a closer look. It had become dulled with age but there was no mistaking this signet ring he had given her when they had last been together in the old Ingram house.

"My god Jenny I…what happened? How is this possible? I don't understand."

"Dearest Adam," she answered squeezing his hand. "I haven't much time left here on earth but I knew I would stay long enough to see you one last time."

She started to cough and appeared to be struggling to get her breath. The nurse came quickly to the bedside and made some adjustment to the apparatus Jenny was hooked up to. The nurse then motioned Adam to the far side of the room.

"She is very low, Mr. Finlay. She is suffering complications from pneumonia. It's fortunate you were able to get here now. She's not expected to last much longer."

He looked at the nurse without answering and then back at Jenny. Her coughing had subsided, so she resumed in a quivering voice.

"The work we began on Ingram Mountain so long ago is growing ever more important to the human race, Adam. You told me back then you would continue and I know that is what you will do. I have with me a briefcase that you must have. In it you will find written material that explains everything about me— and us. There is also a large manuscript in the briefcase that will take you much deeper into the esoteric teachings that are now, more than ever, extremely important to mankind."

She stopped and began coughing weakly again. This time he seated himself on the chair close to the bed and clasped her frail hand between both of his.

"Jenny," he said when her coughing had subsided. "Jenny I…"

Not knowing what to say he stopped and just stared at her. Although dulled with age there was no mistaking the large hazel eyes. "My god," he thought. "This just can't be happening. It can't be."

"Jenny," he began again. "I'm so confused. Nothing…none of this is logical. I…"

"Dear, dear Adam," she said. "Still looking for the logic in everything aren't you?"

She managed a weak smile and for a few moments even the special look that he had become so familiar with.

"It's all explained in the writings Adam," she continued in a voice growing weaker. I don't have enough time left to tell you much except that there is a strong connection between you and I that had it's origin many lives ago. We began a mission a way back in time that we cannot ignore no matter how hard we try and yes we did try, both of us. But as I've so often said the law of karma will bring about restitution. After many difficult physical excursions, we've come to this point where we can now discharge our final obligation to that ancient commitment and continue on our evolutionary pathway."

Her voice had dropped to a whisper so she stopped talking again and drew his hands over and cradled them against her cheek.

"I went back to Ingram Mountain to see you Jenny, to be with you…"

"I knew you would, Adam and I knew the heartache it would cause because I had already experienced it. That was the final challenge I'd mentioned and for that I'm so very sorry but there was no other way to help you back onto your path. You will clearly understand this at some point in the future."

She stopped for a moment, then asked hesitantly, "Is the house…still standing?"

"Yes and in beautiful condition. Henry Meade has taken great care of it. He was keeping it ready for your return."

"Dear, dear Henry," she said her voice dropping to a whisper again. "Did he tell you the whole story?"

"Yes," he answered softly, "and it clarified many things for me."

"Please…" her voice faltered and she was unable to continue.

"Don't try to talk Jenny. Just rest. I'll be right here."

She closed her eyes and appeared to drop off to sleep again. He drew her hand up to his cheek and for a long while just gazed at the most beautiful person he had ever known. It was not just physical beauty, although she had been that too, but a depth of inner beauty, of inner quality that he couldn't adequately describe. She was the epitome of pure goodness and love that made all who knew her eager to say they did.

She's quite heavily sedated Mr. Finlay," the nurse said as she entered the room again. "She will sleep a lot. If you plan on staying…"

"I'm staying as long as she's alive."

"There's a couch in the lounge if you want to lay down later."

"Thanks. I'll be okay right here."

The hours dragged by and Jenny slept. Other than visits to the washroom he remained seated by her bedside. Sleep began to overtake him too and he finally succumbed by laying his head on the bed beside her. Awakening several times with a cramped neck He would check her and then lay his head down again.

Nurses came and went but other than adjustments to the apparatus Jenny was hooked up to, they said little and seemed to be eager to leave as quickly as possible.

At about 3:00 AM he awakened suddenly and sat upright. Jenny was awake too and looking at him with heavy eyelids. Smiling faintly she just gazed at him for a few moments, then slowly parted her lips and whispered, "I have to go now Adam."

"Nurse!" he called tears welling up in his eyes. "Nurse!"

"No Adam," she said tugging weakly at his arm. "They're here now waiting for me. I see them. There's Andy and Jeffery, my parents too. It's time for me to go. Just see me off."

"Oh god Jenny," he said wrapping both his arms around her frail body and drawing her close to him. "My sweet, sweet Jenny."

He could no longer restrain his emotions and for the first time in his adult life, tears ran freely down his cheeks. Within seconds he felt her body go limp and he knew she was gone but he held her close and between spasms of crying kept repeating. "My sweet, sweet Jenny."

CHAPTER 29

He sat staring at the unopened briefcase on the coffee table in front of him. He just stared without moving. He hadn't even removed his overcoat before sitting down. It just seemed like too much effort. He suddenly realized how much strain the events of the past few days had placed on him and now his whole being was rebelling against any more. Weariness pushed him deep into the easy chair and he laid his head back against the cushioned rest and closed his swollen eyes.

Despite his fatigue, thoughts still wandered through his brain. Jenny had left instructions with the hospital staff that upon her demise the briefcase was to be given directly to him and no one else. Her mystical psychic ability was still evident in this last request because she seemed to know they would reconnect with each other at the right time.

Slowly his thoughts gave way to much needed sleep and a dream started taking shape. Once again he was back in the old Ingram house with Jenny but now they were husband and wife and they had an offspring, a son or daughter. In the hazy realm of the dream he couldn't be certain which. A meal was on the table and then he clearly heard Jenny call, "come for dinner Edward." Out of the shadows a figure emerged and as it drew close Adam recognized his deceased son. He felt both elated and bewildered at seeing the boy. Even in this dream state he realized Jeffery was dead, but somehow at the moment he was very much alive.

His sleep was shattered by the roar of a jet plane passing over his apartment, but the impression of Jeffery had been so vivid it remained in front of him for a moment.

"Jeff," he called out not yet fully awake. Then he sat upright and rubbed his eyes as the remaining fragments of the dream dispersed into nothingness. It had been one of those times when being abruptly awakened from a deep sleep, one is disoriented and for a moment occupies both the dream and the waking region. He rubbed his eyes again and then catching sight of the briefcase, his memory came flooding back.

"My god," he thought recalling the dream. "Is it possible?…our son?"

Moving quickly now, he dug the briefcase key out of a pocket and after a few unsuccessful attempts finally coaxed the worn old latch open and raised the lid. A sealed envelope with his name on the front was on top. A leather pouch bulging from its contents was tucked into one side and a thick manuscript occupied the remaining space. He opened the letter and spread the handwritten pages out on the coffee table and began to read.

Dearest Adam,

Since you are now reading this letter it means I have returned home. My last wish was that you could be with me when I left. I do so hope that came about.

I'm sure by now you are confused, upset and possibly angry. For those reasons I am offering this letter in the hopes that it will explain the circumstances under which we came together again. Yes again, Adam. It has not been our first time and will not be our last. For you, that event happened only a few short weeks ago. For me it has been many, many years. Both perceptions are correct which you will more clearly understand if you choose to delve deeper into those wonderful discussions we began in the old Ingram house. In the years prior to your arrival on the scene that winter, I had done an exhaustive inner search in the hopes of finding answers to the most traumatic experience of my life. After isolating myself for extended periods in the solitude of the mountains I began to awaken to my true inner being and the reality underlying all creation. I was given answers to questions that at one time I didn't even know how to ask and ultimately found I could access the universal consciousness that will reveal as much to anyone of us as we are able to receive. In the years after I left the valley I traveled extensively and was tutored by many masters compiling knowledge and revelations documented in the manuscripts you now have in your possession. For those reasons, then, I'm able to explain what I'm sure up to now has seemed to defy logic and recount the many previous lives we had together.

In the distant past you and I have both participated in acts of barbarism that inflicted suffering and sorrow on many people. I won't try to justify our actions by saying such conduct was acceptable in those ancient cultures because at some level deep within ourselves we both knew it was wrong.

As we moved forward through numerous physical lives we finally acknowledged the dreadful error of our ways and united in the common purpose of bringing love, joy and enlightenment in place of the heinous atrocities we had once committed. Taking this new direction has been a slow, arduous struggle because it so radically opposes the old way but we had jointly committed ourselves to a purpose that would not only clear up our own negative karma but assist others on their pathway. This was a sacred vow that would not be denied and only now have we reached the final stages of fulfilling that vow.

I entered this life still needing to experience some very harsh treatment which would clear away remnants of suffering I had once inflicted on others. You returned as Clement Saunders and we both needed that brief encounter to make us aware of the happiness that was possible by following a pathway of love. The tragic ending made us realize we still had to work diligently before we could finally achieve a level of awareness that would facilitate our evolutionary progress.

You probably realize now that there is no reason to mourn Jeffery's death. He is an old soul and needed only a short time on earth to complete a mission of his own which was in part to bring you to a point whereby you would once again embark on your own pathway to enlightenment.

This he accomplished primarily through his death that in turn caused the suffering and sorrow that forced you to seek out truth. It was no accident at all that you found your way back to Ingram Mountain and that you suffered physical restrictions that kept you there for that entire winter.

You see Adam, you, Jeffery and I were together as a family in a past life and during that time knew the joy and happiness that only members of a soul group can experience.

Oh how I yearned to tell you the whole story when we were last together on the mountainside and to relive, if only for that winter, the sweet tender love we once knew, but which had to be left back in a lifetime already lived.

I know you often found my behavior puzzling and for that I apologize. I'm sure you can now understand why. I knew you would soon return to your own time. That brief interlude was for the singular purpose of assisting you back on your pathway to understanding because you and I, indeed all who embrace truth, will play essential roles as humanity enters this new age. It is extremely important you understand your mission from this point on Adam. The human race still teeters on the brink of destruction, and those who will, must work ceaselessly to avert it. Should we be successful, there remains the critical and massive task of ensuring we are properly redirected. If humanity does finally open the right door, beyond that door lies very unfamiliar territory for most. The majority will need strong support from the enlightened minority and this will be the substance of our work for whatever number of lives we choose to still have on earth. It will be both daunting and exciting and will bring us ever closer to an understanding and appreciation of the creator's purpose for the planet and all that inhabits it.

I'm sure by now Henry Meade has told you the entire story of the tragic events befalling the valley so long ago. Hiram Dodds is an entity whom I had mistreated in an earlier time. His bitterness accumulated over many ensuing lives causing him to ultimately use revenge to balance the scales. This created for him a hurdle that he must now negotiate on his own pathway.

You will find in the briefcase a pouch full of money that should cover the cost of my last request. Please take my body back to the valley and have it buried there, for there is where it all began for me in this life.

Although some memories were harsh, there were tender and happy ones I always cherished. In those mountains surrounding the valley I gained a measure of enlightenment that set me on a pathway from which I shall never deviate and from out of those mountains you came to me twice; first as Clement Saunders and then Adam Finlay. This was not by accident but by design because the powerful forces of the universe will not be denied. Our connection to each other has strengthened over numerous lives together and as you go forth now remember that connection is growing ever stronger. I will be with you for the remainder of your time on earth because that is an irreversible commitment we made to each other and the creator long, long ago. Call on me when your path is rough, where you are lonely, when you need support and encouragement. I will be by your side and you will be fully aware of that fact because our love has the strength to transcend all dimensional barriers.

Jenny

The last few pieces of the puzzle fell readily into place. Her strange behavior, his feeling that there was more behind the scenes than what he was aware of. The cat and dog recognizing him because they already knew him as Clement Saunders, the familiar feeling about the old house. It all made sense now. She, in fact, hadn't broken her promise to be there for him when he returned. She would always be there because they had a connection to each other that stretched forward and backward into the mists of timelessness.

CHAPTER 30

"If it's to pay tribute to Miss Jenny and keep her memory alive," Henry Meade said. "I'll gladly sell you the land Mr. Finlay. How much did you want?"

"How much is left?"

"The whole seven hundred acres. I wouldn't ever let logging companies touch a tree on this mountain, even though they made me some fancy offers. In fact a feller by the name of Leo Burns was here about a week ago offerin to buy it and he really got his hackles up when I said no but this is a whole different story. Yer welcome to all of it if you want. There is only one condition; the same one that Miss Jenny asked of my pa and me. Ingram Mountain must always be left in its natural state."

Shaking his head in amazement he realized now what Jenny had meant when she once said the future of this mountain was his business. She knew, even back then, that he would ultimately fall heir to the property and continue the tradition of preserving it.

"You've got it Henry. In fact that is one of my reasons for wanting to buy it."

Adam had mentioned his idea to Henry Meade on the day of Jenny's funeral and the old gent grabbed on to it like it was the most important project in the world. They had agreed to meet up at the Ingram place the next day and discuss the idea further. Talking there now it was evident that Henry would be a willing participant.

"It will be a retreat," Adam explained. "Open to all who want to come and learn Jenny's philosophy. My plan would be to restore the yard, the house, everything back as close to its original state as possible."

"That's just great Mr. Finlay and I'll give you a helpin hand with anything I can. Did I mention we've still a few old pictures of Miss Jenny? Yer welcome to them, just in case you wanted to hang em back up in the house or sumthin."

Adam reached over and clapped the old man on a bony shoulder and said, "I think that's right where they belong Henry."

He looked at Adam for a moment and then tilting the old felt hat back on his head said, "darn near sounds too good to be true. Just wish she was here to know about it."

"She knows Henry. She knows," Adam said and then noticing the puzzled look on the old man's face quickly changed the subject. "We haven't talked price yet. Any idea what you might want for it?"

Henry's response was a blank stare which slowly changed to a chuckle. "Guess I'd never thought about that. Actually this has nothin at all to do with money Mr. Finlay," he said pulling his pipe out of his shirt pocket. After getting it lit he puffed in silence for a few moments.

"The importance of keepin it natural is all that matters cause we made that promise to Miss Jenny long ago and now that responsibility is bein passed along to you. I want only what my pa paid for it back in '48."

"Oh now Henry that's a give away price. I'll gladly pay the going rate."

"Nope. I know you have the money but Miss Jenny would've appreciated that cause she herself never took a speck more of anythin than she needed. It's the least I can do to pay back a little of the good she gave to this valley. That's the deal 'n' I won't take a cent more."

Adam clasped the old man's outstretched hand in a warm shake and after some more conversation he mounted his horse and rode away. Adam watched him until he was out of sight then slowly folded his arms and leaned back against the house.

"If Henry Meade's attitude was any indication," he thought. "This valley had to be the perfect place to start his new mission."

Feeling genuine peace for the first time in many days, he stayed fixed in the leaning position against the old house and allowed his gaze to wander aimlessly over the yard. Suddenly from out of nowhere a soft, cool breeze caressed his face and for a moment he was puzzled because there was not the slightest hint of air movement anyplace else. Then he caught the unmistakable scent of her perfume and with a smile of acknowledgment raised his hand and waved. "Thank you Jenny," he said out loud knowing she had just given her blessings. It truly was time to resume the work they had started in this old house on Ingram Mountain.

ABOUT THE AUTHORS

 Reg Johnston lives and works in rural Northern Alberta.

He is retired from a career spanning forty five years and now devotes his time to investigating and revealing what he believes is a vicious and potentially fatal attack on the environment.

A twenty year involvement in spiritual studies brought him to a point of understanding the irrevocable and direct connection between the natural environment and universal laws.

Reared in an atmosphere dominated by fundamentalist Christianity prompted Johnston to ultimately search for answers that dogmatically restricted religions could not supply.

This book is the result of that background and identifies the direction he has chosen for the remainder of his life.

He has begun work on a second book that probes deeper into the effect that spiritual laws have on our planet's environment.

Melanie Zachoda has been immersed in spiritual studies for many years.

She was able to provide invaluable assistance to the writing of this book and it is her intention to continue in this direction.

Melanie lives in a quiet country setting with her two children and a variety of animals.

Printed in the United States
37879LVS00002B/43-69